BIG
Decisions

A novel based on true experiences from an Amish writer!

LINDA BYLER

BIG
Decisions

LIZZIE SEARCHES *for* LOVE
· *Book 3* ·

Good Books
Intercourse, PA 17534
800/762-7171

Big Decisions includes material originally published by
the author as these books: *Lizzie and Stephen* and *Lizzie's
Married Years*.

Cover design by Koechel Peterson & Associates, Inc.,
Minneapolis, Minnesota

Design by Cliff Snyder

BIG DECISIONS
Copyright © 2011 by Good Books, Intercourse, PA 17534
International Standard Book Number: 978-1-56148-700-4

Cataloging-in-Publication data available from the Good Books website.

978-1-61129-672-3

Table of Contents

Chapter 1

THE LEAVES TURNED SHADES OF BRIGHT orange, red, and yellow, and the squirrels scurried in short swift trips up the rough bark of the trees. Their cheeks were stuffed full of acorns and nuts which they stashed away in a deep, dark, cozy chamber for their winter nourishment.

Lizzie and Stephen walked together on a Sunday afternoon along a creek, kicking the brown leaves and bending their heads to the stiff autumn breeze. Lizzie wrapped her sweater tightly around her chilled body, crossing her arms in front of herself to keep warm.

"I should have worn a scarf!" she said her teeth chattering.

"Hey, Lizzie, I just had a great thought. Thursday evening I'm going archery hunting again. Would you like to come along?" Stephen asked.

"Archery? Bow and arrow? I can't shoot a bow and arrow," Lizzie said.

"No, you don't have to shoot. Just go along and be with me. There's nothing quite like it. Honestly. It is the most exciting, the most intense sport there is. To sit in a tree somewhere, waiting quietly until you hear leaves rustling, or maybe spot a reddish-brown color gliding along through the trees, is an incredible experience. Your heart starts thumping so hard you feel like your head will burst. There's just an unbelievable amount of excitement in all hunting, but archery is my favorite."

That was quite a speech for Stephen, so hunting must be more than a hobby—closer to an obsession, Lizzie thought.

"How can it be so thrilling? Actually, all you do is sit in the woods," Lizzie said, still less than enthused.

"No, that's not true, Lizzie. Come along, and I'll show you."

So that was how Lizzie found herself careening across the mountain at breakneck speed in an old, white work van, driven by a friend of Stephen's. His name was Ryan Gustin, and he was quite a character, speaking the Pennsylvania Dutch dialect as fast as he drove his rattling old van.

Lizzie enjoyed his company, sometimes laughing uncontrollably at his version of a Dutch expression which served to take her mind off the alarming rate of speed he maintained down the winding road.

Stephen seemed quite comfortable in the front seat beside him, so Lizzie decided Ryan must be a competent driver if Stephen was so relaxed.

Turning north, they came to a valley between two mountains. Old buildings and beautiful, prosperous farms dotted the scenery, while simple family dwellings sat along the road. The mountains were colored with every brilliant hue imaginable, and Lizzie was content to ride along and enjoy the beauty. She was just starting to become a bit bored and uncomfortable when Stephen yelled for Ryan to stop. This was the place. Ryan stomped on the brakes.

As the van shuddered to a stop, Lizzie peered out of the splattered window at a dilapidated, old, three-story house. Broken shutters hung from single hinges, the porch railing looked as if it had been ripped from its base, and pieces of gray siding lay strewn across the yard. The porch roof gapped where the wind had torn shingles loose.

Lizzie shivered, wondering if the house was haunted at night. She knew there was no such thing, but old, unoccupied houses always gave her the blues. The real, sad blues. Not that she felt depressed. Not the crying blues. Just the kind of blues where the sun was hidden behind a dark cloud in her feelings.

She didn't really want to get out of the van as she looked a bit timidly at the steep, brush-strewn hillside directly behind the creepy old house. The sloping fields led to dense forest, real mountain woods that suddenly looked quite dark and spooky.

Stephen and the driver were already out, unloading their archery gear, still talking and laughing and having the time of their lives as Lizzie pulled her white cotton scarf tighter under her chin. She sniffed nervously, running a hand hastily across her hair to straighten it.

She wished she had worn some heavy material around her legs, because her thin woolen knee socks were not going to be heavy enough to wade through the unkempt woods. She remembered the hillside along the ridge in Jefferson County and the horrible scratches she and her sisters got every day from the long, spiny raspberry bushes that lined the trail.

She sniffed, squinting nervously to see if she could locate any brambles, but then sighed, gave up, and sat back against the old plastic seat. Stephen would take care of her, she decided, so she would relax.

"Ready?" Stephen stuck his head around the door, extending his hand to help her down. Lizzie took it gratefully, searching his eyes for reassurance. Stephen smiled, and her heart melted as she stood beside him. If your boyfriend was so nice to you, it didn't take much to believe you could do anything at all.

Ryan strode off in the opposite direction, and Stephen swung his bow under his arm as he headed out. Lizzie followed, determined to be a good sport. She would certainly not be a hindrance to him or hold him back by telling him she was uncomfortable.

Stephen parted the tall weeds as they started the gradual uphill slope. Lizzie grimaced as heavy seedpods slapped her cheeks, raining prickly, granular seeds down the neckline of her coat. She slapped at the heavy pods, shaking the front of her dress to get rid of the itchy feeling, her mouth pressed in a line of determination. She would not grumble or complain, knowing Stephen would not appreciate a whiny girlfriend tagging along.

Stephen stopped after a short distance and said, "Whoa."

"What?" Lizzie asked, trying to peer around him.

"These brambles are pretty thick here. Think you can make it without getting scratched too badly?"

"I think so," Lizzie answered, with all the false bravado she could muster.

"I'll try and hold them for you," he reassured her.

He must have forgotten about her the minute that statement was out of his mouth. Lizzie found herself in one of the worst situations of her life, trying to hold back a long bramble with one hand, only to rake a thorn across the palm of her hand, while two more long whips with briars intact tore across her thin woolen socks.

Grimly, she untangled herself, putting the injured palm to her mouth as she tried to free her legs by tramping on the briars. As she bent to hold back the brambles, a long vine yanked her hair, pulling horribly as her white scarf slid around her neck. She grabbed quickly to retrieve the scarf and was promptly scratched by another sharp branch.

"Ouch!" she yelled, completely undone by this thorny predicament.

Stephen's instant response was, "Ssshhh!"

"Why? Why can't I holler? These brambles are unbearable!" Lizzie wailed, close to tears.

Suddenly retrieving his manners, Stephen mumbled an apology and came to her rescue, holding aside the long spiny branches until they came to the forest's edge. Lizzie shook her head grimly, smoothing her hair with scratched fingers and adjusting her white head scarf.

"Okay," Stephen whispered, "step as quietly as you can, and when I come to a suitable tree, I'll motion for you to follow."

"F ... f ... follow?" Lizzie whispered back, aghast.

"Yeah. Up the tree. We have to sit in a tree so the deer don't see us."

"I can't climb trees!" Lizzie hissed, her eyes narrowing.

"Pine trees are easy. Now be as quiet as you possibly can."

That was how Lizzie found herself halfway up a scaly pine tree, positioned so that she had the same view Stephen did. The bark was rough and very uncomfortable. She sat on the side of her leg, holding onto a branch beside her. The first five minutes weren't too bad. She rested from the strenuous climb, breathing in the pine tar and admiring Stephen's profile as he stood alert and absolutely motionless in the tree, waiting breathlessly for the sight of a deer.

The wind swayed the branches as Lizzie strained to see through the thick growth. It would definitely be exciting to see a deer with huge antlers come walking across the pine needles, but who knew when that might happen? Deer roamed acre after acre of woods, but having one walk in front of you seemed about as possible as finding a needle in a haystack, so what was the sense of sitting in this tree? The deer were probably all on top of the mountain or in some farmer's cornfield having a bedtime snack.

Her leg ached and her arm became very stiff, so she shifted her weight to her other leg. Instantly, a small branch broke loose, rattling down through the pine boughs with the noise of a shotgun, or so it seemed.

"Sorry!" Lizzie hissed.

Stephen drew his eyebrows down. "Shhh!" he warned, putting a finger to his lips.

Boy, he was serious. All right, she would be more careful. So she sat quietly. And sat. And sat. Her nose itched, her feet hurt, her whole leg was numb, and still she sat. The sun slid behind the opposite mountain, casting long shadows through the thick forest, and still she sat.

This is a lot worse than council meeting or communion or sitting at Emma's wedding, she thought grimly. A hard bench would seem like a recliner if you compared it to this pine tree. Sitting like this for hours in a darkening woods would be a good form of torture if you wanted to force someone to talk. She would gladly say anything to get out of this tree.

She tried shifting her weight to the opposite side as slowly and quietly as she possibly could, loosening some bark in the process. She looked at Stephen beseechingly, but he only frowned seriously. She groaned inwardly. She wished she had never agreed to go hunting with him. It was the most uncomfortable, boring thing she had ever done in her entire life. She hated hunting and was never, ever going to get herself in this predicament again.

Suddenly there was a decided rustling in the underbrush. Stephen's head turned slowly, and he brought his bow up to a more ready position. The rustling continued. Lizzie listened with bated breath, watching carefully in the direction the sounds were coming from. Would they actually see an honest-to-goodness deer? She didn't know if she could stand to see Stephen put an arrow into the poor, innocent animal.

She didn't know if she wanted to be disappointed or relieved when a busy gray squirrel emerged and raced across the thick pine needles.

"There's your deer!" Lizzie mouthed.

"Shh!" Stephen warned.

What was the use of holding so perfectly still? It was getting dark, and there was no possible way he could shoot a deer now. She was getting very tired and impatient, wishing with all her heart that the night would be over. If Stephen didn't soon come down out of this tree, if he kept up this stupidity of sitting in a tree when it was almost dark, she was going to say no if he asked her to marry him.

What about returning to the van? How would they get through those dreaded brambles again?

"Stephen!" she whispered.

"Shh!"

This time he was serious. Turning his head slowly, he peered intently into the semi-darkness as, much to Lizzie's disbelief, two deer stepped out of the thicket. How could they be so quiet? Lizzie's heart rate increased, but mostly out of fear for the deer's safety. She so definitely did not want them to be killed with arrows stuck into their hearts. They were such beautiful creatures, completely at ease roaming their mountain, so why did anyone have to kill them?

Then as Stephen started to raise his bow to the proper position, they walked just as silently back into the forest. When Stephen finally turned to Lizzie and spoke to her in a normal tone, she knew the whole hunting ordeal was over. Carefully, with aching limbs, she made her way out of the pine tree. Rubbing her back, stretching, and sighing, she regained a sense of normalcy, grateful to be standing on solid ground and able to move at free will.

Lizzie stared at Stephen in disbelief when he turned to her and said cheerily, "That was fun, wasn't it? I bet you really enjoyed it."

"It … it, yes, well, it was all right. Mmm-hmm." That was the closest thing she could say that was honest and still not hurt his feelings. She couldn't say just how tedious her evening was, but he must have known because he laughed out loud quite suddenly.

"Not exactly a hunter, are you?" he said, smiling mischievously.

"Just get me off this mountain safely, and I'll be fine," Lizzie said.

They took a detour under a barbed wire fence, which Stephen held so Lizzie could easily slip through, before walking across a nicely cropped pasture until they came to the old house. Lizzie stared up at the attic windows in spite of herself, wondering who had built this huge three-story house and why it had been left to rot away, the wind and rain and snow all taking its toll on the sturdy structure. Probably the squirrels and the rats had a grand time gnawing at the lumber that held it together.

Ryan appeared shortly and shared his story with Stephen about having spotted a few deer but too far in the distance to have a decent shot. They stowed their hunting gear in the back of the van before climbing in. Finally, Lizzie was on her way home, away from the pine tree, the dark forest, and the creepy, sad, old house.

They turned into a little restaurant, Ryan saying he was starved because he hadn't eaten anything since lunchtime.

Lizzie was only too happy to sit in the tiny booth, eating French fries with plenty of salt and slathered with ketchup. They were the most fattening, most unhealthy thing, Mam said, but one of the most delicious foods in the world. Lizzie enjoyed every one, and then ate her way down the entire length of a tall chocolate sundae topped with whipped cream and nuts.

"Mmm!" she said, smiling genuinely at Stephen.

"Better than hunting?" Stephen asked.

"Much better," she grinned back at him.

That evening, she decided marriage was probably a lot like hunting. You had to take the good with the bad, because God himself knew circumstances would not always be as pleasant as French fries and sundaes. There would be times of sitting in pine trees, but that was only normal. If the good was balanced with the bad, life could be leveled off into happiness. Maybe a mature, quiet kind of happiness, if you learned to care about each other's feelings enough not to always say exactly what you thought.

If she had told Stephen how horrible her evening really was, he would have been hurt. And if Stephen had been as impatient with her as he seemed to be when she struggled through the briars, she would have been terribly insulted.

So it definitely paid to keep your mouth closed when you would love to air your grievances loud and long. After all, Stephen knew hunting was not her favorite thing to do, but she bet anything he admired her for sitting in that tree so long. She had proven to him that she could keep quiet for a good long time. And that was amazing.

Chapter 2

LIZZIE MISSED HER OLDER SISTER, EMMA, A great deal, mostly because she thought about marriage so much herself. She wished Emma was in her bedroom down the hall, ready to talk whenever Lizzie had important questions that needed answers. But Emma had married Joshua last year and moved to Allen County.

Mam and Dat were all right to talk to about such matters. But they were so old, it seemed that when they talked about being newly wed, it was like they had gotten married in the 1800s. You couldn't really compare things, like homes and furniture or anything like that, because things were so different after their wedding than now.

What really alarmed Lizzie is how Mam would throw her hands in the air and laugh about the fact that they had to borrow 50 dollars to buy a kitchen table for their first house. Dat would join in and relate how old and freezing cold their first rented home was, and they would laugh together, as if it was all one big hilarious joke to be so poor and not care one teeny bit about it.

Lizzie wondered everyday when Stephen would ask her to marry him. She needed to talk to someone who got married in this day and age, like Emma. She had nice furniture that Dat and Mam had provided, things like a new hutch cupboard which held the set of china Joshua had given her before their wedding day. She had a brand-new table you could pull apart and put leaves in until you had a table spread clear across the kitchen, and as many as 18 or 20 people could sit around it at one time. Emma even had a new sofa and rocking chairs and a really pretty bookcase with sliding glass doors.

Lizzie didn't know if Stephen had any money or not, so she worried a great deal. For one thing, she hated being poor or having to make do with cheap or broken things, like a torn, wrinkled plastic tablecloth. She wanted a nice new house with new linoleum on the floor and varnished, wooden cabinets with a pretty canister set perched on the Formica counter top. She daydreamed for hours about her new house, and the closer a marriage proposal seemed to be, the more she wondered about Stephen's finances.

Mandy told her airily, in quite a lofty manner actually, that she cared more about her classy new home than she cared about Stephen. "You need to remember, Lizzie, that a nice new house doesn't make a happy home," she repeated.

Sometimes Mandy could be so infuriating with her wisdom and knowledge and always being right, that Lizzie found it easier to talk to Emma about these things.

So when Lizzie came home from school, and there was a long letter from Emma in the mail holder, she was ecstatic. Her excitement increased as she read how they wanted Mandy and John and Stephen and Lizzie to come on Saturday evening.

"Oh, good, good, *goody!*" Lizzie yelled exultantly, waving the letter in the air as she marched around the kitchen.

Mam smiled, and Dat drew his eyebrows down in displeasure. He shook his head and mumbled something about acting your age, before his head disappeared behind his paper again. Lizzie stopped to look at Dat, or rather at the paper he was holding. Dat just was not the same since he had been diagnosed with multiple sclerosis. He was often tired and, of late, irritable and short with his children. He would have laughed in the past, his blue eyes twinkling at them, but now he often frowned or showed his displeasure with a sharp word. Most of the time the girls shrugged it off, but sometimes it hurt, even though they realized he struggled to accept this disease more than they would ever know.

So they hired a driver and traveled to Allen County. Lizzie could hardly wait to see Emma and Joshua, the old farm, and especially their new baby, Mark. Stephen wore a light, cream-colored shirt that made his skin look very tan. His hair was always bleached to a lighter color by the fall after a long summer of working in the sun. Lizzie thought he looked very handsome and wondered if Emma would think so, too.

After you dated awhile, it was much easier to relax and fully accept the fact that your boyfriend really did like you the way you were. It was no longer quite as big an issue for Lizzie to be a bit overweight, because Stephen certainly didn't seem to mind.

Lizzie didn't worry so much about her appearance like she had in the beginning of their relationship. It seemed as if dating for a year or so took care of the flutter of nervousness, the agony of indecision about which dress to wear, or, when you really thought about it, a lot of silly insecurities.

They no longer had strained silences. Instead, it was normal for them to have a good, healthy discussion about something they didn't agree about. But the one thing they didn't discuss was marriage. Of course, Lizzie wanted to get married now. She wasn't really tired of being with the youth, but she wanted to go forward with her life.

For one thing, she was tired of teaching school, of helping Mam at home, and especially of the endless yard and garden work around the old farm. Lizzie wanted her own house, a nice new one, to be exact, with only Stephen to worry about.

The van turned into the farm lane. Emma greeted them from the porch of her brick farmhouse with a huge smile. As soon as they climbed down from the van, Joshua made John and Stephen feel at home with his warm manner as he showed them around the farm, pointing out where the pigs and steers were housed, and walking them to the pastures and the fields.

The sisters sat together in the living room and talked as fast as they could until they all stopped and admitted that no one was listening because all three of them were talking at once. There was just simply no one else on earth like a sister, they all agreed, and before they were aware of it, they were all talking at once again.

They fussed over Baby Mark, admiring the cute shirt and pants Emma had made for him. He was a big boy, toddling around on the glistening hard-wood floor, pulling himself up with a mighty effort as he hung onto a sofa cushion. Emma said the best thing that ever happened to her was having a baby.

"I want lots and lots of children," she said.

Lizzie eyed her a bit skeptically.

"Emma, now you know they won't all be as good as Mark is right now. Suppose you'd have a baby that screams and cries like Jason used to? Or Aunt Becca's baby girl?"

Emma leaned back on her glider rocker, gently massaging Baby Mark's back as she tried to get him to sleep. She laughed easily as she looked at Lizzie in disbelief.

"Boy, you sure haven't changed, have you? Worrying about a colicky baby before you're even married!"

"Not *my* baby. Your next one!" Lizzie shot back. Mandy laughed. "Oh, boy! Here we go. Sounds like home!"

"Don't you ever long to be a single girl at home again, Emma?" Lizzie asked.

"No! Absolutely not. Never. I'd much, much rather be married to Joshua and have a baby boy. Right, Mark?" And Emma proceeded to hug and kiss her precious boy until he struggled to be put down on the floor.

"Come. I have to show you what I made for our snack tonight," Emma said, as she led Lizzie and Mandy to the kitchen. Handing Mark to Mandy, she triumphantly produced two Tupperware containers and whisked the lids off, watching eagerly as Lizzie bent down to see what was inside.

"Emma! You didn't make these. You bought them at a bakery!" Lizzie gasped.

"I made them! I absolutely did. I would never buy something like this at a bakery," Emma laughed, beaming proudly.

Mandy oohed and aahed about the lemon jelly roll Emma held, while Lizzie said the chocolate one looked like a picture in a magazine. It did. Emma had made two perfect cake rolls. The lemon one was piped full of a light lemon filling that smelled so delicious Lizzie's mouth watered. The other cake was a rich chocolate filled with creamy vanilla frosting.

Emma had dusted both with confectioners' sugar. The cakes were perfectly round without a crack or a burnt edge in sight.

"I just can't believe you did that," Lizzie said, absolutely impressed.

"Oh, Lizzie, you know how I always was. There's nothing I'd rather do than spend hours in my kitchen, meticulously producing something like these jelly rolls."

Emma's eyes lit up, and she hurried back to the pantry. "Look at this," she said, holding a perfect loaf of homemade bread. It looked exactly like the loaf of bread in the children's book about the Little Red Hen who baked a beautiful loaf of bread with the wheat she raised.

"Emma, you are genuinely talented at baking," Lizzie said sincerely.

"And having baby boys!" Mandy added, scooping up Baby Mark and squeezing him affectionately.

When Joshua came into the kitchen followed by John and Stephen, there were no awkward moments, no times of feeling ill at ease. That was just how it was when you went to Emma and Joshua's place, Lizzie thought happily. They both loved to have company and made you feel so welcome and relaxed. Maybe it was because Emma was her sister, but whatever the reason, Lizzie loved to go visit them.

They all sat around the kitchen table as Joshua put on the teakettle for hot water. He drank black instant coffee almost continuously throughout the evening—that boiling hot, dark brown, bitter brew that Lizzie could positively not enjoy. She had often tried to drink coffee like Mam did. She tried it with milk, with sugar, with cream and sugar, but no matter how many attempts she made, it just wasn't good. Stephen drank coffee, too. He seemed to enjoy it as much as Joshua did, telling Lizzie he filled a quart thermos with it every morning.

That's why Lizzie found it so fascinating to watch Joshua enjoy his coffee. It was steaming hot, so he would sit back in his chair and stir it for awhile, talking and laughing easily until the coffee cooled enough for him to take the first sip. That black awful stuff.

Emma carefully arranged the cake rolls on a cut-glass oblong tray, putting a sharp stainless steel knife beside it. Her cheeks flushed, she scurried back and forth between the refrigerator and the pantry, slicing cheese and arranging Ritz crackers around it. She poured tall glasses of ice-cold peppermint tea and opened a bag of pretzels, placing them in a dish that matched the oblong tray.

"We don't go to town often," she said breathlessly, "so we can't serve a lot of fancy things like Pepsi and other snacks."

"Emma, that wouldn't seem like being at your house," Lizzie said. "It seems homier and 'farmier' with the food you have."

Emma gave Lizzie an appreciative look, glancing a bit nervously at Stephen and John.

"Don't worry about me. We live very simply at my house," Stephen said.

Lizzie was so proud of Stephen she could have hugged him, but of course she didn't. That was a very nice thing to say, making Emma feel comfortable with the fact that her food was just right exactly the way it was. Emma continued to dash between the table and the counter top, making everyone comfortable, seeing that they had everything they needed, until Joshua told her to sit down and relax or the cake rolls would be all gone before she could enjoy a slice of them.

"Maybe I had better before Lizzie eats all of them!" Emma said, teasing her.

"I could eat the whole thing," Lizzie said seriously.

Joshua's eyes sparkled as he turned to Stephen. "You sure you want to marry her? She may turn out to be expensive!"

"Joshua!" Lizzie cried, horrified.

Stephen thought it was very funny, although his face definitely deepened in color. Lizzie knew her face was bright red, but everyone laughed so genuinely, and Stephen gave her such a reassuring look, that Lizzie could laugh with them. The exchange broke all the reserve they had left, and as the evening wore on they had a genuinely good time playing their favorite card game, Rook.

Lizzie decided during the evening that being married to someone you loved was a very worthwhile goal. It was an exciting idea, one that made her feel happy through and through. She wanted her very own home so she could have her friends over and serve them all her good food, although she knew without a moment's hesitation that it wouldn't be homemade cake rolls like Emma made. She could barely bake a decent chocolate chip cookie.

She sat back in her chair, watching Stephen shuffle the Rook cards. She wondered a bit apprehensively if he could be a good husband and father, and if he had enough common sense to make good solid decisions and protect her. He could be very grown up, especially when he talked about his work, so that Lizzie was sometimes in awe of him. But he could also be hopelessly funny at times, acting as if he didn't have a care in the world.

He turned to smile at her, that secret little gesture of belonging, and Lizzie's heart melted in gratitude that he was her boyfriend. Probably there was no such thing as an absolute, 100 percent, perfect boyfriend, and so far, Stephen was everything she had hoped for.

"No, I'm planning on buying the herd in a few months," she heard John say.

Lizzie snapped to attention, her eyes riveted intently on John's face. She watched Mandy as she blinked her huge green eyes, listening carefully.

The herd! He meant cows! Oh, poor Mandy.

"How many are you planning to milk?" Joshua asked, bending for yet another sip of coffee.

"Around 40, hopefully," John answered.

Forty cows!

"Who in the world is going to help you milk 40 cows?" Lizzie blurted out.

"My brother will help me get started. Then we'll see," he said, turning to scoop up the Rook cards.

Lizzie's eyes narrowed as she watched Joshua's slow grin spread across his face.

"You need a wife," he said, smiling broadly.

Emma and Lizzie exchanged knowing glances and hid their smiles. Mandy cleared her throat nervously and quickly grabbed a pretzel, chewing rapidly.

"Looks as if his wife got hungry for a pretzel very suddenly," Stephen said slowly.

Mandy drew back her arm and threw a pretzel, hard, hitting Stephen's face. He ducked, grimacing, and laughed with Joshua at John and Mandy's discomfort.

Everyone laughed then and settled down to a serious discussion about courtship and marriage. It was no wonder you wanted to get married when you were at Emma and Joshua's house, Lizzie decided. They portrayed marriage as one of the greatest ideas God ever invented. Joshua could go on and on about the merits of living with Emma. He didn't try to hide the fact that she was one of the best things that had ever happened to him, and the time he spent on the farm with his wife were the best days of his life. Emma beamed and smiled, naturally basking in the warm words of praise from her husband.

"Surely, though, there are some things that you would change. Surely you're not always blissfully happy every day," Lizzie broke in, always the pessimist.

Joshua shrugged. "I wouldn't know what!"

"Me neither," Emma said softly.

"Come on. Not one thing?" Lizzie asked.

"Oh, maybe little things like not frying the corn-meal mush exactly as crispy as I like it," Joshua laughed.

"Or watching you eat chocolate cake in your oatmeal," Emma said, smiling.

"What?"

"Oh, he fixes a dish of oatmeal like ordinary people with sugar and milk, then he plops a piece of chocolate cake in the middle, stirs it up, and eats the whole mess," Emma said.

"Now that is definitely different," John said.

"You want to taste it? I've been eating it for years. It's so good it's habit-forming, like coffee. Tell you what, I'll make you some."

With that, Joshua got up and opened a drawer, selected a small saucepan, filled it with water, and settled it on the stove.

By the time the evening was over, they had all had a taste of warm oatmeal with chocolate cake stirred into it. The group gave Joshua's concoction mixed reviews. Stephen liked it, and John grudgingly pronounced it edible. Mandy turned up her nose, but then that was Mandy, skinny thing, about most food, Lizzie decided. Lizzie loved it but didn't really elaborate on the fact, mostly because it was embarrassing the way all food tasted delicious to her.

When it was time to leave, Lizzie wished the evening wasn't over yet. She loved spending time with

Joshua and Emma and told them so.

"You need to invite us again," she said, as Emma hugged her tight.

On the way home, Lizzie sincerely hoped the longing to be married had settled squarely into Stephen's heart and would not let him rest.

Chapter 3

"WHAT REALLY GETS TO ME THE MOST," Lizzie said, waving her arms for emphasis, "is why does a covering have to be a certain size, or an apron belt a certain width? What does that have to do with your soul?"

Her sister, Mandy, didn't say anything, just rearranged the driving reins in her hands as she guided Bess, their horse, toward the small grocery store. Lizzie slumped in her seat as the buggy climbed the hill. That was typical of Mandy, not saying much when she wasn't really sure of herself.

Lizzie and Mandy were about to become members of the Amish church. It was a time of learning for Lizzie, of truly seeing for herself what it meant to be *gehorsam*, or obedient. It wasn't all roses. Not even close.

When they reached the small village of Knobstown, Mandy pulled Bess to a stop. The sisters jumped out of the wagon and tied Bess to the hitching rack before going into the small grocery store.

"How are the girls?" Mr. Tibbs called out, his blue eyes twinkling behind his heavy eyeglasses. His plaid flannel shirt was stretched tightly across his round little stomach, his short fingers ringing up an order as swiftly as any cashier in town.

Mr. and Mrs. Tibbs, who ran the little friendly and efficient store, were always happy to see the "Amish kids," as they called them.

"We're fine," Lizzie said, smiling back at him.

"Speaking for your sister, too?" he called, winking jovially at Mandy.

"Same here," Mandy grinned.

"Good! Good!"

He leaned forward, his palms down on the counter, and asked what he could get for them.

"Mam has quite a list here, so it'll take a while," Lizzie told him.

After the two grocery bags were filled and the items paid for, Lizzie and Mandy each chose an ice cream bar to eat on the way home, even though the weather was bitterly cold. They took big bites of their ice cream as the buggy wound down the hill toward home, Lizzie holding Mandy's bar between bites so she could drive Bess.

Mandy giggled, telling Lizzie that she was getting some strange looks from passing motorists. Lizzie sat on the spring wagon seat with an ice cream bar in each hand, while Mandy, the skinny one, was driving and had none.

"You mean, I look like I eat all the food away from you? Mandy!"

They drove on in companionable silence until Lizzie brought up the subject that was troubling her.

"Mandy, why do the ministers make such a big deal about the smallest things?" she asked.

"Lizzie, just be quiet. I don't understand everything fully. We probably won't until we live to be a ripe old age. You make the biggest fuss about all this. What is your problem with changing some things? You don't want to comb your hair fancy after you're married anyway. Nobody does."

Lizzie thought Mandy was being awfully short with her. She had to talk when something troubled her. Mandy knew that was a vital part of Lizzie's well-being, bringing things out in the open and discussing what lay so heavily on her heart.

"Oh, all right, Miss High and Mighty. I apologize for disturbing Her Majesty's peace," Lizzie said, turning to look squarely at Mandy.

There was no response, only a faraway expression as Mandy looked at Bess's ears.

"Grouch!" Lizzie finished, before turning away to watch the scenery in the opposite direction.

When they brought the groceries into the kitchen, Mam smiled and examined every item before putting it in the pantry or refrigerator. Lizzie made herself a cup of peppermint tea, sat down at the kitchen table, and stared into space. Mandy went straight to her room, with only a few short words to Mam.

Mam lifted her eyebrows.

"What's wrong with Mandy?" she asked.

"I don't know. She was not very nice about my questions on the way home."

"What questions?" Mam asked, sighing as she straightened her covering.

"Oh, just this *ordnung* thing. Joining church."

Mam's eyes narrowed as she watched Lizzie's face closely. "What now?" she asked.

"What does being plain have to do with your soul?" Lizzie burst out miserably.

"Well, Lizzie, obedience to the rules of the church is an outward sign of a change on the inside," Mam said.

Lizzie snorted.

Mam sighed.

"You know a humble spirit is the surest sign of a change in your heart," Mam said. "You want to do what's right, Lizzie. That's why you're joining the church and no longer rebelling against God. After you're baptized, you'll no longer live for yourself and your selfish will, but you'll have started on a journey where God is your Master. Now it's up to you to lead a new and obedient life."

Lizzie sighed. Mam made it sound so easy.

"So, Lizzie, if you can't be *gehorsam* in small things, how can you expect to be willing to obey God in bigger things?" she concluded.

"You mean that's what it's all about?" Lizzie asked.

"Yes. In a way it seems that church rules are all man-made things that God doesn't care about, but if you look at it in a spiritual sense, they aren't."

"What about English people, Mam? How come they can get to heaven so easily and never have to worry about one stitch of their clothes. They polish their fingernails, wear all kinds of beautiful clothes, use make-up, and do their hair, and they never have to worry about obedience and solemnly joining a church with a bunch of rules."

"They were born into that lifestyle. It isn't wrong for them. They wouldn't even think of dressing like we do."

"It still doesn't make much sense," Lizzie said, finishing her tea.

Mandy clattered down the stairs, slumped against the wall on the bench behind the table, and began chewing her fingernails.

"You must be in some terrible mood, chomping down on your fingernails like that," Lizzie said.

Mandy glared at her before she smiled a bit wryly and confessed about being upset, actually a bit more than that.

"John would have liked to get married next fall, but he thinks I'm too young," she said.

"Yes, you *are* too young!" Mam said.

"I'm not too young!" Mandy burst out, her frustration making her eyes look wide and dark.

"I'll say, Mandy! You're way, way too young. I would never want to get married this year, and I'm older than you," Lizzie said, her voice rising.

"Remember, Lizzie, we're not all alike," Mandy sang out in a squeaking voice.

So throughout that winter the girls went to church every two weeks and listened closely as Grandpa Glick and the row of solemn ministers explained the way of the cross, of Christ's suffering, and how to follow his footsteps. The ministers explained to them in minute detail the way they were expected to dress, to behave with decorum, and to learn to be obedient to the rules of the church.

Mostly, Lizzie understood the German phrases and could benefit from the ministers' words. She clearly grasped the concept of learning to fear God, to come before him with due solemnity, and to respect the admonishments of her elderly grandfather.

There was, however, one thing that bothered her during that summer. In the *Light from Heaven* book, the one she had read to her pupils, Joseph Armstrong, the main character, went through great personal anxiety. He searched his own soul deeply and felt a certain transformation after he gave his life to God, as did many young people in other books she had read.

She didn't understand all of this too well. Either the Amish people didn't believe in having an experience like a new birth, or else they were taught to view their spirituality much the same as they viewed everything else—calmly and stoically accepting—kind of like putting a lid on too much joy, too much sorrow, or too much rejoicing.

Sometimes Lizzie wanted to be like the Baptist churches in the South that she had read about where people shouted and sang and clapped their hands, swaying to the "Glory, Hallelujah!" in their soul. They were rejoicing in the Lord, and Lizzie often felt like crying when she read about their religious experiences. It touched a spot in her heart so that it felt right to rejoice with them.

She felt elated, joyous actually, that Jesus had died for her. Mam always smiled and shook her head in that certain way that meant she knew exactly what Lizzie meant. But Mam also told Lizzie she had to be careful. She told her she could rejoice in other ways than clapping and shouting, like when she was all alone and stepped out of the house on a beautiful spring morning and heard the birds singing and saw the sunrise and the green leaves on the trees.

Lizzie promptly informed Mam that it wasn't the same if you didn't have someone thumping on the organ or piano while the people around you sang as loud as they could, just all caught up together in that moment of rejoicing.

Mam's quiet, "Tsk, tsk," was her only response, before telling Lizzie she read too much.

"Contentment and continuing the quiet way of life are the virtues I most admire in Amish people," Lizzie always said. Of course, she wanted to be Amish. She never even thought of not being a part of the Amish way of life. She just wanted to really let loose sometimes.

Being Amish was the only thing she had ever

known. She had no real longing to leave her parents, go into the big, wide world, and try to become an English person. That would seem all wrong. Some Amish people did that, so she guessed they were comfortable with that, but she wouldn't be.

That winter, Lizzie learned in lots of different ways what was expected of her when she became a member of the church. The ministers explained lots of the lessons in the Old Testament, as well as what happened to people when they rebelled openly against God. The ministers also spoke a great deal about the difference Lizzie and her friends would experience when they lived within God's will, serving God and not idols. That was not hard for Lizzie to believe, and she learned to appreciate the stories in the Old Testament, as well as the words Jesus spoke in the New Testament.

But sometimes Lizzie despaired, overwhelmed by the fear that she would never be good enough to be baptized in the fall.

"I'm not *that* different than before, Mam," she repeated sourly as she sat in the kitchen with Mam and Mandy.

"Oh, but you're making an honest effort, Lizzie. That's all you can do. Grace supplies everything, really, in the end," Mam said.

Lizzie eyed her suspiciously. She was just about sure that Mam didn't always know what she was talking about. For one thing, she claimed "all your own righteousness was like filthy rags in the sight of God," and yet, all winter they were instructed to live righteously. What sense did that make?

So now if you tried as hard as you could to do good, to live in the way you were instructed, then it was nothing to God, and it all amounted only to grace? So why didn't people just go out and do what they wanted to? They may as well, if grace took care of everything.

Mam scooped out some cookie batter and dropped it onto the baking sheet, using the back of her hand to brush away a strand of hair from her cheek. Beads of sweat clung to her forehead and the color in her cheeks had heightened as the heat in the kitchen had escalated during the afternoon.

"Mandy, be careful there. You're trying to put too many cookies on that sheet, all right?" she instructed.

Mandy nodded, pushing up her sleeve with one hand and sending the glass mixing bowl full of batter onto the floor where it smashed into a hundred pieces.

Mam gasped, then sighed impatiently.

"Who's going to clean it up?" she asked.

Lizzie thought that was an excellent example right there. "Okay, Mam, so why didn't you get angry and yell at Mandy? You used to when we were little girls. So is that all your own righteousness now, and it doesn't amount to a hill of beans in God's eyes? That's what you claim."

Mam looked sharply at Lizzie, but then she smiled.

"Now there, Lizzie, is the beauty of becoming a Christian. If we are all good and holy, acting righteous and prim and proper so that other people think we are such awfully good Christians, *that* is filthy rags. But if we live to become more like Jesus, if we just have a desire to be good, he quietly, without our knowing, molds and shapes us into a vessel of his own making, and we aren't even aware of it. I would never have noticed any difference at all, girls. None."

"Really? You're a lot different than you used to be," Lizzie said.

"And, hopefully, 20 years from now I'll be so much different than I am now. More patient, more compassionate, not so easy to criticize, oh my, the list could go on and on," Mam answered.

Lizzie fiddled with a cookie, saying nothing. Now that made a lot of sense. She was beginning to grasp only a bit of what it meant to walk with Jesus. It was as if you were only a lump of raw, gross-looking clay, and through life's sorrows, disappointments, and trials—just look at Mam, having to move here to this old farm—you were shaped into a vase or a bowl that pleased him. You never knew what he might make out of the rough beginning, she supposed.

Several weeks later, Lizzie and Mandy were baptized on a cold Sunday morning. There was no doubt or fear, no despair or confusion anywhere for Lizzie. She realized one thing as surely as the sun rose and set. She had set her face toward heaven, promising to live and obey within the Amish church, and she believed very sincerely that Jesus Christ was the Son of God.

She also learned, to her surprise, that Amish people were not as unemotional as she thought. She had been to baptisms before, of course, but now that it was her turn, she saw how the adults cried openly, using huge white handkerchiefs to staunch their tears of joy. They were sincerely grateful that more of the young people had come to the knowledge of the truth, Lizzie knew. It was a moment in her life she hoped to remember as long as she lived, tucked away, kept like a precious jewel.

Her tears ran with the water the ministers used to baptize her and became wet spots on her white organdy cape. She heard small, subdued sobs from the women's side, which was very touching to Lizzie. She guessed Mam and all the aunts and all of the other women in the church must really love the youth who knelt before them. It was a great feeling to know you were accepted into this group of people who had gone before you, setting an example of right and wrong. These people, most of them her family and friends, genuinely cared about her and wanted her to be a part of the growing community of Amish people.

After the service, she ate her bread and cheese, snitz pie, and red beets with the rest of the church just as she did each Sunday. But she knew there was a difference this Sunday. She was now a sister in the church, her sins were forgiven, she was washed clean, and she would learn to apply her faith to the temptations and trials she encountered along life's way. Maybe she was only a shaky new Christian, but she would certainly try as hard as she could. Everyone was just going to have to have patience with her, because, after all, Mam was pretty old when she quit yelling at them.

Chapter 4

THAT WINTER BROUGHT THE USUAL SNOW, frigid temperatures, and ice, which meant skating, tobogganing, and even sleigh rides across the snowy fields. It was one of Lizzie's favorite seasons, and she looked forward to spending time with Stephen and her friends who were now all dating. That winter was a time of relaxing in her lasting friendship with Stephen, a time of contentment and happiness which seemed to radiate through to the children at school. She loved teaching and being outdoors playing sports, almost as much during the week with her pupils as she did on the weekends.

Lizzie decided that the children needed to go skating one more time before the thaw set in and the ice melted. Lizzie announced one morning that the school would take an afternoon at the pond, if the students earned 100 perfect scores on their work.

Every 100% grade, no matter which age group or subject, was carefully recorded with a stroke of the chalk on the farthest left-hand corner of the large blackboard. When they recorded the hundredth 100%, the entire school would go skating.

Lizzie smiled to herself as little heads bent to their goal of 100%. The classroom became so quiet and well-ordered that Lizzie heard the wall clock's homey ticking. Little eyebrows were lowered in their focusing and tongues were bitten as erasers appeared. Students diligently erased work that was not good enough to achieve the prize. Hands held heads and twirled straying hair in concentration. Dictionaries were pulled from the back shelf and put to earnest use by students who normally would have chosen the faster, easier route of guessing when they were unsure of an answer.

She loved her teaching job so much at times like this. Dear hearts, so innocent, responding to such a small prize. It almost didn't seem fair. Lizzie loved ice-skating, and yet she didn't need to work for it the way her pupils did. After about 10 days, Lizzie drew the hundredth stroke with a flourish, turning to her pupils.

"Very good! I do think the first grade contributed almost half of them! It's just wonderful, first grade! Good job," she said.

Anticipation ran high the following morning, as the pupils brought extra food in their lunchboxes. Thermoses of hot chocolate and a large container for water were set on the sleds, cushioned with old quilts. A toboggan, for the little ones, was carefully lined with buggy robes.

Two older boys, Amos and Ben, went ahead of the group, pulling a sled loaded with a box of firewood and newspapers for the fire they would build next to the pond. The upper-grade students would stay warm all day, eventually shedding mittens, coats, and scarves as they heated up from the exertion of skating. But the little ones grew tired and cold, even crying that their poor little feet felt as if they were frozen.

Lizzie bundled up, placing a whistle in her coat pocket. She blew the whistle only when absolutely necessary, but it never failed that some errant person drove her to blowing the whistle as hard as she could. The disobedient person had to sit on a bale of straw for 15 minutes.

The day was sunny, the warmth of it promising spring. The air, however, was still wintry, swirling bits of loose snow across their faces as they bent to walk up the hill, then down the other side toward the pond. The day was so bright, Lizzie squinted against the glare of the snow. She wished she could wear her black sunglasses, but that would seem a bit *gros-feelich*, or conceited, she feared.

Mandy said those big black sunglasses didn't look quite right with an Amish covering, which was something to consider. But the truth was, they made Lizzie feel sort of cool, almost like former President John Kennedy's wife, Jacqueline. She admired that woman so much, and secretly, when she wore those sunglasses, she felt the way Jackie Kennedy looked. Oh, well, no sunglasses today. She was a teacher who commanded respect, and she needed to remain in control.

The pond loomed ahead, a bit grayer than the snow. The top of the ice was not perfectly smooth. There were skaters' marks all over it, and bits of snow, straw, and wood ashes left from other skaters on earlier evenings.

The boys soon had the fire started. They put their skates on and slid across the ice, pushing the scrapers. Scrapers were homemade bits of aluminum fastened to broom handles that smoothed the ice on the frozen pond.

As the boys worked, Lizzie helped the little ones tie their skates, arranged quilts on straw bales, and stoked the fire. Then she sat on a bale of straw and squinted into the sun as the pond became alive with black-garbed figures flying across it, looping and swerving, in a sort of intricate dance.

She decided to drink a cup of hot chocolate before lacing up her skates. There was just something about a steaming cup of hot chocolate on a cold winter day, Lizzie thought, that made your heart so cozy you could hardly stand it. It felt like the softest cashmere scarf around your stomach, soothing it and warming your whole body until you felt fluffy all over.

Hot chocolate tasted even better with a chocolate chip cookie to dip into it. Chocolate chip cookies were funny things, though. They were almost a staple in an Amish child's lunchbox. All the mothers made chocolate chip cookies. They made molasses cookies and whoopie pies and snickerdoodles and raisin cookies, too, but the most popular was always chocolate chip.

But chocolate chip cookies were as unpredictable as the weather. Each mother had a different recipe. Some cookies were hard as a rock, but they were the best to dip in hot chocolate.

Others were high and dry and, the minute they hit that creamy liquid, dissolved into a warm mushy mess. You couldn't get them to your open mouth fast enough before they disintegrated and landed in the bottom of the cup. If you were lucky, a few chocolate chips floated to the top, and you could at least rescue them.

Aunt Becca's chocolate chip cookies were the best, hands down, Lizzie thought. They were firm and chewy and a tiny bit overbaked. If you broke one in half, you could hold it in the hot chocolate for a long time, and then lift it to your mouth with style and grace.

Lizzie never did, though. She just wolfed them down, dripping hot chocolate on the front of her coat. She was dismayed to find that she had already eaten four cookies and probably could have eaten four more.

Sally and Dorothy giggled, sitting beside her on the bale of straw.

"Are you hungry?" Sally ventured.

"Mmm-hmm!" Lizzie said emphatically.

"You ate a bunch of cookies!" Dorothy said, giggling.

"I'll go skating now and work them off," Lizzie said, smiling down at Dorothy.

Energized, she quickly laced up her white figure skates, hit the ice running, and with swift strokes soon caught up with the upper-graders who were already organizing a game of "freeze tag."

That was a game they never tired of playing. When the students who were "It" caught someone, that person had to stand at the very spot where he or she was caught. That student was guarded by those who were "It," while the others tried to dart in and free him or her.

As the sun climbed toward noon, hats and scarves, stocking caps and mittens were flung off near the fire. The owners skated off as fast as they could before being caught. The students dodged, twirled, and sprang away from each other until they were all gasping for breath, their cheeks red from the cold and exertion.

After lunch, the boys were allowed to play hockey, but they had to leave an area of the pond for the girls and smaller children. All afternoon, Lizzie taught the girls how to gracefully skate backward and in a circle, lifting one foot over the other, distributing weight onto the inside skate so that the skater naturally turned in a circle. The girls practiced, fell down, laughed hard, sat on the ice and talked, drank more hot chocolate, and kept trying.

It was all delicious fun. There was no other word to describe it. On the ice, Lizzie forgot the task of being a teacher and was genuinely happy, almost

like a child with her pupils, if only during those precious hours of ice-skating.

The following Monday morning, Mandy flew
down the stairs and literally burst into the kitchen.
Her eyes were wide and very green in the soft lamplight as she told Mam and Lizzie the reason for her
excitement.

"I'm getting married!" she said breathlessly.

Lizzie stopped halfway to the table with a hand-
ful of knives and forks, her mouth dropping open
in disbelief.

"Surely you mean this fall? This coming November?" she croaked.

"No. This spring!"

Mam turned quickly from the sink, her eyebrows
drawn down in a serious display of disapproval.

"Not this spring, Mandy. Amish people have
their weddings in the fall. In November. You can't
get married in the spring."

She turned to stir the scrambled eggs, the subject
closed, swept away by her refusal. She calmly continued her work of getting breakfast on the table
for her family as Mandy glanced at Lizzie, raised
her eyebrows, and shrugged her shoulders helplessly. Going over to the stove, Mandy leaned forward, peering closely at Mam to get her undivided
attention.

"You don't understand, Mam. You really don't.

John wants to get married in March because his—our—herd of cows is arriving the first week in April, so... Well, Mam, we can, can't we?" she implored.

"But... but...," Mam spluttered. Then she did what she sometimes did when she was at a loss for words. She scolded. Clicking the gas burner lower, a bit more forcefully than was absolutely necessary, she said angrily, "Now see, Mandy, you made me burn these eggs. Lizzie, don't just stand there doing nothing. Get the juice poured. There's no jelly on the table."

The subject was closed until Dat had finished his breakfast. Then Mam brought it into the open, abruptly and unexpectedly.

"Mandy says John wants to marry her in March."

Dat's eyes flew open as he stared at Mam.

"This coming March?" he asked.

Mandy nodded eagerly, fairly bouncing on her chair. "Yes! This March, Dat. He's—we're—getting a herd of cows in April, and he thinks it's wiser, smarter, or whatever to be married in the spring so I can help on the farm."

"Will the preachers agree to it, even?" Mam asked.

"Well, I don't know why not. It's done sometimes, although rarely. It's not really forbidden; it's just different." Dat sat back in his chair, adjusted his suspenders, and smiled a watery smile at Mandy. "So I guess if we have to get rid of you, we may as well do it in March as wait until November. It's all right with me."

Mam turned a very light shade of green, Lizzie thought, as reality sank into her head. This was the middle of January, and that meant eight weeks at the most to prepare for the wedding.

Mam threw up her hands. "Oh, dear!" she said, resignedly.

Lizzie gazed unseeingly at her dish of cereal, her appetite gone. Oh, this was just great. Little Mandy would be getting married before her, making her feel like a spinster, an old maid who just couldn't manage to get married in turn. Why couldn't they wait until fall; then she would get married first, the way it should be. John and his cows! That was nothing but a stupid excuse.

She slapped her spoon down on the tablecloth.

"It's senseless that Mandy gets to get married first, all because of a herd of cows," she snapped. "How unromantic is that? So now our whole peaceful winter is over. Mam's nerves will be on edge, and she'll boss everyone around for the remainder of the season."

"You're just jealous, Lizzie," Mam said. "There's absolutely no reason for you to be so childish. If John and Mandy want to get married in March, they can get married then. There is no shame in that. Actually, it is a very grown-up, sensible thing to do."

Lizzie snorted, but she didn't say anything more.

So over the next eight, very short weeks, Mandy glowed with happiness and anticipation as she un-packed and repacked her ridiculously expensive set of china, caressed her linen tablecloths lovingly, hummed, sang, and whistled. It all amounted to an enormous housefly in Lizzie's soup of life. She tried to be generous, happy for Mandy, rejoicing with her, but it wasn't always possible. That's just how Lizzie was. She wanted to marry Stephen, but so far, he hadn't even mentioned getting married. All he talked about was hunting or ice fishing or the boat he would like to buy, and it made her nervous, won-dering if he was not going to ask her to get married until they were old.

Lizzie threw herself into her teaching duties as a way of dealing with the maddening pace at home. The school was full of excitement as they planned a Valentine's Day party. The pupils' eyes shone with anticipation, little beacons of happiness on a dull winter day. They would have cookies and candy and punch, the children decided. The students would each bring a covered dish instead of their usual bor-ing lunchboxes.

Macaroni and cheese would stay hot on the back of the stove. Ham sandwiches, applesauce, carrots and dip, and chocolate pudding rounded out the Valentine's Day menu. Lizzie would supply the paper plates and cups and choose all the games.

Lizzie sat at her desk while the children planned, writing notes to the mothers explaining what their children should bring for the party. The pupils each folded Lizzie's notes and stored them carefully in their lunchboxes.

Valentine's Day was such a big event in the one-room schoolhouse, even if the upper-grade boys pretended to hate it. Many mothers bought Valentines at the K-Mart in town, although some of the more conservative mothers sent homemade cards with their children, deeming the store-bought ones too worldly.

So in the middle of gray February, the school was filled with a festive air as the students took a break from studying to decorate the classroom for the party. The children attached red paper hearts to the windows with double-sided Scotch tape. They stretched chains of pink and red construction paper from each corner to the middle of the room. Red balloons dangled in great clumps above Lizzie's desk.

Little first-graders squealed and clapped their hands, jumping up and down. They spilled their chocolate milk out of their lunchboxes, and chased each other until Lizzie had to tap the bell to quiet everyone. Planning a Valentine's Day party was as much chaos as the party itself, but Lizzie loved every minute of it.

The week before Valentine's Day, Lizzie sat at her desk and frowned at the upper-grade boys near the back of the room. All day four boys had huddled together at Levi Lapp's desk, whispering. Lizzie got up to help the first-graders write their math problems on the blackboard. As she was correcting one of Anna Miller's sums, she heard an almost inaudible giggle, but a giggle nevertheless.

She slowed her writing, every muscle tensed. Yes, there it was again. She whirled, just as Levi quickly opened his desktop and shoved something inside. The remaining three boys bent studiously over their desks, the picture of demure, engaged scholars working on their English.

"All right," Lizzie said loudly.

Four pairs of innocent eyes stared back at her. The classroom became very, very quiet.

"Levi, what did you just place in your desk?" she asked quite firmly.

In the silence that followed, little Rachel Esh picked nervously at her apron, dropping her English book.

"First grade, you may return to your seats."

They sat down quickly, turning to watch the big boys.

"What is it?" she asked, in a voice she hoped was authoritative, even scary.

"Nothing," Levi announced, impudently.

Marching back to his desk, she yanked the lid open and bent to peer inside. Levi leaned back nonchalantly. He didn't seem to have a care in the world, which only fueled her anger. The desk was empty inside except for a matchbox.

"What is in the matchbox?"

"Nothing."

The classroom was as quiet as a lull in a storm, and about as threatening. The lower-graders were terrified, their eyes open wide, their faces mirroring the tension.

"Why did you throw it into your desk in a hurry, then? Give it to me."

Levi grinned as he handed it over.

Lizzie grasped the matchbox firmly and slid the cover off without at any hesitation. Nestled inside was the cutest mouse she had ever seen. His beady, little brown eyes stared up at her, unblinking and quite unafraid. It's fur was brown and so neat and shiny. Perfect little ears protruded from its cute, rounded head.

There were chocolate cookie crumbs in a corner of the large matchbox, and unbelievably, a plastic soda bottle lid filled with water, which had spilled a bit when she pulled it out of the desk. Lizzie's eyebrows lowered, but her mouth began to twitch. It was just so charming! What a darling little mouse!

Lizzie wasn't afraid of mice. She could never bring herself to kill one, and she hated mousetraps. It was the cruelest thing anyone had ever invented. How would people like it if a huge steel bar snapped them to their death in such a horrible manner? She always pitied the mice, hoping they could somehow escape the house, avoiding Mam's broom and Dat's trap.

Lizzie knew she should be stern and strict and punish Levi, while warning the other boys about doing something that distracted the whole classroom. But she couldn't bring herself to do it. Didn't the way Levi had fed this little mouse show real responsibility and kindness? He even gave it water to drink.

"Well," she began, and then her mouth just opened into a smile. She gave up.

"Isn't he cute?" she asked.

Instantly there was bedlam in the classroom as children started giggling, holding their hands over their mouths as they laughed. The students in the lower grades rose in their seats for a better view as Lizzie walked down the aisle to show them, amid oh's and ah's of approval. After everyone had properly seen the mouse, she returned it to Levi.

"Now, why don't we keep him as a pet for a little while? He's a fat little country mouse, and I think he would be very happy with plenty of food and some shavings. Does anyone have a small cage?" Immediately a number of hands shot up, and the children bounced in their seats with enthusiasm.

The rest of the day the entire school was upbeat, except for Levi. Lizzie kept him after school for a serious talk about respect.

"You lied to me when you said there was nothing in the box," she said.

"Well, nothing besides the mouse. Plus, I guess, cookie crumbs and water."

"Still, Levi, no matter how you say it, it still really wasn't the truth. Telling lies, even littler white ones, will land us in a heap of trouble if we're not careful."

He looked at his desktop, avoiding her eyes. Lizzie sighed. Levi had a good heart. He was simply drawn to mischief just as a duck or goose is naturally attracted to water. He thrived on paddling around in his own little pond of schemes and pranks like this one. Harmless, perhaps, but disruptive nevertheless.

A certain quality in Levi spoke to Lizzie's own heart. She had been very similar to Levi when she was in school. When she had gotten bored, she could always think of ways to make life more exciting. Then, when she was reprimanded, she was so embarrassed, until she thought of another prank.

The Valentine's Day party went off without a hitch, although Lizzie ate so many cookies that her stomach hurt. Stephen gave her a beautiful Valentine and a huge box of chocolates. Lizzie couldn't help eating just a few, even after all the cookies she had consumed earlier in the day.

Holiday or not, there was no rest at home. As soon as she sat on the sofa to catch her breath and read the comics in the daily paper, either Mam or Mandy asked her to do something like paint the basement.

For one thing, painting the basement was ridiculous. She had just painted it a nice coat of glossy white paint the summer before. But, oh, no! It had to be done again in the middle of the winter. It was the same all over the house and barn. No rest for mind or body.

No one cared what she thought or paid any attention to her. That was why she ended up at the family doctor's office with a huge infected area on the back of her lower leg.

A week earlier, the winter temperatures had risen enough so that rain fell instead of snow. The rain froze immediately that night when the temperatures dipped, covering the drifts of snow with a slick coat of ice. It was the perfect mixture for wonderful sledding on the steep hill behind Lizzie's schoolhouse.

The children careened wildly down the long, steep hill on sheets of plastic, cardboard, and sleds—anything they could cling to as they raced downward. Lizzie allowed the children an entire hour of extra recess, knowing this sledding was a rare opportunity for some exciting thrills.

Lizzie joined in the fun, flying down the hill with her students until one of Lizzie's knee socks slid down, and the back of her leg scraped on the ice during a wild ride across the snow. She didn't notice that she was injured until the children pointed, shrieking, to a large brush burn that ran down the entire back of Lizzie's leg. She looked and gasped, stunned by the deep scrape. The cold had already numbed her leg, and she wasn't in any pain. She limped back to the warmth of the schoolroom, bandaged her leg, rang the bell, and resumed classes.

That evening, Mam fussed and clucked over the size of the scrape, saying it looked more like a burn.

"Soak it in Epsom salt and put Union Salve on it," she said, her usual, never-fail cure for every ache and injury.

"Now just how am I supposed to soak the back of my leg in Epsom salt?" Lizzie asked, a bit upset because Mam wouldn't help her more.

Mandy glared at her, as if to tell her without words what an absolute baby she was.

"Just fill a dishpan almost full and hang your lower leg over it," she said sternly.

So with a great deal of snorting and displays of her foul mood, Lizzie managed to wet the injured area, spread the dark brown salve painfully across it, and slap a paper towel on top, because, as usual, there was no gauze bandage in the bathroom cupboard.

But now it was only a week before the wedding, and her leg still had not healed. At night, she tossed fitfully, the throbbing pain keeping her awake as she resolved not to make a fuss to anyone. She had actually reached the point where she was truly happy for John and Mandy. Her jealousy had finally dispersed like storm clouds on a sunny day. She had wanted desperately to stop feeling so jealous of Mandy and even prayed earnestly about it. Once she really, really wanted to overcome this, she actually had.

Mandy was so sweet, so easy to like, and so in love with her tall, handsome John that she made everyone else happy, too. Little bursts of happiness shone from her green eyes, and Lizzie told her she reminded her of a fairy scattering stardust.

"Oh, Lizzie," Mandy said sincerely. "I want the same thing for you. I hope with all my heart your turn will be in November."

"I'm about 100 percent sure he'll ask me. I mean, why wouldn't he? Look how long we've been dating."

"Sure he will, Lizzie."

"Look at this, Mandy." Lizzie turned the back of her leg to show her the now-infected wound, and Mandy gasped as she peeled off the bandage. It was clearly a bad infection, and at Mandy's yelp, Mam came to see what all the commotion was about. She took one look at Lizzie's leg and immediately bundled her off to see the doctor.

Armed with antibiotics, salve, gauze, cloth tape, hot and cold compresses, and orders to keep her leg elevated, Lizzie returned to the hubbub of preparing for Mandy's wedding.

By the time the relatives came the next week on the *risht-dawg*, the day of preparation for Mandy's wedding, Lizzie's leg felt much better, and she was able to help get the house ready for the big day. There was the usual happy banter as the food was prepared. Lizzie's aunts baked pies, cooked tapioca pudding, washed the celery, and baked bread until the whole house was a regular beehive of activity. In the living room, the men set up rows of benches and tables.

"When Amish people have a wedding, they even wash their barn windows," Lizzie commented.

"Oh, yes, of course. The cow stable is white-washed, and everything that isn't painted gets a fresh coat," her aunt laughed.

"Our cow stable isn't in use anymore, so it didn't get whitewashed, just cleaned," Lizzie laughed.

Joshua and Emma arrived, all smiles and happy to be waiting on the *eck*. The married sisters and brothers of the bride had the special job of waiting on John and Mandy and the other members of the bridal party, or in the Pennsylvania Dutch language, the *nava-sitza*. It was a very important assignment, and Emma's cheeks glowed with anticipation as she laid out the table linens, china, silverware, and all the pretty cut-glass dishes they would use. Mandy was not allowed to see what Emma and the cousins were doing, because it was all a surprise for her when she sat at the corner table the day she was married.

The women cut butter into fancy wedding-bell shapes, covering it carefully with plastic wrap and refrigerating it for the big day. They made special Jell-O dishes, fruit dip, and all kinds of delicious food for the bride and groom.

"What beautiful china!" Emma gasped.

Lizzie was hurrying past with a basket of clothes and turned to smile at her.

"Isn't it? I was so jealous of Mandy's china for so long that it actually cured me. Kind of like getting a severe dose of the measles. Once it's that bad, you're immune to it."

Emma laughed. "Ach, Lizzie, you couldn't be too envious of Mandy. She's too sweet. Your turn will come."

Lizzie smiled as she hurried up the stairs with her basket of clothes. Dear, dear Emma. She had so much plain-down goodness and common sense, such a well-grounded attitude about everything. She never got too much in a tizzy about anything, just took it all in stride matter-of-factly, never questioning God or fretting needlessly.

She probably didn't even think there was anything to feel bad about if Mandy was married first. That was how God intended it, and Lizzie would just have to be patient and wait until Stephen decided to ask her. Mandy and Lizzie had laughed plenty, sitting in their rooms, trying to decide what you could say to your boyfriend to get him to ask you to marry him. But still, there was no getting around it, the ultimate timing, the big question was all up to Stephen, no matter how many broad hints Lizzie threw at him.

She never said too many shameless things, just coyly suggesting the colors she liked for a kitchen or the style of cabinets. Typically, Stephen never answered or mentioned the fact that he liked a certain type of house or anything at all.

The wedding day dawned bright and clear, a perfect late March day. Buses and passenger vans packed the driveway, mixed with teams of horses and buggies, people hurrying and scurrying everywhere.

John's family and friends were all from the Lamton area, so it seemed as if over half of the crowd arrived in vehicles. Lizzie liked John's parents immediately, a nice-looking, friendly couple who were from an old Lamton family, obviously hard-working and very proper with impeccable manners.

Lizzie told Mam they reminded her of the old Southern families she had read about in books. Mam said, yes, they were probably much the same. They were all well-to-do Amish farmers, though, and not plantation owners, although their ancestors, like the Southern families, probably came from a certain circle of people in England or Germany.

Hmm, Lizzie thought. So now Mandy is marrying into the "gentry" from Lamton. Oh, dear. Next thing, I'll just be her common servant, and she'll snap her fingers to have my absolute obedience.

When John and Mandy stood before the minister from Ohio, they looked so sincere and serious, pronouncing their vows with such quiet solemnity, that Lizzie was quite overcome by emotion. Unexpectedly, a huge lump formed in her throat, and quick tears sprang to her eyes at the thought of Mandy's serious step, this embarking together on life's river with John by her side.

John was as handsome as he had been the first day Lizzie saw him. It had taken her a while to accept that John wasn't interested in her, but instead in skinny, big-eyed Mandy. Lizzie glanced over at Stephen who sat straight and still on his bench. Well, things had worked out for the best, just as Mam had said they would.

Still, Lizzie didn't want Mandy to be married. First Emma, now Mandy. The thought of life without sisters, except for her twin sisters, KatieAnn and Susan, who were still too young to be much fun,

was depressing indeed. But this was a day of happiness, of joy and celebration, so Lizzie put aside
all thoughts of losing Mandy to John and his dairy
farm. There was no sense in becoming absolutely
morose on Mandy's special day, so she did her level
best to smile brightly, talking and laughing happily
with all the guests after the service was over.

But once the buses and vans motored out the
drive, and the tired aunts and uncles finished washing dishes and putting benches and chairs away, and
she could finally collapse into bed, she cried great
tears of genuine self-pity. She wallowed in her sad
feelings like a pig in its mudhole, actually enjoying
the fact that she could release her pent-up emotions after spending all day with that artificial smile
pasted on.

She wished with all her heart that Mandy
wouldn't have married so young. Now she'd never
be the same. She'd turn into this proper walking
stick who didn't laugh hilariously and kick Lizzie
out of bed or do other unladylike things that were
so ... so sisterly and had long ago secured a bond
between them that no proper Lamton family could
even touch.

Oh, she could just see it. Now, when she'd go visiting Mandy on the dairy farm, she'd open the door,
her hair combed sleek and smooth, not even a trace
of any stray hairs, her covering ironed to perfection,
and she'd inquire with genuine warmth about her
trip. And Lizzie would stand on her doorstep and
feel like a genuine hillbilly, fat, with her hair going

in every direction and her covering crooked, and say, "Fine, thank you. Isn't it a beautiful day?"

They would never again, not once, throw back their heads and laugh uproariously or go swimming in the creek or drive Billy. Mandy was *married*. A great wave of regret and nostalgia carried Lizzie along until she thought she would just stop breathing with the awful pain in her chest.

And another thing. Stephen hadn't even been very romantic at the supper table. He was having too much fun with Marvin and Aaron, who sat across the table. He was having a great time, laughing and teasing poor Sara Ruth until Lizzie was embarrassed. He could at least act as if he planned to grow up someday and seriously ask her to be his wife.

Well, I'm not going to live here alone without Mandy, she decided. If he doesn't ask me to marry him, I'll have to ask him myself. It had been hard when Emma left home to live in Allen County, but Mandy getting married was even worse.

Why hadn't Stephen tried to give her some special attention and hint about it being her turn to be the next bride? Not a word, not a serious look, nothing.

She punched her pillow, flipped on her side, and groped for the box of Kleenex in her nightstand drawer. Blowing her nose loudly, she wiped her eyes, rolled over, and resumed pitying herself. The next morning, when Mam asked her what was wrong with her eyes, Lizzie glared at her and told her she had eaten too much wedding cake.

Chapter 5

JOHN AND MANDY MOVED 10 MILES AWAY TO their dairy farm soon after they were married. Lizzie went back to school where she was quickly swept up in her teacher's duties again. The easy routine of teaching made it easier for her to accept the fact that Mandy was married and that she had gone to live with John.

It wasn't that she didn't miss her; there was just nothing else to do about it. Life went on as usual, the sun rose and set in the same sky, and Mandy lived under the same sky with the same sun and moon, except now she was 10 miles away. Emma was even farther away, and Lizzie had soon become accustomed to that, so she would survive.

Dat's health seemed fairly stable in the spring. He loved the challenge of building. Mam said that his giving up farming was one of the best things that could have happened. He was always eager to go to work, he was happy while he was there, and he had only minor frustrations, like stumbling occasionally or bouts of blurry vision.

One warm Sunday evening, Stephen and Lizzie decided to sit under the old apple tree in the pasture instead of sitting as they normally did in the living room. The grass was soft and cushiony, so after their walk, they sat side by side in the soft, warm darkness.

Stephen was acting a bit strange, Lizzie thought, having less to say than usual, which really, on ordinary days, was never very much at all. Lizzie tried gamely to keep up a lively conversation, but she didn't get a very positive response from Stephen.

Finally, she could stand it no longer, so she blurted out, "Why don't you have anything to say this weekend? You're much quieter than usual."

Stephen didn't answer until Lizzie became quite uncomfortable.

Then, all he said was, "I'd like to build a house someday."

"A house!" Lizzie squeaked, her heart plummeting to her stomach.

"Yes."

"You mean to sell? Or for yourself, or... I mean, where would you build it? Do you know how to build a house by yourself?"

"Of course. That's what I do."

"Oh, yes. I guess."

There was a soft silence as dogs barked in the distance. Headlights created an arc of light as a car rounded the bend, the kitchen door slammed as someone went out to the front porch, and still

Stephen said nothing.

Lizzie gnawed at the corner of her thumbnail, cleared her throat, sighed, glanced nervously in Stephen's direction, and wondered what was going on. Surely he wasn't contemplating marriage this weekend, as he had been having the time of his life with all of his friends, playing baseball, going on day trips, talking about walking that dreaded—in Lizzie's opinion—Appalachian Trail again. Stephen's first trip had just about ended their relationship, and Lizzie wasn't sure she could handle it if Stephen went hiking for a month again.

And then, oh sickening thought, she wondered if he wanted to end the relationship, to have absolute freedom to go on long trips or just do as he wanted. He had acted like it lately, now that she thought about it.

She held her breath as he reached down and took away her hand.

"Don't do that. You'll chew a hole in your thumb."

There was a space of a few heartbeats as his hand tightened on hers, and he leaned closer.

Then, very softly, he said, "Lizzie, do you think we could build a small house on an acre of your dad's land?"

"W...We?"

"Yes, we."

"I...I don't know. I guess we could ask him sometime."

"No, not sometime. Next week. We have to

know if we want to live in our house this winter."

Lizzie drew a deep breath. "You ... you mean ... ?"

"Would you live in a new little house with me, Lizzie?"

"We'd ... I ... we'd have to get married first?" she breathed.

"Of course. If I asked you tonight, would you marry me?"

"Well, are you asking?"

"Yes."

Lizzie sighed happily, turned to him, and said, "Yes, I will. I will marry you and live in a little house with you."

Stephen laughed happily. "All my hopes and dreams have come true, Lizzie!"

Lizzie, as usual, felt awkward and wasn't sure how to answer. For one thing, she was so happy she had to fight back her tears, and for another thing, the lump in her throat threatened to choke her, so she just sat there and swallowed. She couldn't speak at the moment, although a thousand questions rained in from every direction, wherever thoughts came from. For once in her life, she was absolutely speechless. She wanted to tell him it was a dream come true for her, too, which it was, but to be perfectly honest, she was a bit afraid. How did they know the dream come true would remain a good dream?

So she said, "We'll be very happy, I'm sure."

There was nothing wrong with that, was there? Of course not. Of course they would be very happy together. Maybe not 100 percent of the time. Like all the Amish preachers said, they would have their rainy days and their sunshiny days.

Stephen got to his feet quite suddenly, pulling her up with him. His hands closed firmly around hers, and she felt the difference in him as he placed her hands around his waist. Her own heart beat with his, and it was the most natural feeling she had ever experienced. This beating of two hearts together was as light as a moth and as powerful as a large magnet.

Lizzie raised questioning eyes to him. The lights from the back porch reflected the love in his blue, blue eyes. As naturally as their hearts beating, he slowly bent his head, and their lips met in an honest-to-goodness kiss of love.

It wasn't that the world stood still, the way the books said. But the dark sky, the apple tree, the soft summer night's breeze, disappeared for a very short time. In that moment, there was only Stephen and this all-consuming love she felt for him.

"Lizzie, I love you so much," Stephen said, his voice shaking. "Thank you for promising to be my wife."

"I do love you, too, Stephen," she said.

And she did.

The spoken words, that mutual kiss empowered Lizzie, drowning any doubts or fears she had ever felt. They would stand together, in love, with God at the helm, and even if they stumbled and fell sometimes, he would pick them up.

After a moment, Stephen pulled back.

"You know, Lizzie, I don't have a lot of money. I have very little saved up, but I think if we had a bit of land, we could borrow the money from the bank to build our house."

"Do you really think we can borrow the money?" Lizzie asked. "I mean, how do you know we could even qualify?"

"We probably won't unless we own an acre of land," Stephen answered.

Then he laughed softly. "Here we are, planning our house as if our life depended on it and acting as if our relationship—actually getting married—is of no consequence. Do you think we can get along?"

"Oh, of course," Lizzie said airily. "We don't always agree on everything now, so I'm sure there will be times when we don't agree in the future. And you know me. I can't keep my thoughts and opinions to myself, and I might get a bit loud and judgmental, don't you think?"

Stephen laughed. "Yes, definitely."

"And," Lizzie continued, "you'll just stay quiet and never say what you think but do exactly as you please, no matter if I fuss and carry on like a wild person."

"Not always. Not if I love you as I should," he said soberly.

Lizzie was amazed at that statement. He must have read his Bible about that subject as well, which was very good. Stephen was not the type of person to be verbal about God or what certain passages in the Bible meant. He was taught to keep his faith to himself, as most Amish youth were. They were instructed to live their beliefs and let their lights shine, which was good.

Stephen did not think highly of himself or his opinions, especially when it came to spiritual matters. Lizzie had realized early in their relationship that he was not comfortable with speaking about God. Lizzie had mentioned this to Mam, and Mam said that it was nothing to worry about. That would come in time, as he matured spiritually, which was comforting to Lizzie.

Lizzie clasped her hands, sighing joyously. "Oh, I can hardly believe this! Really, Stephen, are we actually going to live in a new house? How did you know I always wanted a new one? You know I'm not like Emma. She always wanted an old house with old quilts and stuff. I'll even have new kitchen cupboards, won't I? And I'll get to pick out the color of my linoleum, no, not *my* linoleum, *our* linoleum," she said, laughing happily.

So they sat and planned, talking about many different subjects, until Stephen said it was past his usual time to leave.

"You ask your dad about the land, all right?" he concluded.

"No, you come over Wednesday evening, and we'll ask him together," she corrected him.

"You know, it's funny about your dad. I don't know how often I've heard him say he would gladly have all his married children live on the farm, and so far, they've all moved away to farms of their own. I always thought he'd probably be glad to offer us some land. Do you think I'm right?" Stephen asked.

Lizzie laughed. "Oh, you know how Dat is, Stephen. He talks almost as much as I do!"

She helped him hitch up his horse, and as he drove out through the darkness, his lights blinking as they always did, Lizzie thought they blinked a bit faster and brighter than before. She and Stephen were so happy that even the buggy lights felt it, she thought, then told herself to stop being so downright silly.

Wednesday evening Stephen was a bit late, which had Lizzie in an absolute dither. For one thing, she had tried so hard not to talk about the marriage proposal and the acre of land to anyone, but unable to help herself she had confided in Mam the very first thing on Monday morning.

Lizzie thought Mam seemed quite pleased, especially about their plans to build a house somewhere on the farm. So that made Lizzie feel good inside, thinking how happy Mam was to welcome Stephen warmly into the family as a new son-in-law. Of course, she reasoned, Mam and Dat had always approved of Stephen, she was sure of that.

When Stephen finally did turn into the drive, she breathed a sigh of relief. Dat had just finished the barn chores and was sitting on the porch for a minute's rest. He looked questioningly at Lizzie as

Stephen pulled up to the barn door.

"This isn't Saturday evening," he said bluntly.

Lizzie ran lightly down the steps, calling over her shoulder, "I know. He has something he wants to ask you."

"Hello, Stephen," Lizzie said, smiling up at him warmly as he walked toward her.

"Hello, yourself. Did you tell him?"

"No."

She hadn't told him, that was the truth, but she was almost certain Mam had said something to him about it.

"Hi, Stephen," Dat called. "We didn't expect to see you this evening."

Stephen grinned at him.

"How are you feeling?" he asked Dat.

"Oh, I'm fine. I would hardly know I have MS, except my legs don't always want to do what my brain tells them to do. My eyesight is largely improved by the new prescription from the specialist in Warm Springs. He knows what he's doing. It took him two whole hours to thoroughly examine my eyes, and he found some things an ordinary doctor would never have found. I got a new pair of glasses. Almost fell over backward when he told me the price. Three hundred dollars! I almost told him to keep the glasses. That's ridiculous."

He stopped for breath, but before Stephen could get a word in edgewise, he started rambling on again.

That was Dat, Lizzie thought, smiling to herself

as she walked to the porch with Stephen. As long as he had someone who listened without saying much, which Stephen was very good at, Dat would talk.

"You ought to start working with me and Jase. We need a good block layer right now. Are you familiar with masonry?"

Dat barely paused long enough to hear Stephen's "Mm-hmm," before launching into a lively description of a concrete job they were doing.

Stephen sat down next to Dat and listened, nodding his head, or shaking it in disbelief, and laughing at appropriate times. His eyes were crinkled at the sides, and he looked as if he was enjoying the whole conversation, although Dat was doing all the talking.

Jason came up on the porch, greeting Stephen with a quick smile.

"Are you mixed up, Stephen? It isn't Saturday evening," he asked, interrupting Dat.

"I know. I came to ask your dad a question," Stephen said quietly.

"What? What?" Dat was fairly hopping up and down on his lawn chair, if it was possible to hop up and down while still sitting.

Stephen took a deep breath, and Lizzie could tell he was nervous. He wasn't good with words, long speeches, or talking when he felt embarrassed, so she felt a bit sorry for him.

"I guess ... Did Lizzie tell you we want to be married in the fall?" he started.

"No! Really? She didn't tell me!" Dat leaned

forward, slapping his knee. "But do you think a secret like that would survive 10 minutes in this house? Of course, I know. Annie told me."

"Well, anyway," Stephen said, grinning shyly, "we wondered whether you would be able to give us some land if we want to build a house."

"Land? Would I give you land? How much?"

"Oh, just a small plot, enough for a house and barn. Maybe an acre."

"An acre? Oh, of course. We could do that. I don't know how much money you have, but you know if you have an acre of ground, that's enough collateral to be able to acquire a loan to build your house. Did you know that? And if you don't build a very big house, you know not a real big one—you don't really need it the first five years that you're married—you can always add on later, you know."

Stephen nodded.

"And another thing. If you build your house close enough to ours, you won't have to build your barn right away. You can always use our barn to keep your horse in. But then, maybe you wouldn't want that either. Where do you want to build? Surely not down in the flats. If we get another flood like Hurricane Agnes, your whole house would be under water. No, that's not going to work, building your house in the flats."

Stephen nodded.

"You could build your house along the road, there where those three ranch houses were built recently. That would work. The only thing is, it's on top of a hill. Do you mind building your house on a hill? Now me, I always liked a view. To be able to look around and see for miles. That's a good feeling, a real good feeling. If you don't mind living on a hill, I'll give you an acre. Do you want to walk up there and see it?"

Stephen looked at Lizzie, and she nodded her head eagerly.

"All right," he said.

"Let me get my hat," Dat said on his way to the kitchen.

"You sure you're not too tired?" Stephen asked when Dat returned.

"Nah."

Lizzie smiled to herself, thinking how self-assured and confident Dat sounded. He probably felt proud to be able to be Stephen's benefactor, the person who made it possible for them to build a house. He was all excited, waving his arm for emphasis as he talked almost continuously while they walked behind the barn and up over the alfalfa field adjoining the pasture behind it.

"Yes, it spites me not to be able to farm this land anymore, but I guess it's like Annie says. If you're not cut out to be a farmer, you never will be one. I guess that's me. I still can't figure out what happened, but the cows died, we had dry weather, and in no time flat, we were struggling to keep our heads above water. Then I got this MS, and I knew it was time to give it up."

Stephen nodded.

"Another thing. Not farming makes me grateful for my job, too. A farmer never gets done. He just quits in the evening, and the way my legs are now, I can relax in the evening when I come home. Now, here. Right about here."

Dat stopped, waved his arm, and asked, "What do you think?"

They stood in the middle of an alfalfa field on top of a rounded slope that led gently down to the small country road below. There were three new ranch-style houses out farther along this road, but a good distance from where they stood. There was a field across the road, a low one that led to the creek and was filled with small locust trees.

Stephen looked around without saying anything. Lizzie was so thrilled, she was afraid if she said anything at all, it would break this wonderful, too-good-to-be-true feeling of standing on this hill, thinking this would be the exact spot where her new house would be. So she didn't say anything.

"It looks all right," he said finally. That was all. Just that.

So Dat started talking again, waving his arms while Stephen smiled. Lizzie wrapped her arms tightly around herself and took a deep breath, straightening her shoulders as she did so. The sun was setting behind the distant mountain, casting the green hillside in a soft orange glow. Birds twittered in the brush, and a car passed slowly on the road below, the driver honking his horn softly as he waved to someone in the lawn.

How perfect! How absolutely unbelievable! Mam and Dat lived just down over the hill and would always be there for them if they needed them. There were English neighbors to the right of their acre, and their house would be on a hill overlooking a sweeping little woods and fields.

What kind of house would Stephen build? Would they agree on the size, the color, the layout? Well, of course, they would. She was so happy to have a brand-new house of her own, she would let Stephen do exactly as he pleased. Yes, she would. Surely good intentions, coupled with a sense of pure happiness, would be sufficient for her to be a quiet, submissive wife. Lizzie's thoughts swirled around in her head, and she vowed to be everything she should be for Stephen, very much the same as counting a flock of chickens before they are hatched.

Chapter 6

LIZZIE PULLED ON THE REINS, PRESSING HER lips together to make a buzzing sound.

"Come on, Bess, hurry up," she said aloud as she sat alone in the buggy on her way to John and Mandy's farm.

She didn't want to push good, old, faithful Bess too hard, as the morning was already warm, and she still had about half the distance to cover.

She could hardly wait to see dear Mandy again, so the drive down to their farm seemed twice as long as usual.

Route 842 wound across the rolling countryside and past large dairy farms and chicken houses. Some of them were homes where Amish people lived, and when she saw someone at the wash lines hanging out laundry, she smiled and waved.

The cornfields looked richly green with young tender stalks standing about as high as a person. She wondered if there would be sufficient rainfall, since Cameron County land with its deep shale deposits tended to lose its moisture faster than some areas. She hoped sincerely, for John and Mandy's sake especially, that God let lots of rain fall on the cornfields, and the alfalfa fields as well, so their dairy farm could prosper and give them a good start financially.

She was grateful all over again that Stephen was not a farmer. She was afraid she couldn't stand the suspense of not knowing if it would rain enough to grow a decent crop to feed the cows so they could make their farm payment. Wouldn't it just be sickening to stand outside hanging up clothes week after week, while the corn curled its leaves and changed in color from a brilliant, healthy green to an olive-colored dryness, and you knew that was your profit?

She was afraid her nerves would not be able to hold up under such a strain, so it was very good she was marrying Stephen and that Mandy was married to John. Probably she'd snap, almost like losing her mind but not quite, and do a rain dance in the front yard, which would look awfully suspicious. She grinned to herself. She wondered what Mandy would say when she told her about Stephen asking her to marry him and about the new house.

"Come *on*, Bess," she hollered, slapping both reins down hard on the poor, unsuspecting horse's rump. Startled, Bess took a few fast steps, then settled down to her usual slow, steady trot. Lizzie sighed.

She didn't know why Dat didn't let her drive Red, his fiery sorrel gelding. They had a horse named Red when she was a small child, and now Dat owned a horse almost like him and had named him Red. Lizzie begged Dat to let her drive him to Mandy and John's house, but the answer was always the same. Her arms weren't strong enough. No. So here she sat, watching the cornfields and thinking of rain to while away the time, as Bess hung her head straight out like a cow and took her good old time getting there.

Finally, at the bottom of a sloping hill, "Bigler Road" appeared on a flat green road sign, and Lizzie tugged slightly on the left rein. Only a mile anymore, and she would top the familiar little rise before the road sloped down to Mandy and John's farm.

A small, red-brick house was situated under towering maple trees with two barns behind it. John had built the new round-roofed dairy barn next to the old structure, but both were painted red, so the new one looked as if it had always been there, really. There was an implement shed on the left, opposite the house, and various corncribs and other outbuildings here and there.

Lizzie looked appreciatively at Mandy's neatly mown grass and the growth of new petunias arranged neatly around the flower beds. Mandy was a good little worker, she surely was, Lizzie noted happily. That was all the time she had to think anything, because the door of the brick house was flung open and skinny little Mandy appeared, her smile stretched across her face as far as it could go.

"Lizzie!" she yelled in a tone of voice that conveyed gladness and disbelief at the same time.

Lizzie leaned forward as far as she could, as if that would get her there sooner.

"Surprised you, didn't I?" she called, savoring this moment she had been waiting for.

Bess stopped, and Lizzie hopped out of the buggy as Mandy ran to meet her.

"Oh, Lizzie, I'm so-o-o glad to see you. I didn't have real homesickness—not really. I just wished so much one of you would come see me today or tomorrow, because I'm not really busy this week."

Mandy helped her unhitch Bess, chattering happily as they led her to the water trough for a long drink. Barn swallows swooped and chirped about the forebay, as Lizzie looked around at the almost, but not quite, finished barn.

"John still busy?" she inquired.

Mandy was tying Bess in a new box stall, but Lizzie could hear her sigh as she said, "I mean it, Lizzie, he works all the time, constantly, steadily, except to eat his meals."

Together they walked back to the house, and Lizzie admired her neat lawn.

"Of course, you know it was you and me that kept our yard looking nice, so what would you expect?" Mandy said, batting her long, thick eyelashes.

Lizzie slapped her arm playfully.

"*Gros-feelich*, are we?" she laughed.

"Just a little."

After touring Mandy's house, which was small, but filled with new furniture and pretty accessories, Lizzie pronounced it the cutest, homiest farmhouse she had ever seen.

"Do you like it?" Mandy asked, clasping her hands together eagerly.

"Oh, I love it, Mandy. It's so cute, it's almost like a little doll house."

"We're going to need an addition built on if we have children, though."

They settled on Mandy's new sofa facing each other, Mandy with her blue dress smoothed over her pulled-up knees, as she always sat. Her thick, heavy brown hair was smoothed back tightly, like married women wore their hair, which only accentuated her large, heavy-lashed green eyes. Lizzie thought she looked better than ever, with a rosy glow on her cheeks, a picture of health and contentment.

"You look so nice, Mandy. Almost beautiful. Marriage becomes you, I suppose. Are you as happy as you look? Like Emma?"

Mandy smiled genuinely. "Of course, Lizzie. There you go again, asking me a million questions in that worried, eyebrow-tilted expression of yours."

"Well, see, I guarantee you that things can't be absolutely perfect after you get married. How can you move away from Mam and Dat and Jase and never get homesick, never wish you weren't married? Mam told us over and over, there's more to marriage than a happily-ever-after story. And here are you and Emma, acting as if it's the greatest thing that ever happened to you, living on your farms!"

Mandy laughed long and heartily. "What a pessimist!"

"I'm not!"

"Yes, you *are*!"

Lizzie shrugged and then sat straight up, remembering her big news.

"Hey, Mandy, guess what? Just guess!" Lizzie leaned forward, her gray eyes alight as she searched Mandy's face.

"You're getting married!" Mandy said positively, without a doubt.

"How do you know?"

"You told me to guess."

"Well, guess what else."

"You're going to live close to us."

"No!"

"He's building a new house for you!"

"Yes! Oh, Mandy, I mean it. Can you just imagine how excited I'll be? Mam will live just down over the hill from me."

Mandy clasped and unclasped her knees, trying to remain genuinely happy, but like headlights on a car, she had hit the dimmer switch. Lizzie instantly caught on.

"What? What's wrong with that? Huh? Your smile kind of melted to a smaller one."

"No, no, Lizzie. That's just *great* that you'll live

close to Mam in a new house. I'm really, really, genuinely happy for you."

Lizzie watched her with narrowed eyes. "That's not all of it. What is it?"

Mandy picked up a cushion and pulled at a button that was sewn in the middle of its top as if her life depended on it, her head lowered, averting her eyes. Finally, she sighed and looked up, straight into Lizzie's eyes, honestly. "All right, here goes. It's just that, well... nothing."

"Mandy, stop it. If you don't stop that and tell me what's on your mind, I'm going to go home."

"No, don't. Don't. All right. Okay. When we were little girls, and Mam bought us something, like a new scarf—actually, it *was* new scarves that I'm thinking of. You *always* and, Lizzie, I mean *always,* got to pick the best color, then me, then, of course, Emma. These three scarves were bright pink, yellow, and a dull green. Guess who got the pink one?"

"Me. I remember," Lizzie said flatly.

"Okay. See what I mean. You're used to getting what you want, right?"

"No!" Lizzie protested vehemently.

"I'm just saying you've always wanted a new house, and now Stephen is building you one. You never wanted to live far away from Mam, and now you don't have to. Which is good, but just so you aren't... aren't..."

Mandy floundered for the right word, and Lizzie sighed, rolling her eyes.

"Selfish."

"Yes."

Mandy said it evenly and meaningfully, not unkindly, just dropping the word like the colored little pill you drop into warm vinegar water to dye Easter eggs. It was only one little word, but it immediately changed the ordinary water into one brilliant with meaning.

"So you think I'm selfish?" Lizzie asked, her eyebrows drawn low, suspiciously.

"Not always, Lizzie. Just sometimes. I'm afraid you'll be selfish with Stephen. Like expecting him to do everything perfectly and on time, and just ... well, Lizzie, marriage is just not for you to sit on a pretty cushion and expect your husband to keep you happy."

"I know that," Lizzie spat out, thoroughly riled now.

"I'm sure you do."

"Well, I do. I don't care what you say."

"Let's not argue," Mandy said agreeably, gazing unseeingly out the window.

"I'm not arguing, Mandy. I'm not selfish, either. Well, I know what you mean, though. It seems as if I get my own way in lots of things, and that I don't appreciate it enough but just expect more. I'm sure that's the way you see me from your perch on top of the Himalayan Mountains with the rest of the little grizzled men who dish out wisdom to us failures!"

Mandy laughed genuinely, then jumped up and tugged on Lizzie's sleeve.

"Come on, let's eat an early lunch. I'm starving. John isn't home today. He's helping his brother with hay and will eat there. So let's make those huge sandwiches like we used to make on Saturday evenings before church."

They went to the kitchen, finding Swiss cheese, leftover chicken, tomatoes, and mayonnaise, which they slathered thickly on two slices of soft, chewy, homemade bread. Heating the griddle, they slowly toasted them while Mandy poured peppermint tea into two tall glasses, adding ice cubes from the refrigerator.

Mandy told Lizzie that she was indeed very happy, and John was a sweet, kind, and loving husband. But like Mam told Emma before Baby Mark was born, having a baby is more than a woolly pink blanket, so it is with marriage. There were days, of course, when things went wrong, and your husband was not always the way you thought he should be. But when you averaged everything out, she would much rather be married, living right here on the farm, than anything else in all the world. Lizzie took a bite of her sandwich and chewed thoughtfully while she listened. Of course, Mandy was right, just as she almost always was about important matters.

When John came home that afternoon, Mandy begged Lizzie to stay and watch them milk. John agreed laughingly, knowing her dislike of cows and anything that went with them.

So Lizzie tagged along with Mandy while she tied her *dichly*, the little triangular bandana most Amish women wear to do chores or help with farm work. She watched as Mandy went to the milk house and started assembling milkers, looking around at the brand-new interior of the large building.

"Wow!" she breathed. "Classy farmers!"

"You think so?" Mandy asked, pleased at Lizzie's compliment.

"Of course. Our old milk house wasn't even half as nice as this one. Maybe I wouldn't have minded milking so much if our facilities had been better."

She watched as John let the cows in who walked as ungracefully as any other cows, new cow stable or not. Cows didn't change, that was for sure. John worked with deliberate swiftness, if there was such a thing. He didn't seem to move fast; in fact, he hardly moved, and yet, he did everything at once. Mandy went from cow to cow, washing udders, exclaiming over the amount of milk in the milker from one of their best cows. They worked together in complete unison, and Lizzie could tell that Mandy had a genuine interest in the cows' well-being, which in turn made John feel proud to have such a good helper.

Well, Lizzie thought wryly, God sure doesn't make mistakes, does he? As much as I wanted to marry John, I could never be Mandy and love to milk cows the way she does. She doesn't have to pretend one tiny bit. She truly enjoys her work on the farm.

They talked and laughed while they worked, the milkers clicking away in their usual ka-chink, ka-chinking rhythm. It reminded Lizzie of her mornings with Dat, which she never once had felt even a twinge of nostalgia about now that the cows were all gone. Milking cows was just not something she enjoyed, and she probably never would.

John was awfully good-looking, though, in his straw hat and everyday work clothes, and his small dark beard. She told Mandy about her observation after chores were done, and Mandy laughed agreeably.

"Of course, Lizzie, he's the most handsome man in Cameron County, you know."

As Lizzie drove out the driveway to start her long trek home, she looked forward to the time alone, driving Bess. She needed to think. No use looking back, that was one thing sure. Life went rolling along like a gigantic wheel, and all human mortals had to go along, whether they wanted to or not. But did she really want to go back to when Mandy and Emma were still at home, before Joshua and John were part of the family? Probably not really.

She did so look forward to the time when she would live in her own house with Stephen, even if she was worried about marriage sometimes. If there were trials and troubles, everybody got through them. Well, Amish people did anyway. Some English people were divorced, but they were allowed to be, and Amish people weren't. Although when Mam heard of some far-off people who were having marital problems, she would shake her head and say, "They should live apart for awhile." Stephen was quiet, that was one thing, so Lizzie would probably do most of the talking, but that was all right. She did that now, and Stephen listened. He liked to hear her talk.

Oh, there were countless things to look forward to when she got married. Stephen would buy her a set of china, a water pitcher and tumbler set, and silverware in a nice wooden chest. Mam would go furniture-shopping with her. It was all just too good to be really true. Already, Mam was piecing two quilts for her, and one was a yellow and white Dahlia pattern that she would put on her guest bed. If she had one. She didn't know how many bedrooms Stephen was planning on having in the house.

She missed her pupils, thinking back to the last day of school a month earlier. She wasn't sure if she wanted to try and keep on teaching in spite of getting married or not. They had asked her to return in the fall, but she really hadn't decided. The money she made would be nice, but maybe it would all prove to be too stressful with the new house underway and planning her wedding.

Mam was really the one who carried most of the stress when it came to having a wedding. Lizzie often wondered what kept her from popping like a balloon when you blow it up too far; that's how nervous she became about the day before the *risht-dawg*. Oh, well, a lot of Emma and Mandy's wedding-day tensions could have been avoided if they hadn't cared so very much about things like the amount of guests they invited, the menu, or who did what.

It didn't matter a whole lot to Lizzie, because a wedding was just a wedding, and then it was over. Who knew or remembered who was invited and who was not, or what they ate, for that matter. She slapped Bess and told her to hurry up. It was time to get home.

Chapter 7

Stephen spread out the sheet of paper with blue markings all over it. After he turned it the proper way, it resembled a rectangular pattern of sorts, the lines running every which way, outlining walls, doors, and windows.

"There. Hold that corner," he said.

Lizzie held down the one side of the drawing to keep it from rolling up and peered eagerly at the sketch of their house.

"Here's where the front steps go up to a small porch," Stephen explained. "This door goes into the kitchen. You said you wanted the floor plan open— kitchen, dining room, and living room in one, or almost. What do you think?"

Lizzie drew down her eyebrows, concentrating intently on the small squares that were rooms.

"Do that porch and door face the road?"

"Mm-hmm."

"Oh."

Two bedrooms made up the back of the house; the bathroom sat on one side with the basement stairs across from it. An open stairway in the living room divided it from the back bedroom. The dining room and kitchen seemed like one room except for a small wall on each side that separated them, and the living room was off to the left, creating an L-shaped living area.

Lizzie loved the sensible house plan. For a small house, it was very open, the space flowing together in a way that allowed for the maximum amount of light and air on summer days.

"We don't need two bedrooms, though," Lizzie said doubtfully.

"I thought we'd use the one to put my desk and gun cabinet and all my hunting and fishing things in until we need it," Stephen said.

"How many bedrooms are upstairs?"

"Three small ones. It's only a story and a half, you know. The dormers out the front allow for extra space for windows."

"What color is our house going to be?" Lizzie asked eagerly.

"What color do you like?"

"Brown."

"We'll have brick halfway up to the windows, so we'll need to decide what color we like. I like white bricks with brown mortar. I think that will look nice with that brown siding that resembles wood."

Lizzie looked at Stephen. She was incredulous.

White bricks! White! He couldn't be serious. He liked white bricks. She knew in one swift moment that she shouldn't say anything, but she so desperately disliked the idea of ruining her dreamed-about little brown house with white bricks, that she blurted out, "White? I hate white bricks."

Stephen turned to look at her, his eyes narrowing. "You do?"

He was surprised at her outburst, Lizzie could tell. Well, he's just going to have to be surprised, because I won't have my dream house ruined by that strange idea.

Her own will overrode her common sense, even the things Mam had tried to teach her about being submissive. Like a gray storm cloud across the sun, the atmosphere between them became a bit chilled as Stephen cleared his throat.

"Yes, I do. They look like a prison or a doctor's office," she said emphatically, completely sure of herself now that Stephen was wavering.

Her heart sank as she saw Stephen turn to the drawing, his jaw setting as he worked the muscles along his face.

"Well, that's too bad, Lizzie. I happen to like them. The light-colored bricks set against the dark brown mortar look neat."

Lizzie's mouth literally dropped open in disbelief. He was openly disagreeing, without considering her point of view at all! How could he do that? Wasn't he supposed to love her enough so that her every whim would be his command?

She panicked. She didn't want to have white bricks on the house, so she burst out, "Well, then I guess you'll have to live in it alone, because I won't live there if you use white bricks."

"Lizzie!" Stephen said sharply.

She crossed her arms in front of her, leaning back against the chair. Stephen stared at her, and she glared back defiantly. Silence stretched between them like a taut rubber band, ready to snap in either direction.

Stephen sighed.

Lizzie breathed quietly, her heart hammering in her chest. She knew she was hurting his feelings, but she so hated the idea of white bricks that she didn't care how he felt.

He rolled up the drawing, stood up, and said, "Well, I may as well go home then, if we're going to disagree."

"No! No! I don't want you to go," Lizzie said, gazing up at him with eyes that she hoped would melt his heart. Maybe if she whined and begged, even shed a few tears which were very close to the surface anyway, he would give in to her.

"I'd better go. It's getting late. Your parents will think I shouldn't be here anyway, the middle of the week like this."

"Are ... Aren't you going to talk anymore about the ... the bricks?" Lizzie implored him.

"There's no use. Lizzie, I'm a builder, and I know what looks nice. You aren't used to building houses, so how could you understand what I'm talking about?"

That was like throwing kerosene on an already smoldering fire. Lizzie completely lost all sense of right and wrong, of caring whether she hurt his feelings, of anything at all. She was so angry she leaped to her feet, her eyes flashing as she faced him squarely.

"Oh, you! You make me so angry. You don't have to be a builder to know what looks nice and what doesn't. Women have more taste than men, and they always know what looks pretty. Men don't, and you don't either."

All he said was, "I think white bricks would look best," and then walked out to the kitchen, through the door, and out to the barn, while Lizzie fumed and sputtered all by herself.

All right. Let him go. She was not going to go help him with his horse or say good-bye. Good for him if he had to go home like this. She watched, barely breathing, as he backed the horse and buggy out of the forebay and gathered up the reins. Switching on the headlights, he climbed in, and gravel spit against the wheels as he turned to drive out the lane at a fast pace.

He meant what he said! Surely he'd turn around and come back to her. He'd pity her and tell her brown bricks were the best choice just because she thought so, and that he loved her much more than the house, and that she was the light of his life and he would do anything in his power to make her happy. Then she would feel so adored and be so happy in her little brown house that would look exactly as she had always pictured it.

She stayed by the window, watching and peering anxiously into the darkness for a glimpse of the bluish white lights of his headlights as he returned to apologize to her. Crickets chirped steadily, and the night sounds remained exactly the same with no horse's hooves clopping on the road. Sighing, she smoothed back her hair in agitation, chewing on her lower lip as a lump began forming in her throat. Her nostrils burned and quivered, and tears stung her eyes.

Turning, she marched up the steps to her room, determined not to give in to her absolute misery with a display of emotional tears. He was completely out of his rightful place. She had every right to choose the bricks for her house. She was the wife, or soon would be, and who would live in the house the most? She would. He would be away at work over half of the time anyway.

See, that's how Dat was, she thought angrily. If he wanted to move somewhere, he just said he was moving, and it was up to Mam to go along. Men were all alike. *Gros-feelich*. Conceited. How could he think that just because he was a builder, he knew what looked good?

Lizzie fairly snorted as she buttoned her nightgown and turned down the covers of her bed. Climbing in, she pulled them up to her chin and stared wide-eyed at the ceiling.

Dear God, she tried to pray. Please make Stephen see his big mistake.

That didn't work.

Her prayer seemed to bounce against the ceiling and come back down, landing like a great crushing weight on her chest, making her feel worse. She was so miserable that she didn't feel like getting married at all, especially if he was going to be so stubborn about bricks.

She rolled over, punched her pillows, and squeezed her eyes shut. Then, like cold, hard little hailstones, she was accosted by doubts and fears. Her thoughts ran completely rampant, as she lay all alone in the dark with only her own will and anger to keep her company. It was not a peaceful or restful kind of company.

How much were you expected to give up after you were married? Bow before your husband, the king, and say in a quiet, hushed, humble tone, "Oh, of course, Your Majesty, white bricks are beautiful." Stuff all your own wants and desires in a deep recess of your brain, like a garbage bag full of forbidden fruit, stuck away into the darkest corners of the attic?

And so her rebellion raged, fighting off any hope of ever falling asleep. What was best? Living in a house that didn't even come close to what she had imagined and submitting to the will of her husband. Or, like a fiercely determined warrior, sword and shield drawn, hack her way through until he finally relented? Oh, she so wanted to have her little brown house encased in brown bricks with pretty shrubs growing around it, exactly as she had always pictured it.

Maybe her whole life would be easier if she never married but remained single and taught school until she was 70 years old. She could hold Emma's and Mandy's babies and eat all she wanted, because she would not have to worry one tiny bit about her figure if she had no boyfriend or husband. For one thing, she could do exactly as she pleased. If she ever saved enough money from teaching school, which was highly unlikely considering teachers' wages, she would build her own house and use brown bricks. Just like the last little pig in the "Three Little Pigs" nursery rhyme, she thought grimly. The wolf could not get in.

Maybe I'll just break up with Stephen, she thought. Immediately his dark face and long brown hair with blond streaks in it, his blue, blue eyes, and just him, the image of Stephen, appeared in her mind. She knew without a doubt she could never be happy without him. A quiet sob tore at her throat as she buried her face in her pillow and cried great tears, soaking the pillowcase in the process.

Suddenly there was a soft knock on her bedroom door. No, it couldn't be. Nobody knocked on bedroom doors in the Glick household, especially in the middle of the night.

Knock, knock.

Her heart leaped to her throat and cold shivers chased each other up and down her spine. Grabbing her woolly housecoat, she wrapped it tightly around her body, her arms crossed over the front protectively.

"Who is it?" she called weakly, her mouth as dry as if it were full of cotton.

There was no answer, then in the space of a few seconds, a quiet, "Me."

Stephen!

Lizzie drew a sharp breath, and in one rush, she was at the door.

"Stephen!" she gasped, "you're not supposed to be up here."

"I know. Can we talk?"

Placing her hand firmly in his, she crept down the stairs, carrying the kerosene lamp from the bathroom. She set it carefully on the kitchen table and turned to face him with red, swollen, questioning eyes.

"What is it?"

In a gesture of helplessness, Stephen raised his hands beseechingly, then let them fall to his sides.

"I...I'm not real good at expressing my feelings," he said in a quiet tone of voice, "but... well, I got home and just couldn't unhitch my horse. I had no right to be so bullheaded. You know how much I love you, and I want to be able to do anything for you. But I'm self-willed, too, and if I want something, I think that's how it has to be. I'm sorry. That wasn't right."

Lizzie tried to laugh softly, to float lightly over the top of his unaccustomed deep emotion. But her tears were still too close to the surface, and her laugh, when it did emerge, was more like a sob, followed by more dreaded tears.

"It's all right," was all she could manage before she walked across the kitchen to the box of tissues.

Stephen sank into a kitchen chair, then looked at her across the lamplight. "No, it isn't all right. I was being mean to you."

Lizzie wiped her eyes, and this time her low laugh was genuine. "No, Stephen, I was the one being mean. I should have tried to picture the house the way you did. It really is not so significant, either, whether we live in a house made of white or brown bricks."

"Why did we have that senseless disagreement?" Stephen asked.

"Because we're us. You and I are so much alike." Lizzie shook her head, feeling very wise at that moment.

Stephen leaned forward.

"Lizzie, you pick the color for the bricks," he said. "I don't mind either way. Honestly, I don't. I don't know why I acted so sure of myself in the first place."

Lizzie watched his face, his eyes soft with emotion, and thought that if he ever did seem like a king, it was at this moment. She loved him with her whole heart and knew without a trace of doubt that white bricks were going to look absolutely fantastic. Oh, she wanted to be a sweet, submissive wife when he was so unbelievably kind and good.

"So," he finished, "it's up to you."

Clasping her hands in her lap, taking a deep breath of pure happiness, she said, "I think white bricks would look very nice."

Stephen laughed. "You don't."

"Yes, I do. Stephen, when you are so kind, it's easy to want what you want. Don't you think that's very important after we get married? We just have to remember to consider each other's feelings instead of saying outright anything we want."

After a while, Lizzie asked him how he even got up the stairs without waking Mam and Dat.

"You have the creakiest stairs in Cameron County," he grinned. "It took me a long time to get to the top step, believe me."

She laughed. "I'm sure Mam and Dat never heard you."

How different she felt as she hung up her housecoat and climbed into bed. Her prayers were now of thanksgiving and praise. It felt as if God beamed down on the old farmhouse, straight through the ceiling to her heart and soul. How light her heart felt!

Finally, she understood this submission thing, this giving and taking, and it seemed very possible that she would be able to be happy and submissive at the same time. Oh, they would have their flare-ups, their disagreements and sad times, same as all couples who were married, but wasn't it just something? Wasn't it just unbelievable?

She bounced onto her back, patting the covers into place. Imagine! He said he couldn't unhitch his horse until he drove all the way back, he felt so bad because he was mean. He wasn't really being mean, just ... well ... And here she was, thoroughly miserable, unable to sleep because they had parted coldly, without wishing each other well. She felt as if she had been rescued out of a pit of quicksand full of despair, her feet planted now on firm ground while birds and butterflies twittered and darted around her.

A house made of white bricks, filled with love and understanding, with peace and submission, was so much better than one with brown bricks, filled only with her own determination and her lack of love. Maybe she would be as old as the hills before she understood everything or learned to be submissive in all things, but this much she understood. It was easy as pie to submit to a kind, loving husband.

The following morning she hid her smile when Mam said she declared there were some strange creaks in the night. Dat told her when the nights became cool, the aluminum siding on the new part of the house expanded and contracted, causing creaking sounds.

"No," Mam said wisely. "It was the stairs."

When Dat left to go to work, Mam's eyes bored into Lizzie's, and she said, "All right. Out with it. What was going on?"

Lizzie burst into happy laughter, telling Mam everything. Mam's eyes became soft and watery, and her nose turned red as it always did when she became emotional. "Ach my, Lizzie, I would say you're off on the right foot." It was like a large pat on the back, hearing Mam say that.

Chapter 8

LIZZIE UNHOOKED THE BUGGY WINDOW FROM the ceiling and lowered it into place with a decided click. Rubbing her hands across her sweater sleeves, she shivered and said, "Brrr."

Stephen smiled at her.

"I wondered how long you'd keep that window open. This is real hunting-season weather."

Lizzie slapped his arm playfully. "That's all you ever think about."

"Oh, no. Not this fall. I'm thinking about you, then the house, then hunting. See? Hunting is way down on the bottom of the list."

"Don't you ever think about getting married? About the wedding?" Lizzie asked, smiling happily.

Stephen's face became quite sober, and he watched the horse's ears intently. "Yeah, I do."

"You don't sound very thrilled about it."

"Oh, I am, Lizzie. You know I am. It's just that I'll be glad when the actual wedding day is over. I don't like crowds of people all packed together in one house, even if it's our wedding. I mean, I don't want to make it sound as if I don't want to marry you. I just wish there wouldn't have to be quite so many people there."

Lizzie patted his arm reassuringly. "I know, Stephen. I know very well how you dislike crowds of people. I'm just the opposite, aren't I?"

Stephen nodded quietly.

"I'll just love all the attention, the relatives, the gifts, the food! Actually, I can hardly wait for our wedding day."

The horse picked up speed without being urged when it spotted another buggy on the road ahead of them. Horses did that, Lizzie thought. They could be clopping along, a bit bored, and suddenly, their ears would prick up when they spied another team ahead of them. Instantly, their ears turned forward, and they surged ahead, no longer content to amble along by themselves. Stephen pulled back slightly as his horse lunged into his collar, racing toward the other team.

They were on their way to Ben King's house to a supper for the youth. It was one of the farthest places they had to travel in their district. Stephen had let his horse walk up a few of the steepest hills to save his strength for the miles ahead. At the rate the horse was traveling now, it certainly looked as if he had conserved more than enough energy.

The gap between the two teams narrowed until Lizzie could see someone waving and a face in the mirror peering back at her. "Rebecca," Lizzie laughed. "The only person who waves like that!"

Stephen grinned.

Rebecca was Stephen's sister, as well as Lizzie's closest friend now that Mandy and Emma were both married. She had a great sense of humor with an endearing manner that made her easy to talk to and so much fun to be with, Lizzie thought.

Rebecca had been dating Reuben after they had gone on a camping trip together with Lizzie, Stephen, and other friends. Now they were making their own plans for their wedding. Lizzie's Uncle Marvin and Sara Ruth, as well as her friends, Amos and Sally, were also planning their weddings in November or December. This would be one of the last youth gatherings that Stephen and Lizzie would attend since most of the group was getting married.

They reached a steep hill that wound through a wooded ridge, so both horses slowed to a walk. Lizzie gasped as Rebecca hopped lightly out of Reuben's buggy while it was still moving and stood in the middle of the road, grinning at Lizzie.

Lizzie slid back the door of Stephen's buggy.

"What are you doing, jumping out of the buggy like that?" she asked.

"I'm tired of sitting. Jump down. Let's walk the rest of the way."

Glancing questioningly at Stephen, who was busy keeping his horse from balking on the hill, she hopped out of the buggy, almost stumbling before she stood beside Rebecca.

"Hi!"

"Hi!"

They both burst out laughing for no reason at all.

"Rebecca, you know what? We shouldn't be quite so silly anymore. We're both getting married soon. Can you imagine? We'll be old married ladies, sitting at our quilts, sighing about our arthritis way too soon!" Lizzie laughed.

"Just because we're getting married doesn't mean we can't laugh," Rebecca cried.

Lizzie caught her breath, grabbing her side. "Don't walk so fast. I have side stitches."

"What are they?"

"Not so fast!"

Quite suddenly, Rebecca headed straight for the leafy bank and sat down so fast that little puffs of dust rolled from under her skirt and leaves whirled away with the dust. "Okay then, we'll sit."

Lizzie plopped down beside Rebecca, gasping. "I don't know how you can walk up a hill that fast and keep talking at the same time," Lizzie said wryly.

"That's because I'm skinny," Rebecca announced.

"Do you think I'm fat, Rebecca? Seriously, tell me honestly, am I too fat to be getting married? Would you go on a diet if you were me? Huh? Tell me."

"Well... let me see. Hmmm." Rebecca leaned back, eyeing Lizzie carefully. "Yes, you're fat."

Lizzie pinched her hard on her upper arm. "Stop it."

"Well, you are."

"What?"

"Fat."

"I'm not! Do you think so, for real?"

"Yes, you're fat."

They both doubled over with laughter before Rebecca wiped her eyes and said, "You're not skinny. You're a bit heavy, but Stephen likes you like that, so I would never, not even once, worry about it."

"Did he ever tell you he likes me a…a…bit heavy?"

"No, but I know he does. He likes you."

"I would hope so. We're getting *married*, Rebecca."

"We are, too."

"Do you want to?"

"What?"

"Get married?"

"Why do you ask such a silly question? Of course."

Lizzie smiled, but the smile kind of slid downward into a soft sigh, like an ice cream cone that was melting in the hot sun.

"Don't you ever wonder if you're doing the right thing? I mean, what if…after a couple gets married they suddenly decide they really don't like each other all that well, and they're Amish and can't get a divorce and are miserably unhappy all the rest of their lives."

"O…o-oh, Lizzie. You think of the dumbest things."

"Do you know of one couple, just one Amish couple that that happened to?" Lizzie asked, peering anxiously into Rebecca's face.

Their conversation was brought to an abrupt end by the appearance of two teams coming up over the hill. The first one was Marvin and Sara Ruth, followed by Amos and Sally.

"Jump out!" Rebecca shouted, gesturing to the approaching women to join them. Both women leaped nimbly out of their buggies as Marvin and Amos waved and said hello before moving on up the hill to follow Stephen and Reuben.

Sara Ruth and Sally were both small and blond. They were each only a bit over five feet tall, weighing slightly more than a hundred pounds. Lizzie always envied their slim figures, looking so little and girlish, so light-haired and dainty. But she guessed not everyone could be so perfect.

After saying hello, Sara Ruth felt the sleeve of Rebecca's dress. "Is it new?" she asked.

"Yes, I made a few new dresses for the weddings this fall. We'll all be going in with the 'young married ones,' so we have to look nice and neat and a bit plainer, you know. Comb our hair flat."

They all laughed at Rebecca, but each one knew what she meant. The "young marrieds" were the couples who were engaged. They got special treatment at each wedding. They were seated first among the youth, which was always an honor. Even if you weren't married yet, only engaged, you were still seated first. These girls combed their hair more demurely, like the married women, and looked very mature and ladylike, Lizzie always thought.

She tried to savor every moment here on the leaf-strewn, wooded hillside, chattering as only young women can. This was almost their last time together at the youth's supper, and it all took on a surreal quality as Lizzie listened to Sally and Rebecca, smiling to herself as she tore a brittle leaf into many pieces.

It was a bit sad to think that there would be no more weekends of running around with her friends. Not really sad, just nostalgic maybe, kind of wishing you could go back and be 16 all over again. Would there ever be another time in her life quite as exciting as going to Allen County with Emma that very first weekend just after Lizzie turned 16? Probably from here on until she died, nothing would even come close to it. She would just grow old and fat—fatter, according to Rebecca—and have a whole houseful of children with runny noses and bottles dripping milk all over the floor. In a brown house with white bricks, instead of a brown house with brown bricks.

Suddenly she wanted to never, ever get married. Like a dark cloud hiding the sunlight, all of her happy anticipation disappeared. She pulled up her knees, stretching the blue fabric of her dress tightly around them, resting her chin on her folded legs.

Rebecca stopped talking and looked at Lizzie. "You're being very quiet."

"Don't worry about it."

"Grouch!"

Lizzie smiled.

The other girls chattered on, Sara Ruth giving them a vivid account of sewing her own wedding dress. They talked about how nervous they were about their actual weddings when they would stand facing the minister in front of hundreds of pairs of eyes.

"Mary Ann is lucky!" Lizzie said finally.

"Why?" Sally asked.

"Because she's been married for almost a year, living in her cozy new home in Lamton, and all this nerve-racking stuff is behind her."

"You think getting married is nerve-racking?"

"Well, kind of. In a way."

The truth was that while Lizzie looked forward to all of the food and attention on her wedding day, she also got very nervous whenever she thought about it. Would Stephen know how to do everything right? She remembered Joshua and Emma, and also John and Mandy, practicing the day before their wedding, each turning the proper way so that the groom never turned his back to his bride. Things like that. She knew Stephen was completely ill at ease in a crowd, so the whole wedding day was something that gave her a severe case of butterflies in her stomach.

"Oh, it won't be so bad when the time comes," Rebecca comforted her.

"Come on, let's go. It's almost time to eat," Sara Ruth said.

So they walked the remainder of the way up the wooded hillside, the four of them in their bright dresses making a colorful scene against the back-drop of green leaves. As they neared Ben and Lydia King's home, they all remarked over Lydia's perfect flower beds and garden.

"She even has cabbage and lettuce that looks absolutely healthy!" Rebecca said excitedly.

"What's so thrilling about that?" Lizzie wanted to know.

"Oh, a lot. We're moving onto a produce farm, you know, so I'll be busy helping Reuben with all kinds of vegetables and things. Imagine! We'll have about a hundred times the amount of this garden."

Lizzie looked at Rebecca closely. Sure enough, the enthusiasm shining from her pretty blue eyes was genuine. Unbelievably, she did look forward to all that work.

Lizzie shook her head incredulously. "Rebecca, I can't believe you. How can you look forward to toiling in a huge garden every day?"

Rebecca stopped and stared at Lizzie. Then she spread her hands wide and laughed. "See, Lizzie, you just don't get it. Not everyone is alike. Look at Mandy, way down the 842 on her dairy farm. Is she happy? Huh? Is she?"

Lizzie burst out laughing. "Stop it, smarty."

"Well, just because you don't like cows and get depressed thinking about growing produce doesn't mean Mandy and I do, too. We're just not all alike."

All the girls burst out laughing. It was just Rebecca's way, turning an ordinary sentence into a statement.

Lizzie slipped her arm through Rebecca's and squeezed her hand. "All right, I understand. Stop acting like Mandy."

Rebecca grinned at her, and Lizzie's heart swelled with love for her true friend, because that's what she was. Stephen's sister or not, she would always be a special friend, one whom she hoped to remain friends with all the days of their lives.

That evening on the way home from the hymn-singing, Lizzie felt so much love and gratitude for having Stephen in her life. He was not a dairyman or a produce farmer, and he was building a new house for her, albeit with the white bricks he had chosen. She sighed happily, thinking how perfect he was for her.

"Tired?" Stephen asked.

"No, just happy. Stephen, I'm so glad you're not a dairy farmer or a produce farmer, I mean, a person who grows vegetables on one huge acre after another. I don't think I would marry you if you were. Can you imagine Reuben and Rebecca?" she asked.

"Sure, I can imagine Rebecca. She loves to garden."

Lizzie slipped her arm into his and said softly, "But, oh, Stephen, I'm so glad you're a carpenter."

They rode together in silence for a short time before he asked her if that was the only reason she had agreed to marry him.

"Of course not, Stephen. There are many other reasons. But you know as well as I do that I could never look forward to slaving in a produce field or milking cows. I would give up to it if I had to, but I probably wouldn't be very happy, at least sometimes."

Stephen laughed wryly. "Likely not. Giving in is not one of your strong points."

"Ouch!" Lizzie said, smiling.

"That's all right. I will probably like a wife with a little spunk."

Lizzie smiled to herself. Stephen was so right for her. She wondered what had taken her so long to see it. Life was amazing, or rather, God was amazing, the way he worked things out. Even if you resisted his will at first, he just did what was best for you until you were ready.

Like knowing Stephen was the one for her. How could she have known if he hadn't gone away for a while? And how did he know she had to have that time without him? Probably God, same as always. He put in people's heads things that were right until his perfect will was made manifest, like the Bible said.

"Stephen, you know what, though? Sometimes we so barely manage to find the Lord's will. You know? Kind of like a needle in a haystack? If you keep searching and want to find it with all your heart, you will. Right?"

"Sometimes you know where it is, you feel deep down that you found it, and then, you can't have it," Stephen said very quietly.

A slow smile spread across Lizzie's face. "You mean me, don't you?"

"Yes, I mean you. Although you're a lot bigger than a needle in a haystack."

Lizzie laughed.

Chapter 9

A FEW WEEKS LATER, ALL THE BUILDING permits had passed through the network of township ordinances, the bank had obligingly loaned Stephen and Lizzie the amount they needed for Stephen to get started on the house, and the bulldozer was scheduled to arrive.

Dat was fairly dancing with excitement. Mam said she declared he was getting better, MS or not. His mind was fully occupied with Stephen and Lizzie building a new house on the acre of ground Dat and Mam had given them. It was still a one-way street when Dat and Stephen were together, Dat doing all the talking, or rather, the greater portion by far, and Stephen quietly deciding things his way without much ado.

Mam said she was afraid Dat was a bit pushy, shoving all his own ideas on Stephen, but Lizzie assured her that Stephen could take care of himself. He just didn't say much, then went ahead and did exactly what he wanted to do in the first place.

When Lizzie stood on the hillside and watched the huge bulldozer backing down off the trailer that had transported it, she put both hands to her mouth to hide her excitement. KatieAnn and Susan were with her, their eyes big with awe around this noisy, rattling monster.

Stephen and Dat walked over to them and grinned.

"Think he can dig your basement?" Dat asked.

"He's certainly big and noisy enough!" Lizzie yelled above the clanking and chugging of the big machine.

The driver waved down at them, pulling levers and working pedals as he turned the bulldozer toward the four wooden stakes with plastic orange streamers tied to them, outlining where the house would be built. And then, just like a gigantic spoon over a dish of hard, frozen ice cream, he scooped up a layer of sod and set it aside.

Lizzie felt a bit sad for the poor warped little alfalfa plants which were taken from all the rest of the alfalfa plants on the hillside and cast aside by the bulldozer to die. It didn't seem right. The little plants had to sacrifice their lives so she could live in her house on the hill. Sorry, little alfalfa, but you'd have to withstand the winter winds anyway, and then only to be cut and dried and eaten by a cow, she thought.

The huge yellow machine kept chewing and scraping at the alfalfa-covered hillside until a decided hole appeared, which swallowed up parts of the bulldozer as the driver dug away, or so it seemed.

Stephen stood and watched, his blue eyes alight, as Dat kept walking here and there, swinging his shovel and talking fast and loud whenever he passed by Stephen. Stephen smiled at Lizzie over Dat's head, and she burst into laughter of pure joy. That was Dat! That was just how he was.

"I'm cold!" KatieAnn said, grasping Lizzie's hand tightly as she burrowed her head into her sweater.

"Are you?" Lizzie asked, glancing at the twins, surprised to find their noses red with the brisk wind.

"Okay, come on. We'll go down to Mam. This is long enough now. We know what he'll be doing the rest of the day, right?"

Susan nodded, and turning, Lizzie walked briskly down the hill, the twins hopping and skipping along on either side, clinging to her hands.

They burst through the kitchen door. Mam stood at the stove, stirring something that smelled wonderful, the steam enveloping her face. She stepped back, lifting the spoon and knocking it against the rim of the kettle before smiling at them.

"Cold, isn't it?" she said.

"Mam, you should see the big hole he's digging..." Susan shouted.

"With his big yellow digging machine!" KatieAnn finished.

Mam gasped in mock excitement, her eyes opening wide. "Really?" she asked.

"Mm-hmm."

"Stephen and Lizzie's house!" KatieAnn exclaimed.

Lizzie sat down at the kitchen table, eyeing Mam eagerly. "Mam, how long—usually how long, anyway—does it take to finish a house? I mean from the time the bulldozer starts digging until we can move in?"

"Ach my, Lizzie, I forget. We only built one house, and I can't remember the actual time it took. But, my goodness, you're not married yet, you know. You still need to have a wedding and buy your furniture and lots of other things."

"But I want time to go faster. Mam, do we have to live at home here with all of you in this house all winter? Why is that an Amish custom? Stephen doesn't say anything, but I guarantee he doesn't want to do that. Why do we have to?"

Lizzie got up and lifted the lid from the kettle, taking a deep sniff of the bubbling contents. "Mmmm!"

"Chicken and dumplings," Mam said. Then she sighed and said, "Ach, I don't know why either. It's not done that way where I come from. In Ohio, the custom is to move right after the wedding, and you don't have to run all over the creation 'young married visiting' either. Whoever thought up that scheme must have wanted an extension to the wedding. Same as Easter Monday."

"Now, Mam!" Lizzie chided.

"I know. You can't change an old chicken, can you?"

"'You can't teach an old dog new tricks' is the actual saying."

"I'm not old. It's just hard for me to conform sometimes. Guess I'm too thick-headed, as Melvin would say."

She got up and headed for the stove, taking up the wooden spoon. She peered closely through the steam and held it lightly over the dumplings. Lizzie knew exactly what she was doing. She would insert the spoon into a dumpling to test the middle of it, and when it was light and fluffy the whole way through, it was done. Mam made the best chicken and dumplings in the world. Not that Lizzie had ever traveled very far to taste many other varieties, but she knew Mam's were just delicious.

A week later, the footer for the house was poured and the first concrete blocks laid. Dat and Jason, as well as Stephen's father and brothers, helped Stephen with the construction. Stephen's dad was a thin man, about Dat's age, who owned a farm and raised lots of pigs. He enjoyed farming, working hard from sunup to sundown as most dedicated farmers do.

Stephen's two brothers, Daniel and Henry, were a merry twosome, especially Henry who was always laughing about something. Dat said when Stephen's brothers were both there, it was almost less help than if there were only a few people working, because they were always distracting everyone with their stories.

Lizzie discovered she had one huge problem, which quickly ballooned quite out of proportion. Her eyebrows were drawn up in the middle, which is what happens if frustration is allowed to rule your face, she thought. She wished it wouldn't take so long to lay the block basement walls. Every time she walked up to the top of the hill, the brothers were either sitting somewhere talking, or Henry was throwing mortar at Stephen, which caused Lizzie's eyebrows to shoot straight up.

At the rate they were going, they wouldn't move into that longed-for house until next summer. With all the stress of the upcoming wedding and no furniture, or hardly any yet, this was ridiculous. How could Stephen be up here on the hill acting like a 12-year-old with his brothers?

So she became increasingly irritable, trying to keep her lack of patience from showing, especially when she was around Stephen. She tried to keep her eyebrows straight, which was an awful job, giving her a constant headache. She had to think continually or remember to flatten them, pasting a make-believe smile on her face when Stephen was near. Lizzie's impatience turned the much-anticipated time of building their house into a long, weary ordeal.

Lizzie's undoing came that Friday evening when they were sitting on the hillside, Stephen covered with dirt and mortar, his eyes tired. He took off his hat and ran his dirt-covered fingers through his hair, sighing wearily.

"Guess I'll take tomorrow off and go squirrel-hunting with Daniel," he said, replacing his hat and turning to look at her.

Lizzie was caught totally off guard. Her eyebrows shot straight up as an alarming note crept into her voice. "Why?" she squeaked, determined not to become hysterical.

"Why? Because I'm tired, Lizzie. I work during the day, go to the livestock auction on Tuesday evenings, and then work some more, besides spending every spare moment over here building the house. So don't ask why," he said flatly, a bit irritably even.

Lizzie knew instinctively what to say. Of course, he worked too hard and was tired. He deserved at least one Saturday off to go squirrel-hunting. But her impatience had taken over her life, and like a bird flying out of its cage, and Lizzie making only a half-hearted attempt at catching it, she turned to look at him

"Aren't you worried one bit about getting this house finished? At the rate you and your brothers are going, we won't live in it until next summer," she said.

The look in Stephen's eyes drove home the fact that she had said something awful. It was a lot worse than letting Mam's parakeet out of a cage; it was more like throwing some precious item into a deep, swiftly-moving river where it could never be retrieved. She knew her words had done a lot of damage, and she could not bring them back. They were out. Said. Done.

"You think I'm not working fast enough?" he asked, disbelief in his eyes. "Well, if you're going to act like a regular taskmaster, then I'm going hunting for sure."

Lizzie sat up straight, fuming. She didn't care if she had said something to hurt him now. He was being ignorant. Throwing all caution to the wind, she burst out, "Oh, go ahead. If you think I'm so difficult, maybe you'd better not marry me at all."

Stephen snorted. He actually snorted, and it was not a nice snort.

"As tired as I am, maybe I won't."

"Fine."

Stephen turned and headed down the hill in the gathering darkness with short, swift strides, so that Lizzie knew he was very angry. Quickly she got up and followed him, hurrying, knowing she had to make this right. He had only told her innocently that he was going squirrel-hunting. He had not intended to get into an argument. It was all her fault, all her own stupid fault, because she had no patience.

Catching up, she caught his arm, but he shook her off.

"Stephen!" she cried.

He walked straight ahead, down to the drive and into the forebay of the barn. There was nothing for Lizzie to do but stand there like some senseless person and watch him go.

"Oh, dear. Oh, dear," she said out loud to no one

in particular except herself. "He is really mad."

That thought spurred her into action, and she ran after him, stumbling on some rocks at the bottom of the hill. Before she reached the barn, she slowed to a steady walk so that he wouldn't think she was really racing after him. She had her pride, after all, and he was not going to see how worried she was.

He was placing the bit in his horse's mouth when she sauntered into the barn. She put her hands behind her back and cleared her throat for attention. Stephen said nothing, just fastened the chin strap on the bridle as if his life depended on it. Turning to walk past her, he never slowed or looked at her, so she had no choice but to step out of his way.

Turning, she held the shafts for him while he backed his horse between them. She helped him hitch up, fastening the proper straps to the proper hookups. She watched in disbelief as Stephen climbed into the buggy and without as much as a "Good-night" or his usual "See-ya," he was gone.

They had just argued like this before about the white bricks! A giant wave of despair washed over her until she felt tumbled about, soaked, drowned in the maelstrom of feelings that encircled her heart. She wasn't fit to become his wife. Well, he wasn't acting very mature either. Big baby!

Turning on her heel, she marched across the gravel driveway and up the steps, yanking open the kitchen door before throwing herself into a chair. Jason looked up from the magazine he was reading.

"What gives?" he asked.

"O ... o ... h, that *Stephen*!" Lizzie said, two red spots in her cheeks showing her anger.

"Why?"

"He plumb went home without saying good-bye or good night because he's all upset about me saying something or other about him going squirrel-hunting. Can you imagine? He's going squirrel-hunting, and those concrete blocks will never, ever be finished. Does he care? Oh, no. Not as long as his silly brothers are around."

Lizzie looked up to see Mam in the doorway, her thin white scarf tied around her head, wearing her old light blue housecoat, smelling as she always did of soft, flowery talcum powder. Mam smiled a very small smile and shook her head ruefully. Turning to sit in the chair opposite Lizzie, she looked straight into her eyes until Lizzie flinched, dropping hers.

"What did you say to make him mad?" she asked softly.

"Nothing!"

"Yes, you did."

"Just that ... well, how can he go squirrel-hunting when the house isn't coming along as fast as it should? He doesn't even *care*!" she burst out.

"Boy, Lizzie!" Jason said loudly. "Big baby. I wouldn't marry you if I were him. Can't you see how hard he works? I mean, he looks almost haggard. He sleeps so little from working two jobs besides trying to get this house built."

"Jason's right," Mam said, softly and not unkindly.

"So you're both on his side?" Lizzie burst out.

"Now you listen to me, Lizzie. I saw your eyebrows go steadily higher all week, and I figured it would come to this. You're going to have to learn to give up if things don't go exactly as you plan. I know I can talk about it until I'm blue in the face, but you're going to have to learn the hard way if you don't listen to me. Stephen is doing more than enough, and to have you nagging at him about hurrying with this house is simply not going to work. You're going to find out after you're married, mark my words."

"It takes a long time to build a house, Lizzie," Jason said.

"I know that. I do. I guess I'm just panicking."

"Now, if Stephen said he wanted to take you shopping for your china and silverware on Saturday, would you have said 'no, the house is being built too slowly'?" Mam asked wisely.

"Of course not."

"See, it's called being selfish, Lizzie. How can we enter marriage and figure it's going to work as long as we hang on to our own selfishness? Never wanting Stephen to go out and do something fun, because you think he should stay home and please his little princess."

"Stop it, Mam. You're being mean."

"No, I'm not being mean. I'm being truthful."

Jason got up and stretched, running his fingers through his mop of curly hair, yawning. "I'm not going to get married for a long, long time. Girls are a big bother."

Lizzie said nothing as he slapped her arm playfully, peering closely into her face, saying in a high,
singsong voice, "Good night, sweetheart!"

Lizzie punched his arm and laughed in spite of
herself. "You better fix that hair of yours before you
ask anyone for a date," she teased.

Mam sat quietly after Jason went upstairs. The
clock ticked steadily as a warm, companionable silence settled over the two of them. Lizzie caught a
soft whiff of Mam's talcum powder and was instantly
transported back in time when she was a very worried little girl, checking on her kitten, Snowball, in
the middle of the night, certain that she was hungry
or scared. Then Mam had smelled the same, a warm,
comforting, clean Mam smell that never ceased to
make Lizzie feel loved and comforted, secure and
safe in the middle of a very uncertain world.

"Mam, am I going to make a decent wife for Stephen, if I have all this impatience and—what do you
call it—'Wanting what I want and wanting it right
now'?"

"Why, of course, Lizzie. I don't doubt for one
moment that you and he are meant for each other.
I always felt that way. He's the perfect one for you.
You're not going to walk all over him. You might
not have the easiest road, which, for some reason,
we mothers want for our girls. I mean, we've had
some tough times, your dad and I. Yet I think that
each daughter, as she gets married, will have this
perfect little love story and live happily ever after,
when I know real life just isn't that way. We struggle;

all of us do."

"Well, if it's so tough, why bother getting married in the first place?" Lizzie asked, a bit wearily.

"It isn't tough. It's what we make of it. Getting along with a brand-new husband is the first serious step in putting all that love and romance to the test. We *think* it's all roses, and we're so in love. But just wait until he does something, like now, squirrel-hunting, that you think is absolutely unnecessary. So what do you do? You tell him, and probably not in a very peaceful or kind tone of voice."

"Whatever is a 'peaceful voice'?" Lizzie snorted.

"Not exactly 'peaceful.' More like a 'peace-making,' understanding tone of voice. I do it too, Lizzie. You're not alone in this. I hurt Dat's feelings at times by being critical or unsubmissive. But once we learn, and often, actually, by trial and error, we see that our unkindness is often what starts an argument in the first place."

"That's quite a speech, Mam, and it comes dangerously close to that dreaded king and his humble servant theory."

Mam laughed deeply and genuinely. "Yes, I guess it does, Lizzie, but at least it brings a lasting kind of happiness. The kind of happiness where you start singing in the middle of doing something you don't even want to do, not knowing or understanding why. You're just happy. That comes from doing God's will, which is more often than any of us care to admit, from submitting to our husbands."

"Who are out traipsing around in the woods

shooting squirrels while the house is on hold?" Lizzie asked.

"Exactly."

"Hmmph."

"Well, if you don't believe me, try fighting against Stephen and everything he does, and see how often you feel like singing."

Lizzie looked at Mam, clearly understanding what she meant. The difference between the white bricks and the coveted brown ones.

"All right, I get it. So if you hear me singing tomorrow, you'll know I'm in my rightful place."

"In order to do that, your rightful place is on your knees this evening. Only God can give you the power to overcome your own selfishness."

Dat appeared in the doorway, buttoning a clean shirt, his hair wet from the shower.

"Very good speech, Annie." He laid a hand affectionately on her shoulder. "When I hear you talk like that, I think of all the times I required too much submission from you. You've been a good and faithful wife to me."

Quick tears welled up in Mam's eyes, and she blinked with embarrassment. "Oh, not always, Melvin. Not nearly always."

"Take care of Stephen's feelings, Lizzie. It's worth it," Dat said, clearing his throat gruffly at the unaccustomed emotion he felt.

When Lizzie dropped to her knees beside her bed, she could only thank God for two parents who were often imperfect, but who had gone the way before her and wanted only what was best. That was a huge thing, really.

Chapter 10

When Stephen came with a driver to go to Falling Springs the following week, Lizzie was waiting eagerly on the porch swing, her sweater wrapped closely around her body with her arms folded. It was getting close to their wedding date, and they had to choose the remaining furniture they needed to furnish their small house.

She was quite beside herself with anticipation. She had very seldom gone shopping with Stephen, as he certainly did not enjoy doing that, he had informed her firmly. But today he had no choice, she told him. He had to buy her china and her water set, which was really a water pitcher and six glasses she'd use on the day of their wedding. She also needed a set of silverware and a nice wooden chest to put it in.

Mam had given her all the money left in her savings account to buy kitchen chairs and a rocking chair for her living room. She had frowned about Lizzie's determination to have captain's chairs for her kitchen table, telling her those "furniture store chairs" don't last. They're not built as well as the Amish-crafted ones. But Lizzie was adamant. She loved the look of the low, round back and the arms you could rest your elbows on when you sat back in the chair.

Their first stop was the furniture store. Lizzie hopped out of the vehicle almost as soon as the wheels had stopped. Stephen laughed and shook his head at her.

"Why don't you just calm down a bit? At the rate you're going, you'll be completely worn out long before we're finished selecting our things."

"Oh, okay," Lizzie answered, trying to walk slower and act more demure, which really, if she thought about it, was how a girl who would soon be married should act.

She stopped at the big glass door, and Stephen reached around her to open it for her, allowing her to walk in first. It impressed her so much that he knew how to behave politely in the presence of English people. Besides, it made her feel special, cherished, even a bit queenly, when he allowed her to go first. She glanced up at him with a look she hoped conveyed her appreciation of his good manners. She was rewarded with a warm smile that melted her heart.

How could they forget their argument about squirrel-hunting so soon and love each other so much again? That was one of life's greatest mysteries, she supposed, how angry you could become and how soon you could forget that emotion when love came flooding back, like the sun warming you after it had been hidden by dark clouds. She wondered how long it would keep working like that, or if eventually, if you got too angry too many times, that the love wouldn't work anymore? That was scary to think about.

The salesman came over to them, danced over, actually, Lizzie thought, and asked them quite eagerly what he could help them with. He introduced himself and shook hands with Stephen, which was a bit too friendly when he was only a salesman in a furniture store. He looked like the cat in the Pinocchio book, so Lizzie took an instant dislike to him. She bet anything his chairs were expensive and very low quality.

He showed them different dining room sets, hovering over them like a bothersome mosquito, reciting the best merits of every set. He works on my nerves, Lizzie thought. I wish he'd go away.

As if reading her thoughts, Stephen asked him politely if they could have a bit of time by themselves to decide which chairs they wanted.

"Oh, of course! Certainly! Certainly!" and he was off as if his shirt was on fire.

Lizzie stifled a giggle, and Stephen grinned.

"All right. Now with him gone, do you like any of them?"

They looked at each one, compared prices, and finally decided to buy four oak captain's chairs, but no table. Mam had ordered their table from an

Amish furniture shop in Lamton, one that you could stretch out far enough to add 12 leaves and seat as many as 20 people at one time. That's the kind of table all Amish women owned, a very necessary and practical piece of furniture with all the company they would serve over the years. Some women had their tables for 50 years, that's how well they were built, Mam said.

They also bought a Boston rocker which was a wooden rocking chair with a high back and two pretty beige and brown cushions. When the over-enthused salesman totaled the bill, the amount was still 100 dollars less than the amount Lizzie had in her purse. She was so happy because she could buy something more now, maybe a coffee table or some extra dishes. After Stephen made arrangements to have the furniture delivered in a month, they were on their way to the little shop on Main Street to buy a wooden silverware chest.

Lizzie was a bit apprehensive, not knowing how to let Stephen know that he didn't have to spend an exorbitant amount of money on her without making him feel as if he didn't have enough money to buy her pretty things. He opened the door for her, and a little bell tinkled above their heads. A small, heavy-set man on a wheelchair turned to greet them, an easy smile spreading across his round face.

"Hello, there!" he greeted them.

They both answered with hellos of their own before looking around the tiny shop. The walls were covered with cut-glass or crystal dishes, displays of silverware, and wooden chests to store them in. There were also clear glass cases of jewelry and glistening gold and silver trophies, awards for having won a certain sport or event.

"If there's anything I can help you with, please let me know," the man told them in his soft, polite manner.

Lizzie's eyes lit up, and she pointed to a clear glass water pitcher set. The pitcher was round and a bit low with the most wonderful-looking handle coming up from the bottom, shaped into a graceful arc with the rounded end resting against the top of the pitcher. There were eight tall glasses, each with a clear glass bottom and one delicately stemmed flower etched on it. The set was beautiful, absolutely perfect, but she hesitated before she could summon the courage to look at the price.

"One hundred thirty-nine dollars!" she gasped.

Turning to look at Stephen, she said, "You can't buy that for me. The price is outrageous!"

"Do you like it?" he asked.

"Oh, I love it. It's so beautiful! I never saw anything like it. I wonder how they can make a handle like that out of glass." She bent over the set, lifting a glass and turning it against the light.

"Well, you said you don't mind getting inexpensive china, didn't you? I could buy this set for you if you don't mind less costly dishes then," Stephen said, as she watched the sunlight playing on the clear glass.

Lizzie returned it to the shelf, clasped her hands

together in excitement, and said, "Of course! That's what we'll do! You can buy this ridiculously expensive water pitcher set, and we'll go to K-Mart for my china. That's exactly what we'll do!"

When they emerged from the quaint little shop, Stephen carried a box containing the beautiful water set, and Lizzie carried one which held a oak silverware chest. It was lined with beige-colored felt and had different compartments to hold knives, spoons, and forks, with a small drawer beneath.

"Oh, Stephen!" Lizzie breathed. She couldn't think of one thing to say other than that simple statement. She meant to say, "Thank you," but it seemed so inadequate. She was, quite easily, thrilled beyond words.

However, they had not bought the silverware to put into the chest because it was simply too expensive. Lizzie didn't mind at all. She knew that at K-Mart there was a set she had often admired for about one-fourth the price, which really was smart, because how often did you use your good silverware?

Before they went to the big K-Mart store, they stopped for their favorite treat—pizza. That was one thing they never disagreed on. Pizza was their favorite restaurant food. Lizzie knew that pizza and all the big sandwiches, French fries, fried mushrooms, and whatever, were terribly high in calories and everything else that was not good for you, but she never cared, figuring a few such meals weren't going to hurt her.

Lizzie liked going to restaurants with Stephen. He always told Lizzie the same thing—that he didn't know how to pronounce the words, so she should order for him. Then he would show her the item he wanted and pronounce it in some outrageous fashion, so that she always laughed when the time came to order.

Over piping hot slices of thick pizza, loaded with mushrooms, sausage, and pepperoni, just as Stephen loved it, they talked of their house and how much they looked forward to arranging their new furniture in it.

"I just wish I could buy china like John gave Mandy," Stephen remarked.

"Please don't, Stephen. I wouldn't even feel right, knowing you're putting every penny you have into our new house. To tell you the truth, I'm not interested in dishes much anyway. If a set of china is arranged in a hutch cupboard, who can tell if it's expensive or not?"

That was how she felt, too. K-Mart china was just fine for her and perfect for Stephen's budget. She knew that sometimes she would run her hands over the unbelievably smooth surface of Mandy's plates and cups, marveling at the luster of those dishes, but she never once wished she could have some just like them.

They were pushing a cart up the long aisles at K-Mart when Stephen began showing signs of impatience. He said something about where they kept their hunting stuff, then leaned against a shelf and tapped his foot while Lizzie browsed, or he whistled a slow tune under his breath. He sighed, asked Lizzie where the clock was, and asked if she couldn't choose silverware without him.

"No, Stephen, I want to get my things with you!" Lizzie said, sharper than she had intended.

"Oh." That was all he said, and afterward he started looking at the ceiling, humming and tapping his shoe against the tile floor.

"Stephen, look. Which design do you like best?" Lizzie held up three different knives to show him the handles.

"That one!" he said, so quickly that she knew he hadn't even considered.

"You didn't even *look*!"

"They're all nice. I like them all. Just buy all three."

Lizzie laughed. "You don't even care!"

"Why would I? You don't see the handle of your fork while you're eating. You look at your food. Just get whatever you like best."

He resumed his humming and foot-tapping routine, which was soon accompanied by drumming his fingers against the shelf he was leaning against. Lizzie tried hard not to let it bother her, but she was starting to feel a distinct twitch in one eye. Her back began to ache with tension, and she chewed her thumbnail.

She liked the design that looked as if little blocks were hammered into the handle, but then, what about the rose design? Of course, there were no roses on her water pitcher set, so maybe that wouldn't look right either. She simply could not decide, and Stephen was acting like some huge dolt by this time.

"Let's go look at the china," she said evenly, although she had to clench her teeth so she wouldn't lose her temper.

He followed her meekly, saying nothing, leaned against another shelf, and looked at the ceiling. Then the foot-tapping began again.

"Stephen, do you like this design?" she asked quickly. Anything to stop that incessant foot-tapping.

He walked over and peered down at the plate she held in her hands. "That's pretty. Actually, if your mashed potatoes covered that one row of flowers, and the gravy ran over to the opposite side, it would look exactly like every other set of china."

"If you don't act normal, I'm going to break this plate over your head," Lizzie said, trying to joke but falling a bit short.

"You would, wouldn't you?" Stephen said.

"If you don't stop tapping your foot and staring at the ceiling, I will."

"Lizzie, I hate to go shopping. Why do I have to stand here so long? Just buy something, anything, so we can go home. I want to work on the house," he said beseechingly, spreading his hands for emphasis.

"I'll tell you what. You go to the sporting goods section and look at fishing rods or guns or whatever it is that holds your interest, and I'll choose my china all by myself."

"You sure?"

"I'm sure."

She had never been more certain of anything in her life, letting out a huge sigh of relief the minute his tall form disappeared around a corner. Men just weren't made to go shopping. Mam said the very same thing about Dat. After he left, she calmed herself considerably and chose the hammered design for her silverware and a beige and gold flower pattern for her china. A salesperson helped her with the two boxes of china, and she wheeled it toward the sporting goods section, hoping both boxes would stay intact until she found him.

Sure enough, there he was, bent intently over the gun case, muttering to himself. She stood and waited to see how long this would go on. He didn't look up or notice her for a few minutes, then caught sight of her from the corner of his eye.

"Oh! There you are! Sorry!"

He looked at her closely to see if she felt any resentment or anger toward him. But, oh no, Lizzie was smiling serenely, determined not to ruin the rest of this outing.

"I'm not a very good shopper," he admitted wryly.

"You're doing just fine, Stephen. It did take me too long to decide," she said, smiling sweetly up at him.

She felt no resentment because it made her very happy to think of future shopping trips when he would be at work, safely away from any store where she needed to go. She knew the reason Stephen tried his best to be apologetic and very helpful, loading the boxes of china onto the checkout counter, was because he was thanking his lucky stars that you only got married once, and from now on, it was up to her to go get the things they needed. Large stores gave him a severe case of claustrophobia, and he couldn't breathe very well if he didn't look at the ceiling.

What a clamor when they arrived home! The twins squealed and jumped up and down, and Jason asked Stephen dozens of questions about turkey-hunting before they had even finished unloading all of their purchases from the buggy. Mam exclaimed over and over about the beautiful water set, and Dat sat at the kitchen table and shook his head, smiling at Stephen.

"Aren't you glad you'll only be getting married once?" he asked.

"Funny you say that," he said. "That very thought is the only thing that kept me going through all this!"

Dat threw back his head and laughed. "Oh, how well I remember that very same feeling! Although back when we got married, we didn't buy all these fancy things like they do nowadays. I would never have been able to afford it. I wasn't even 21 years old yet."

Lizzie sat down beside Stephen and smiled. "Was it really that bad going shopping with me?" she asked.

"Not the first part of the trip, no. I enjoyed buying the kitchen chairs and the rocking chair. It was the china and silverware that fixed me!"

Jason laughed uproariously, which didn't impress Lizzie at all. She glared at him and told him to wait and see how much he would like to go shopping with Sharon a few years from now.

"Sharon!"

"Don't act so shocked," Lizzie said in a singsong tone of voice.

Jason very seldom blushed, but Stephen laughed when his face turn a decided shade of red.

"Now, Jason!" he said.

Lizzie unpacked her plates and showed Mam the pattern and texture of her silverware. Mam told her she had done very well and that she was proud of her for being careful of Stephen's money since he was building the new house and all, until Lizzie's heart swelled with love and gratitude.

Why, even when you had a boyfriend and were getting married, did your parents' approval still mean so much? Was it something you sought your whole life long? She supposed it must be so, because even with loving Stephen and having him in her life and looking forward to getting married, she cherished her parents more than ever.

Maybe love was just like that. The more you loved, the more you were given to love, until your cup was full and ran over and even splashed on the floor. It was a wonderful thought, and Lizzie hoped it would never end.

Chapter 11

LIZZIE WAS UPSTAIRS ON HER KNEES, BENDING over to paint the wide, heavy piece of baseboard in Jason's room. The wedding was only a week away, and they were putting the finishing touches on the freshly painted and cleaned upstairs.

She dipped her brush into the gallon of thick white paint, than ran the brush carefully along the bottom of the board, very slowly so she wouldn't ruin the linoleum. Sighing, she sat back on her heels. Time and a bit of paint had certainly made a huge difference in this old house, especially in the rooms that had new flooring.

She heard the kitchen door banging and wondered if it was already lunchtime. She sure was getting hungry, but it seemed too early to be noon. Then she heard the stairs squeak in protest as Mam came up at a fast pace. She appeared at the doorway, her scarf coming loose, her hair windblown, and a hand over her chest as she struggled to regain her breath.

"What is it, Mam?" Lizzie scrambled to her feet, her face ashen.

"It's Mandy! She had a doctor's appointment today, and they have a pair of twin girls!"

"No!" Lizzie screeched.

"Yes, they do!"

Then she was laughing and crying, and Lizzie was laughing and crying and dropping her brush and picking it up again. Mam was gasping and fixing her scarf, trying to speak, but all that came out were little gasps and hiccups. Finally, she dug in the pocket of her dress, found her handkerchief, and blew her nose. Then she handed it to Lizzie, and she wiped her eyes and blew her nose.

"S ... s ... six weeks early! Oh my goodness. *Siss ken fa-shtant!*" her favorite Pennsylvania Dutch phrase which means there's no sense. Mam used the only way she knew to fully express her feelings at a time like this. It didn't make much sense, but Lizzie knew exactly how she felt.

Then the thought hit Lizzie like a slap in the face. "The ... the ... my wedding!" she screeched again.

"Yes, the wedding! No, we can't have a wedding without John and Mandy. We'll just have to move the date to December sometime."

"Ma-a-m!" Lizzie wailed. "What will Stephen say?"

"It can't be helped, Lizzie. You're going to have to give in. Mandy will need help and lots of it, so there's no way we can have this wedding in a week."

Lizzie struggled to give in to this unexpected turn

of events. The doctors had assured them that Mandy
would be fine to attend the wedding. Why did she
have to go have those twins now? Lizzie stopped
that ugly thought, knowing it was completely selfish and uncaring. Dear, sweet, big-eyed Mandy. So
young, with such an awesome responsibility placed
on her shoulders. She took a deep breath and stead-
ied herself as Mam watched the display of emotion
move across her face.

"Stephen will be all right with this, Lizzie. He's
not the kind of guy who gets all upset about having
his wedding a few weeks later. He's not that childish," she said firmly.

So that evening Lizzie's family all took early baths,
changed into clean Sunday clothes, and got on their
way in a van to the hospital in Falling Springs. Their
first stop was at Stephen's parents' place.

Lizzie was met at the door by his mother, a small,
round person with big blue eyes like Stephen's. She
wore glasses and was dusting her apron with her
hands, removing the flour that clung to it.

"Lizzie! This is a surprise!" she said.

"Yes, it is, isn't it? Is Stephen at home?" she
asked.

"I think he's upstairs. Let me call him."

She turned to get Stephen, and Lizzie smiled at
Daniel who was seated on the wood box.

"Hi!" she said.

"Hi, yourself," he answered and grinned at her. He is almost better looking than Stephen, Lizzie decided. That dark hair and those blue, blue eyes.

Stephen appeared with his mother.

"John and Mandy have twin girls, Stephen! That means we have to postpone our wedding for at least two more weeks."

Stephen's mom held both hands to her mouth and said, "Ach my! *Siss ken fa-shtant*!" exactly like Mam.

In typical Stephen fashion, he didn't say anything at first, then he smiled and shrugged his shoulders. "So I guess we'll be getting married later then."

"I guess. We're going to have to write a bunch of postcards and make a pile of phone calls."

Stephen's mom bustled out to the van to congratulate Dat and Mam, and Lizzie stepped closer to Stephen, putting a hand on his arm. "Stephen, I feel so bad about all this. I'm sorry."

"It's all right, Lizzie. Really. She couldn't help it. At least we're still getting married, and you're not here to tell me you decided against it."

He looked down at her with so much love shining from his blue eyes that quick tears sprang to Lizzie's own.

"I would never decide against it. You know that."

She hurried out to the van as Stephen's mother stepped back, and Lizzie and her family were on their way to the large hospital in Falling Springs.

KatieAnn and Susan's eyes grew very large at the sensation the climbing elevator gave them. When it clunked to a stop on the fifth floor, they both suppressed their giggles. Mam was in a fine tizzy. Two bright red spots appeared on her cheeks, and her nostrils flared the way they always did when her excitement ran high. She hustled the twins off the elevator and into the waiting room, giving Jason quiet orders to stay with them until the rest of them found Mandy's room.

"We could stay here by ourselves," KatieAnn snapped, shrugging off Jason's hand from her shoulder. Jason laughed and steered the twins toward a set of chairs.

Lizzie smiled to herself as she walked down the hallway to find Mandy's room. She was surprisingly nervous. Would Mandy look the same? Would she be awake? Was she in pain? How would she react to being the mother of twins at such a young age?

"There it is," Mam said much too loudly. Mam always spoke loudly when she was nervous or agitated, but nobody told her to quiet down. Dat winked at Lizzie. Hospitals put them all a little on edge ever since Mam's long stay several years earlier when she had pneumonia. Lizzie smiled at Dat, glad that they had a happy reason for visiting the hospital this time.

Lizzie followed Dat and Mam into the room.

There was Mandy, lying sound asleep in an elevated hospital bed, her head sagging a wee bit to one side. The curtains were drawn, casting a quiet evening shadow across the room. There were no babies in sight.

Mam walked up to Mandy's bedside, and Mandy's eyes flew open in an instant. "Mam!" she exclaimed and then burst into tears as Mam hugged and hugged her, fussing like Lizzie had never heard her.

"Honestly, Mandy. Ach, my. *Dess iss net chide*," she kept saying, laughing and gasping while tears rolled down her cheeks. Dat kept wiping his eyes, and Lizzie hugged Mandy, becoming quite undone as she tried to congratulate her.

"Where's John?" she finally asked.

"He went home to milk the cows and change clothes. He should be in soon," Mandy said in a soft voice.

When everyone calmed down, Mandy grinned mischievously at Lizzie and announced, "So, my twins and I thoroughly messed up your wedding plans!"

"You *would* do that to me, wouldn't you?" Lizzie grinned back. Knowing how well Stephen had accepted this made things much easier for Lizzie. What were a few weeks to wait if they could spend the rest of their lives together?

They all walked to the nursery and peered through the glass at the tiny cribs containing the smallest babies Lizzie had ever seen. There were white cards put in a holder that only said "Zook," so they didn't know what their names were. They hadn't even thought to ask Mandy.

The twins weighed almost five pounds each, although Lizzie had a hard time believing this. They were so skinny! Their little hands looked too fragile to be real, and their faces were actually almost gaunt. Mam said that was because they were born prematurely and weren't filled out yet.

Lizzie could not imagine being the mother of those tiny, fragile, little human beings. It would be too much responsibility for her. She could never do it. She knew she couldn't. She became very quiet and sober, pitying Mandy so intensely she could barely make herself go back to her room.

When they got back, John had arrived, greeting them all with so much genuine warmth and enthusiasm. There were tears in his brown eyes.

"Congratulations!" Dat said, beaming warmly.

"Thanks. Thanks. Isn't it something though?" John answered.

"Their names, Mandy! We forgot to ask their names," Mam gushed.

"Sarah and Sylvia!" Mandy announced happily.

Everyone talked and exclaimed about the birth of these tiny twins, but Lizzie sat on the wide window ledge and became steadily depressed, thinking about being a mother to two tiny babies all at once. What in the world would Mandy do if they both cried at the same time during the night and there was no one to help her, especially if John was out milking cows? What if they were both hungry? How could she feed two at once?

Like a soft, stifling vapor, the thoughts of inadequacy enveloped her until all the bright, happy moments from just a few minutes earlier were obliterated. She stared at the floor, chewing her lip and scuffing the toe of her shoe against the nightstand. She wasn't completely sure she was normal where babies were concerned. They quite simply gave her a sense of helplessness, of weary, endless responsibility.

Did you ever want babies? Was it normal to get the blues about having babies? She shrugged her shoulders, shaking off the feelings of despair, and decided she was just tired and struggling to accept this sudden change in plans. Of course, she wanted babies, and, of course, she would be a good mother. Anyone that could teach a roomful of children and thoroughly enjoy it could surely take care of one harmless little baby.

Mandy and John brought the twins home the following Friday, and Lizzie was there to greet them on their arrival. She had hustled and bustled, cleaning every corner of Mandy's small house, doing the laundry and raking some of the lawn that was strewn with maple leaves. Mam brought another small crib, and they set them up side by side in the living room. They fussed with and arranged the tiny baby clothes, sleepers, tiny socks, and T-shirts. Lizzie loved the smell of the baby lotions and powders, spreading some on her arm to keep the scent close by.

"See, Mam, it wouldn't be so bad if you had one baby at a time. I do love babies, honestly, I do, and, of course, I want children after I'm married. It's just that I can't see how in the world Mandy is going to manage," she said worriedly.

Mam shook her head wisely. "Well, let me tell you, Lizzie, having a baby is more than a woolly pink blanket. Indeed it is. But I so love babies, and I thoroughly enjoyed the twins. I'm hoping Mandy will feel the same way. No doubt, two babies are a big responsibility, but I enjoyed every minute."

Lizzie watched Mam in amazement, thinking how capable and courageous she really was. Everything that happened in her life, she took in stride. She made the best out of each situation. Moving, old farms, sicknesses, twins, whatever, Mam always stayed the same. She just marched up each hill as it was presented, in her high-strung, take-charge kind of way. That is just how Mam was. Lizzie wished with all her heart she could be more like her.

As if Mam read her mind, she stopped folding the snowy white diapers and said, "See, Lizzie, you think too much. You're always supposing this or supposing that about the future, making yourself extremely anxious when it is absolutely unnecessary. You should learn to place your trust in God and not in your own power. If God thinks you're capable of managing a pair of twins, he'll give you a pair."

Lizzie dropped a tiny T-shirt. "Mam!"

Mam looked up, surprised. Seeing the expression on Lizzie's face, she burst out laughing, a real deep laugh that shook her stomach.

"It's not funny!" Lizzie burst out, which only increased Mam's mirth.

"Oh, my! Yes, it is funny."

"Mam, seriously, what are the chances of me ever having twins? How many daughters, I mean, genetically, have a pair of twins if their mothers have some. I don't ever, ever want two babies at one time. Surely God knows that. Should I pray not to have twins?" Lizzie asked anxiously.

"I don't know," Mam chuckled. "As long as I can remember, from the time I was a little girl, I prayed for twin girls."

"Whatever for?" Lizzie asked incredulously.

"Oh, I wanted them. Here they come!" she said all in the same breath. Lizzie ran to the window just in time to see the van pull up to the sidewalk. John bent his head to pay the driver, and Mam and Lizzie hurried out to Mandy and the babies.

Mandy looked pale and tired, but she smiled happily when she saw Mam. Lizzie climbed up to receive one of the babies. It felt as if almost nothing was in the blanket, the baby was so tiny. For a moment, Lizzie panicked, worrying which end of the blanket held the head and which the feet. She lifted a corner of the blanket, and sure enough, she had the wrong end up! Glancing hastily at Mandy, hoping she wouldn't see, she switched ends, hurrying into the kitchen, red-faced. See? That just proved how hopelessly inadequate she was with babies.

There wasn't much time to think about that, with getting Mandy settled on the sofa and finding a cool, clean white sheet and pillow for her. John was hungry, and it was getting close to milking time, so Mam hurried around the kitchen, fixing toasted ham and cheese sandwiches and tomato soup while Lizzie unpacked the accumulation of things from the hospital.

The twins just slept. That's all they ever did, Mandy said, because they were born so early, and that's what premature babies did.

Lizzie sat in the rocking chair opposite Mandy's sofa and marveled at her good spirits and her calm demeanor. She didn't seem nervous that her twins just slept and that sometimes she could hardly waken them when it was time for a feeding.

"The nurses in the hospital were a great help. Sometimes they had to take their sleepers off so they'd cool off and wake up. They showed me lots of ways to rouse them out of their deep sleep when their feeding time comes."

Her voice became quieter and quieter and, to Lizzie's astonishment, Mandy drifted off to sleep. Imagine, she thought. How could a person be so relaxed after bringing home two babies to care for? What Lizzie didn't know was how utterly exhausted Mandy really was. There was not much time for sleep in a hospital with all the IV lines, the check-ups, and tests. They had no mercy on a sleepy young mother.

So Lizzie rocked all by herself as Mam and John had supper. She was hungry, but her wedding was only a few weeks away, so it was high time to lose some weight. She watched Mandy's pretty face, her eyes perfect half-moons in sleep, and hoped with all her heart she would remain strong and optimistic as she accepted this major responsibility.

Suddenly, a high-pitched squeak pierced the air, and Lizzie jumped straight out of her rocking chair. "What was that?" she cried.

Mam turned to look at Lizzie, saw one little bundle in the crib moving, and burst out laughing. There was another high-pitched squeal, and Mam laughed until she had to get out her handkerchief and wipe her eyes. John's laugh rang out, and Mandy's eyes fluttered open, followed by a smile when she heard everyone laugh.

"One of the babies is awake," Mam said, coming over to the crib and lifting her out. Bending her head, she cooed and fussed, saying all kinds of things to this tiny infant who, Lizzie was sure, could not understand a word she said.

"What? What's wrong with my little girlie? Huh? Do you need a clean diaper? I bet you do! Little squirrel. You know, Mandy, they look like little squirrels with their thin faces," she said, misty-eyed with love for these tiny babies.

Lizzie still felt weak from her scare. Watching

Mam with narrowed eyes, she wondered how a mother and daughter could be so completely opposite. She guessed she would just have to charge into marriage like Mam did and trust God about babies.

Chapter 12

THE FOURTEENTH OF DECEMBER DAWNED bright, clear, and cold. Of course, the entire Glick household had been awake long before dawn, because this was Stephen and Lizzie's wedding day.

Lizzie was upstairs, her hands clammy with nervous perspiration as she tried to pin her white organdy cape perfectly. Her royal blue dress had been made to perfection, but her difficulty with putting on an organdy cape sure never changed, wedding day or not.

Stephen knocked on the door of her room, then came in to have his bow tie adjusted, just as she finally put the last pin into her cape. She forgot all about her frustration, catching sight of Stephen, her handsome husband-to-be. Doesn't he look so good? she sighed to herself. His tanned face was cleanshaven, his streaky brown-blond hair cut and combed neatly, and he was wearing his new black suit with a crisp white shirt which set off his dark skin.

Lizzie reached up to secure the bow, straightening his collar a bit, as he watched her face intently.

"Nervous?" he asked.

"Oh, yes. Actually, more nervous than I thought I would be. Are you?"

He laughed a bit ruefully. "Afraid so."

"Just be glad you don't need to pin on a white cape and apron."

Stephen came over to stand beside her, telling her she had nothing to worry about—that she looked lovely just the way she was. "You are just perfect, Lizzie," he said soberly. "I feel like a very lucky— no, blessed—young man today."

Lizzie didn't say anything; she just let her eyes tell him what was in her heart. If she ever had any doubts at all, they were completely banished on this morning of their wedding day. She understood deep insidethe exact meaning of "meant-to-be," the rock-solid assurance that this day, this time in her life, was where God wanted her to be.

Emma dashed up the stairs, her cheeks pink with excitement. "Hey, you two. Mam says you're supposed to be down in the kitchen sitting on that bench in 15 minutes."

"Oh, dear!" Lizzie whirled around to grab her white apron from the bed.

"Emma!" she hollered. "You have to help me with my apron."

Rolling her eyes at Stephen, Emma came in and began adjusting the apron for Lizzie. Joshua and Emma had come from Allen County the previous day to help on the *risht-dawg*, the day of preparation before an Amish wedding, just as they had done for Mandy.

Baby Mark toddled around and squealed with excitement most of the day until he wore himself out completely, falling asleep on a corner of the couch in the dining room. The whole house had been in a frightful uproar, same as the previous weddings, but Mam seemed a bit more unruffled, not quite as upset about things, as this was, after all, her third wedding.

Dat was always the same at wedding time. He loved it, thriving on the action and the attention from relatives on both sides, but most of all, he loved the singing. He would always lead quite a few songs on the day his daughters were married, just for the pure joy of "getting the singing going real well."

Mam and Lizzie hardly argued or disagreed on anything. Mam was much calmer, and Lizzie wasn't particular about little details, like who was invited, or how many of the youth were included, or what kind of pies they served.

Aunt Vera made mountains of date pudding at home in Ohio, bringing it all the way to Pennsylvania with buckets of whipped topping for the big day. Date pudding was Lizzie's favorite dessert, ever since she had first tasted it as a little girl in Ohio. It was a soft, moist cake baked with dates and nuts, then cut into tiny squares and layered with a caramel sauce and whipped topping. It was rich and creamy with a nutty texture that was simply delicious. They served it on every table throughout the house, with small squares of red and green Jell-O on top, because their wedding was so close to Christmas.

Lizzie's room soon filled up as the remainder of the bridal party moved over from the adjoining room. During the wedding, Jason would sit with Rebecca, and Daniel would sit with Lizzie's cousin Esther, who, along with Lizzie's sisters and their husbands, made up the six individuals who would be the honored guests.

"Hold still, Lizzie; I mean it," Emma hissed around a straight pin in her mouth.

"Get that pin out of your mouth, Emma!" Lizzie hissed back.

Emma straightened up, giving the smooth white belt an extra pat and said, "There!"

Lizzie stepped up to the mirror, surveying the finished attire, her eyes wide with apprehension.

"Do…I…I…Does it look all right? Emma, you made a nice covering for my wedding day. Thank you. You are a dear. Honest."

"You look lovely, Lizzie, and I'm glad you like the covering, because I sure went to enough pains with it. I must have opened and redone that one side three times."

"Ready?" Stephen asked.

Lizzie looked around her room wildly. "Where are the decorative throw pillows for my bed?" she asked.

Jason produced them from behind his back,

grinning, and Lizzie pounced on them, arranging them carefully, making certain everything looked just right.

"Do we remember who goes first?" she asked.

"Of course," Jason said airily, and they all filed solemnly down the stairs and sat side by side with their backs against the stairway wall, as straight as stickmen on a hard wooden bench in the kitchen.

Suddenly Lizzie thought she would be sick to her stomach from sheer nervousness. The house was already full of people, and every minute another horse and buggy or van load of people arrived. Where would they all sit? Suppose there was not enough room for everyone? Maybe this would actually be the first wedding the Amish people could remember that didn't have enough seating space. People would talk about it for 50 years. Like the story of the bride who changed her mind at the last minute and would not join her groom to stand in front of the minister to be married. The minister asked if there was anyone else in the room who would marry this man, and the bride's sister got up and married him, and they lived happily ever after. Was that really true? No one seemed to know who these people were, so Lizzie always doubted the story.

Why did she sit here on her wedding day, thinking all these ridiculous thoughts? She was so nervous this minute that she felt like crying. She wished she could hold Stephen's hand for comfort, but then she was so clammy with sweat he probably wouldn't want to hold her hand. This was awful.

Oh, dear, a whole load of people Lizzie had never seen before walked up to them, and she didn't have the slightest clue who they were! She swallowed hard, glancing wildly at Stephen, but he was smiling genuinely at a tall, plump lady and greeting each strange person who shook his hand.

Lizzie wondered what would happen if she panicked and burst through the door and ran down across the flat pasture to the fencerow by the creek and hid. Would they come looking for her? Why did she think these thoughts? She had to calm down, really seriously calm herself, and remember what day this was. Her wedding day. After today she would no longer be Lizzie Glick. It was high time people started calling her Elizabeth, now that she was a respectable married woman who combed her hair sleek and flat.

After shaking more hands than she had ever shaken before, at least in one sitting, she took a few deep breaths to calm herself so she could smile at bustling aunts and greet her friends as they filed into the room. She began to feel comfortable enough to enjoy her wedding day.

The singing started, which was the official signal that the ceremony was now in progress. The ministers all filed upstairs to hold conference, with Stephen and Lizzie following them. The ministers each took turns speaking to them about marriage and what was expected of them in their life together.

As Lizzie listened, she knew that beginning with this day, she had entered into a permanent union, one rooted as deeply as the largest oak in the forest. Seasons would come and go, the heat of summer, the winds of autumn when every branch moved in the gale, the ice and snow in winter, which bent every branch to its limit, sometimes even breaking sturdy limbs, and yet she and Stephen would endure.

When spring came, new growth would replace the broken limbs, strengthening the tree, just like their argument about the color of the bricks on their brown house had deepened their relationship.

There was no turning back now.

She peeped at Stephen beneath lowered lashes, overwhelmed by happiness and her faith in him. He was so serious, his tanned face so solemn, his hair shining, and cut in the proper *ordnung* for this day.

All she needed to do was place her hand in his and follow him back downstairs as the singing congregation waited. He would lead her to the minister who would unite them in holy matrimony. With the singing wafting up from the house below, Lizzie felt like crying again because of the interest of these kind ministers, and well, just everything.

When they were finished, Lizzie and Stephen filed slowly and solemnly into the living room with the rest of the bridal party, sitting across from each other on the new wooden chairs that Stephen's grandfather had made for them in his little woodworking shop. They had been a gift from Stephen's parents and pleased Lizzie immensely.

Lizzie kept her head bowed demurely, her hands folded in her lap. She couldn't look up—she didn't dare look at Stephen—so she just looked at her lap. It felt as if hundreds of eyes were staring intently at her from every direction, so the safest thing to do was keep her head lowered.

The singing stopped and someone chose another song—that familiar tune that had been sung at hundreds of other weddings. It was a very cozy feeling, Lizzie thought, to know that this ritual, this form of *ordnung* or set of rules the wedding was based on, had been the same for Mam and Dat, for Stephen's parents, and their parents before them, and on and on for generations. That was a good and calming thing, the realization that everyone in this house knew what to expect and how to go about running this wedding.

It certainly had not seemed very orderly yesterday. The whole house had resembled a chicken house after a fox makes an appearance. Well, that was a stretch, perhaps, but how could 10 or 15 women get anything accomplished and all talk at the same time? Because talk they did. Laughed and planned and stood in small bunches with pieces of paper, writing down who did what, and who was seated where, and how many platters of chicken and filling went on which table, and on and on.

Sometimes Mam got a little snorty if the rules were a bit stringent, and she would shake her head and say, *Ach, voss machts aus?* What does it matter? She was from Ohio, so she was no stickler for tradition, although she had a few practices of her own from her growing-up church that Lizzie didn't particularly like. But when all the dust settled from the *risht-dawg* and the sun rose on a perfectly prepared wedding day, who knew what an unbelievable fuss had occurred there the day before? That's just how it was.

Now the preachers all walked into the room, quiet and solemn, and took their seats in the same row as the bridal party. After the singing was finished, the first minister stood up, cleared his throat, surveyed the crowd of people, and began to speak. After his sermon was over, there was a short prayer, the scriptures were read, and then the bishop from Mam's home church in Ohio stood up to preach the long sermon. He was in his 60s, Lizzie guessed, according to his white hair and beard. He proved to be a good speaker. He touched on many interesting aspects of marriage, including living together in harmony with your neighbors, as well as with each other.

However, Lizzie became fidgety, her palms began to perspire again, and her back started aching. She knew the minister would talk about the Tobias story, the tale from the old German storybook where a young man of God set out on a journey for his father and discovered love and then marriage. It was a good, rather touching story, but after the bishop mentioned Tobias's name, Lizzie's heart never really slowed down. She knew that soon the bishop would call Stephen and her to stand before him.

Her heart jumped in one frantic flutter when he started the Tobias story and went racing on until he stopped to announce that today there were two who were prepared for matrimony. He announced their names, and Lizzie ignored her swiftly beating heart and her nervousness. She solemnly did what was required of her, getting up from her chair, holding Stephen's proffered hand, and following him to stand in front of the bishop.

The minister cleared his throat and asked the congregation if there was anyone who wished to put a stop to this wedding. Of course, there wasn't. Then he asked Stephen if he wished to take Lizzie as his wife. Would he promise to love her and take care of her, through sickness and other trials of her life? Stephen quietly answered, "Ya."

Then the minister asked Lizzie the exact same questions. Lizzie's voice shook only the tiniest bit as she said, "Ya." The minister asked them more questions of faith, to which they both responded in turn with another "Ya."

The minister covered their joined hands as he pronounced them man and wife, then spoke a blessing in the name of Jesus Christ. Lizzie and Stephen turned and sat down across from each other. Only then did Lizzie take a deep breath, and her heartbeat slowly returned to normal. Only after the ministers had given testimony, another long prayer was read, and the last exultant song was started, she dared to sneak a look at Stephen's face. His eyes were very blue, and he gave her a small, special smile, which she returned before lowering her eyes properly to her hands in her lap.

The singing rose and swelled around them. Of all the slow, old German tunes that were sung, this was the most lovely of them all with its words about God and a bride and groom. Lizzie pressed her lips firmly together to hold in her emotion. The song was sung so beautifully.

Joy flooded her heart, and a sure feeling enveloped her soul. She had sought God's will in her own fumbling, unsure way after many errors. But now she had come home, securely bound to her husband by her love and, most importantly, by God.

The last soaring note of the song died away. It was almost time for the celebration to begin. Finally Lizzie could look at Stephen and see only him, hold his hand, and go back upstairs to change her covering from a black organdy to a white organdy one. She and Stephen also changed from their borrowed, old-fashioned, high-topped shoes to their afternoon slippers.

Then the festivities of an Amish wedding day officially started. Men quickly rearranged the living room, carrying in long tables and setting them up around the room. Lizzie and Stephen were told their dinner was ready in less than half an hour after the service was over. The wooden benches where people were seated during the ceremony were placed around the tables, tablecloths were put on, and dozens of hands passed out plates, water pitchers, rolls, butter, jelly, applesauce, coleslaw, filled doughnuts, trays of cookies, fruit, and hot platters of food before the guests were again seated.

Lizzie tried hard to keep a mature, serene expression on her face, but her smile just kept sliding out of control. She was deep-down, really happy, genuinely pleased to have become Stephen's wife, to spend this wonderful day of celebration as the honored guest who sat in the most important seat, the *eck*, or corner.

Her nicest tablecloth covered the table, and it was set with her china, silverware, and, best of all, the expensive water pitcher and glasses Stephen had given her. A cut-glass bowl held fruit, two cakes sat on glass cake stands, and a variety of fancy dishes were filled with good things to eat. Even the butter was molded into wedding bells with little sprigs of parsley adorning it. The whole corner table looked so grand. Joshua and Emma, John and Mandy, and Aunt Vera's two children, Leroy and his wife and Mary Ann and her husband, served as their waiters.

After finishing their delicious meal, Lizzie and Stephen went upstairs to Lizzie's bedroom to open the gifts that were piled on Lizzie's bed. Many of the aunts and cousins came up to watch them open the beautifully wrapped presents.

After the gifts were unwrapped, Lizzie couldn't imagine what she would do with all the stuff! She would need a large pantry and plenty of cupboards in her new house, no doubt about that. She smiled.

"Where will we keep all of this?" she asked Stephen.

"We'll have plenty of kitchen cupboards, Lizzie," he told her, which made Lizzie glad and happy all over again.

After that, the afternoon singing began, and Lizzie and Stephen and the rest of the wedding party all filed back to the *eck*, their table, again. Each of the single young men chose a young girl to sit with him at the table, and they shared a songbook between them during the hymn-singing. All the older folks stopped their dishwashing and other various duties to watch "the *youngie* go in." There were quite a few giggles and rib-punching and some whispering among them, as they watched to see who had picked which girl.

Stephen told Lizzie he was so glad he never had to do that again, and Lizzie could very easily agree with him. The singing started again, slow hymns and also faster ones which the youth led, while candy dishes, fruit, drinks, and other delicacies were passed from person to person.

There was lots of talking and visiting going on, and one part of the table became a bit rowdy, with some of the young boys tossing small pieces of candy or celery at each other. Their companions either giggled or looked horrified, depending on the type of girl. It was all familiar and very dear to Lizzie and Stephen.

The last event of the day was pairing the boys and girls for the evening meal. This was Lizzie's duty. Each boy took a girl to the table. They would eat supper together and join the hymn-singing later in the evening. This was a big event in the life of a teenager. Sometimes, after being taken to the table, a couple would begin dating, so it was considered a good way to meet a companion. It was the hardest part of the day for the bride, because after thinking that she had everything down pat, finished up, and that everything was fine, a few of the boys would refuse to accompany the girls she had paired them with for the evening.

The air had turned sharply colder after a snow shower that afternoon. Lizzie was getting tired and a bit irritable with some of the couples' slow response to her pairing. It was getting late, she was almost in tears, and she couldn't find Stephen.

Finally he appeared, and she made a dash to be at his side. "Stephen, where were you? I need help badly. David and Lee won't take Susie and Fannie. Now what do I do? Everyone else seems to be okay with the partners I assigned."

Stephen put his arm around her waist and held her firmly, soothingly, while Lizzie struggled to keep her emotions in check.

"Let me take care of it," he said and marched her along with him, confronting the two boys who were acting reluctant to join their dates.

"If you don't want the girls she gave you, I guess you won't be getting any supper then, will you?" he said in a firm voice.

"Aw. Come on!" Lee wailed.

"Sorry. It's either Fannie or no one," and he steered Lizzie away.

"You mean ... Can you do that?" she asked.

"Sure. I can act as stubborn as they are."

Lizzie giggled.

"They'll get over it," he finished. And that was that.

Lizzie decided on the way to the *eck* for supper that she had better appreciate Stephen all her days. What would she have done without him?

The buttered potatoes, corn, and meat loaf tasted good to Lizzie after a day of traipsing around in the cold, trying to keep everyone happy. She soon forgot her frustration after all the youth filed in and they sat eating the good food and listening to the singing. Lizzie looked for David and Lee but couldn't find them, so she figured they must be all right.

Stephen sat back, his blue eyes drooping with sleepiness after the tension of the day. Lizzie watched him, then asked if he was glad the whole day was over, or almost.

"Oh, am I ever! Even if it's my wedding day, all these people really make me tired in a hurry!"

Lizzie laughed. "You look beat."

"I am."

After the guests said good-bye, and Lizzie and Stephen were wished congratulations one last time, the aunts and uncles started washing dishes, filling garbage bags with candy wrappers, leftover apple cores, and celery tops, all the while still smiling and joking. Some of the relatives continued singing heartily, although Lizzie wondered how in the world they could keep going without their voices wearing out.

For the last time the bridal party left the table, glad to have had a wonderful time together, but at the same time, grateful it was all over, and that they could get on with their normal lives. Of course, life for Lizzie would be a new "normal." She was no longer a single girl at home, helping Mam and being one of the family. She was Stephen's wife now, whatever that entailed, though all she felt was joy and anticipation.

Even if marriage was a bit like jumping off a cliff, never completely certain where you would land, there was no other place she would rather be than here in this torn-up, messy house that had just held such a joyous celebration.

She loved Stephen. Wasn't that amazing? Each disagreement, each time one of them hurt the other's feelings, actually brought them closer as they forgave each other, which in turn, brought them a deeper affection. So what was there to be afraid of? Nothing really, unless, of course, the disagreements became too serious.

Chapter 13

Stephen climbed into the buggy. He wrapped the blue and green plaid buggy blanket around Lizzie's legs before settling it around his own. He lifted the reins and chirped to George, the horse. The buggy rolled forward.

Outside, the air was frigid with gray clouds scudding across a backdrop of dull blue and white sky, as if the sunshine had frozen along with the rest of the world. The buggy wheels screamed that thin high squeal of metal on frozen snow, which always set Lizzie's teeth on edge. She shivered and snuggled closer to Stephen, glad for the warmth of another person and the heavy blanket wrapped securely around them.

They were on their way to visit yet another family in the community and to receive the wedding gift that awaited them. It was the custom among the Amish of Lizzie's community for newlyweds to visit the home of each guest who had attend their wedding and receive a gift, becoming better acquainted with each other in the process. Sometimes the new couple stayed for a meal; other times only for a short visit or a "call." Lizzie couldn't understand why some families went to a lot of work preparing a meal, while with others, you sat for a short time, collected your wedding gift, and kept going. Kind of like a drive-through gift collection. She thought the short variety was pretty dumb.

But, being Amish, Lizzie knew that it wasn't up to her to say how things were done or not done, no matter what she thought. She was a member of this Amish church, and she never even thought of being anything else. She was perfectly content to follow its customs and dedicate her life to living happily within the church's rules. Well, not always. She still wanted nice things. Sometimes she wished she didn't have to comb her hair like all the other married women, so completely flat and smooth and up off her forehead with only thin, flat rolls along the side of her head.

No wonder everyone waited until they were married to comb their hair like that. Suddenly the unsuspecting husband found his wife looking quite different, and there wasn't a thing he could do about it. He was married to her. Of course, Lizzie reasoned, she had combed her hair almost the same way on their wedding day and Stephen still went ahead and married her. Mam said looks had nothing to do with love, but deep down, Lizzie knew that wasn't completely true.

Her mind wandered to the table set up in her bedroom with gifts stacked on top, beneath, and on both sides. Gifts everywhere. In her opinion, it was time to move into the little house on top of the hill that Stephen was building. She didn't like living with Dat and Mam and the rest of the family for the first months after she was married. But that was how things were, so there was no use fretting.

Mam wasn't too enthused about it either, but she never let on, except when Stephen and Dat were at work. Then she would tell Lizzie how it was done in Ohio where she was born and raised, the newlyweds moving the day after the wedding, the way it should be, she said, her eyes snapping behind the wire rims of her glasses. But she never said much to anyone else. She packed Stephen's lunch along with Dat's and Jason's, cooked delicious meals, and in general, seemed quite thrilled to have them in the house, in spite of the newlywed tradition in Ohio which she preferred.

Mam was a good sport about most things in life, a trait that Lizzie had come to appreciate as she became older. Actually, when she really thought about it, Mam was more dear to her with each passing day. It seemed especially so since Lizzie knew she would soon leave their farmhouse, the place she had spent the past seven years of her life.

Lizzie slid a sideways glance at Stephen, wondering what he was thinking, and wondering, too, if he truly was the exact right person for her to spend the remainder of her life with, now that she had promised to love, honor, cherish, and obey him. She sincerely hoped so.

The thing about Stephen, though, was his inability to talk very much at a time, which kept her chattering on, kind of like a fish out of water, flopping around on the bank until it flopped its way back in. Sometimes when he became too quiet it worked on Lizzie's nerves, and she said senseless things that annoyed him, she could tell.

His head was turned as he stared intently out the window of the side door, watching for deer again, the way he always did on the Water Mill Road. He should know that there would be no deer in broad daylight, especially in the frigid weather, and most of all, with the squeal of the buggy wheels that could be heard a mile away.

"You're not going to see any deer," Lizzie said, flatly.

"I might."

"Not in this weather."

He didn't bother answering, so Lizzie toyed with the fringe of her black woolen shawl under the heavy blanket and felt nervous. He didn't look very happy, and she was almost 100 percent sure she knew why. He simply didn't enjoy this going from one place to another the way he should, and that made Lizzie feel very anxious, afraid that he might no longer want to go. What would people think?

After the last meal they had had almost a week ago at Aaron King's house, Stephen had definitely been subdued, shrugging his shoulders noncommittally when she asked him why he was unhappy.

"I'm not, really. It's just that ... well, nothing."

"What?"

"Nothing."

"Come on. You didn't enjoy tonight, did you?"

"Well, your Uncle Marvin says everything, so there's nothing left for me to say."

Marvin and Sara Ruth and Amos and Sally were the other two couples who went visiting with them through the winter months, and Lizzie enjoyed them immensely. It was a bit of a shock to hear Stephen talk about her beloved Marvin that way. He was a very sociable person, easily conversing with anyone about almost any subject, which Lizzie thought was an extremely admirable quality. It was the way most of the Glicks were.

She thought Stephen was acting like a baby, but knew she shouldn't say so because it simply wasn't nice. She wanted to though.

"Marvin was always fussy and outgoing."

"I know."

So that conversation came to an end in a hurry, and Lizzie glanced at Stephen again. She still wondered if she should tell him he was being childish and that she couldn't understand why he couldn't enjoy listening to Marvin talk. Suddenly she remembered when she was 15 years old at a pajama party at her friend Sharon's house, and how terribly left out she had felt, all because the girls loved Mandy. She had even cried all alone in the bathroom and had never told one single soul, certainly not Mandy.

Maybe that was how Stephen felt now, like going to the bathroom to cry all by himself because no one had noticed him. Sometimes you couldn't help it when you felt like that, even if it was terribly childish and dumb. It wasn't Marvin's fault, not one bit. He was just being Marvin, oblivious to the fact that Stephen wished he'd be quiet and let him say something occasionally.

They pulled into the driveway, and John Miller's wife, Suvilla, stepped out onto the porch and waved. While Stephen tied up the horse in the barn, Lizzie picked her way across the frozen ground to the house. Suvilla welcomed Lizzie warmly, holding the door open and shaking her hand over and over before directing her to the bedroom. A kerosene lamp offered its cozy glow in the quiet room. Lizzie took off her black shawl and bonnet, unbuttoned her coat, and slid her arms out of the sleeves. She laid her coat on the bed and took her covering out of the covering box, pinned it securely on her sleek hair, and tied the strings, gazing disapprovingly in the mirror.

The thing was, her forehead was twice as high as it used to be with her hair pulled back so severely now. She looked like that picture of a turtle in the *Tommy Turtle* children's book. No matter how she tried, she just couldn't get used to seeing herself with that high forehead.

She heard Suvilla chattering on as she returned to the hallway just as Sara Ruth and Sally arrived. Lizzie smiled with the familiar pleasure she always felt when she was with her two dear friends who had also just gotten married. Visiting was twice as much fun when you had good friends to share the evenings with. They giggled and laughed together, shivered and commented on the weather, all agreeing how glad they would be to have homes of their own and to be able to stay at home on evenings such as this.

Their husbands came into the house, and they all sat down around the dining room table. The supper was delicious. Lizzie enjoyed everything thoroughly, running her hand worriedly across her stomach under the table. Oh dear, this will never do, she thought unhappily, as she finished a whole piece of chocolate cake with peanut butter frosting. I have to stop eating so much this late in the evening.

She glanced at Stephen, who seemed to be enjoying himself, talking to Marvin and Amos. John was getting into the conversation as well. Good, Lizzie thought. Maybe it was just that one evening that was a problem and everything will go well from here on.

After the dishes were done, the Millers gave the couples their wedding gifts—stainless steel bowls for the young women and pitchforks for the men. These were good, useful items they were grateful for, and Lizzie thanked her hostess genuinely, telling her she didn't have that size bowls at all. Aaron would not let them leave before they had played a few tricks, including "Where's Jack?" a game where a blindfolded player stumbled across the kitchen, trying to reach his opponent. It was as hilarious as always.

Lizzie left the house with Stephen, filled with a warm happy feeling, thankful for the gifts, and appreciative of the good meal and secure relationship with older members of this close-knit group of Amish people. As they left this home, Lizzie felt keenly the strong ties of love she had for each family, never wanting to say anything bad about these evenings.

So she was relieved when Stephen seemed happy on the way home, talking more than usual. He told her that Marvin and Sara Ruth were planning to move into temporary living quarters in their new shop, and then take their time building a new house, instead of rushing as he had to for his and Lizzie's house.

Rushing along? Lizzie lowered her eyebrows and tried not to say what she thought, she was so incredulous. Rushing? In her opinion, the house was coming along at an unbelievably slow pace, so she couldn't understand what Stephen meant.

"Rushing? Do you think we're hurrying on our house?" she asked.

"Why, of course!" he said, loudly.

"But...?"

"Oh, I know. It's not fast enough for you. But to think we're only working in the evenings and on Saturdays, I think we're pushing it."

"But... but... at the rate the house is going, we won't be moved in till spring!" Lizzie said in a voice that tried very hard not to be a wail.

"We can move before that. I was thinking of moving into the basement anyway, now that we have running water. If I do a bit of plumbing, and if we bought a heating stove and some carpet, we could move."

"Really?"

"If you want to. I'm ready to live by ourselves, even if it means living in an unfinished basement."

"Oh, goody!" Lizzie clutched Stephen's arm excitedly. "That will be so cozy!"

"You won't think all the sawdust seeping through the ceiling is cozy, Lizzie," he laughed.

"I don't care. You can wipe sawdust away. Oh, let's do! Let's move in a week!"

"We could."

❧

And so they did. The following week, Mam helped Lizzie clean and scrub. Dat and Jason put up temporary shelving for Lizzie's dishes, they laid pieces of carpeting on the fresh concrete, connected the plumbing, and generally made the basement quite livable.

On the day they moved the new furniture to the basement, the weather turned surprisingly warm and balmy for February. Lizzie thought happily that this was very likely a good omen. Perhaps they were being a bit impatient—unwise, actually—but, oh, it would be so good to have a home of their own.

The gas stove sat beside the makeshift sink with enough counter-top space to prepare a meal and wash dishes. The refrigerator stood beside the sink. The hutch, or "combine," as the Amish called it, stood against the opposite wall, with the new table and chairs in the middle.

It was all very cozy, and Lizzie chattered happily all the while she unpacked her brown ironstone dishes, setting them in the combine. They strung sturdy wire from the chimney to the back wall and then over to the north wall, hanging old sheets to partition off a bedroom. The men brought in Lizzie's bedroom suit from the farmhouse to fill the temporary room.

Joshua and Emma had not been able to come because their children were sick. Their absence almost ruined the day for Lizzie. She felt sorry for Emma, who, she was sure, would have loved to help arrange furniture the way Lizzie had helped her. But there was nothing to do about that now, so she tried not to pity Emma, knowing she probably didn't mind as much as Lizzie did.

John and Mandy arrived late because of doing the morning chores, having two babies to bundle up, and then driving 10 miles with their horse and buggy. Lizzie squealed with excitement when they arrived, running over to Mandy and grabbing her arm, while Mandy's grin spread the whole way across her face as she looked about the new basement.

"Lizzie, I can't believe you're going to live in this

groundhog hole," she said.

Lizzie stopped in her tracks, truly insulted.

"It's not a groundhog hole!" she protested.

"I know," Mandy smiled. "It's just…"

"Not finished!" Lizzie completed the sentence rapidly.

Mandy laughed.

Mam didn't think Mandy's twins should be in the new house. Susan and KatieAnn kept them in the farmhouse so Mandy could be with Lizzie. The sisters worked side by side down to the last detail, hanging curtains over the small windows and putting a new tablecloth and place mats on the table, before they all trooped down the hill for Mam's late dinner of chicken stew and dumplings.

Halfway through dessert, Lizzie could hardly swallow because of the lump in her throat. This was it. This was truly it. She would never live at home again with Mam and Dat in the old farmhouse with the new addition and Mam's porch filled with "cheraniums" in the wintertime, all kinds of seedlings and transplants in the spring, and bountiful houseplants in the summer.

Now who would mow the grass and trim along the flower beds? That had been her job as long as she could remember, although Susan and KatieAnn had begun to do a lot of the mowing the previous summer. It certainly wasn't Mam's job. She never mowed lawn. She cooked and baked, cleaned the kitchen counter, tended her flowers and quilted, and the girls did the remainder of the work.

It wasn't that the family couldn't survive without Lizzie's help, she knew. It was just sad to think that it was all over now. Her new life with Stephen would begin this evening when they were all alone in the funny little unfinished basement on the hill behind the farm. Lizzie looked up to see Mandy gazing intently in her direction. She lowered her eyes, willing herself to finish this last piece of butterscotch pie.

In Mam's wise way, she opened the subject when the men returned to the new house and Lizzie stayed to help with the dishes. Dumping leftover applesauce into a Tupperware container, she turned to face Lizzie.

"So, this is it for you, huh?"

Blinking rapidly, Lizzie answered. "I suppose so."

"Well, it's the way God intended, Lizzie," Mam said, sighing a bit as she wiped the container where she had spilled some of the applesauce. "He didn't mean for us to be tied to our mother's apron strings after we reach a certain age. Nature, the animals, everything God created, has its times and seasons. Birds leave the nest, baby calves are weaned, and on and on."

"I know, Mam, but I just hate to think of this part of my life being over. All the closeness we shared as sisters..."

"I know exactly what you mean, Lizzie," Mandy broke in. "And let me give you a bit of sisterly advice. Prepare yourself, because marriage isn't all roses, no matter how much you love your husband. I'll never forget the almost overwhelming nauseas before the twins were born, and..."

She giggled, holding a hand to shield her eyes for a minute. "I mean it, when I think back to those first months! What a baby I was—upstairs crying, wanting desperately to be home again, just wanting to be one of Melvin Glick's girls again, and poor John was downstairs eating cold sandwiches for supper. All alone! Oh, how horrible."

Mam threw her head back and laughed long and genuinely. Taking off her glasses, she wiped her eyes, still shaking with silent laughter, and said, "Ach my, Mandy. I remember that very same feeling. It's all a part of life, of growing up and learning to become a more mature person."

Lizzie leaned back in her chair and glared at both of them. "You think it's funny, Mam. Well, I don't. And I'm not going to have one moment like that. Stop talking such things. It gives me the blues."

"All right, Lizzie. But really, it isn't all roses and sunshine, just like Mandy said. You'll have days when you wonder why you ever got married in the first place."

"I don't believe that," Lizzie said staunchly. "I refuse to think that could be possible. You just weren't... well, maybe you didn't love John the way you should have."

Mam's eyebrows went straight up, followed by Mandy's, and they had a genuine, "She'll learn" look between them. Lizzie was so angry that she got up and said it was time for her to go back up to the house. So much for a tearful farewell, she thought, as she stalked up the hill into her little basement that promised to be a haven of pure marital bliss.

Chapter 14

Aᴄᴏʟᴅ ғʀᴇᴇᴢɪɴɢ ʀᴀɪɴ ᴘᴏᴜʀᴇᴅ ғʀᴏᴍ ʟᴇᴀᴅᴇɴ skies, driving in from the east in long, wet slashes against the small basement window as Lizzie pinned her cape once again for another visit. This evening they would be going to visit Elmer and Malinda Esh, a young couple who rented a farmhouse about six miles away. Lizzie looked forward to the evening since the Eshes were not much older than they were.

She was grateful for a good woolen shawl and the bonnet that afforded some protection from the freezing rain as she climbed into the buggy.

"Whew!" she gasped. "This weather!"

Stephen nodded.

"I'm worried about leakage in the basement, no spouting on the house, and the cement blocks offset the way they are, for bricks. I just hope the ground will contain the seepage."

"Oh, it'll be all right," Lizzie said airily.

"I'm not so sure," Stephen replied.

"Well, what's the worst that could happen? Some water on the floor that will surely go down the drain?" Lizzie asked.

Stephen didn't reply, only grunted, so she remained silent, although the thought of rain water coming into the basement made her bite down hard on her lower lip. Her eyes darted nervously to the rain streaming against the buggy windows.

She forgot the pelting rain, the basement home, or anything worrisome after she entered the cozy farmhouse kitchen and found the table set with Malinda's prettiest dishes. The only light in the dining room came from real candles burning in their delicate holders.

Oh, but that was just about the classiest thing Lizzie had ever seen! She clasped her hands in front of herself excitedly. How romantic for newlyweds to eat by candlelight, which was always flattering to anyone's looks. The imperfections of your face were well hidden by the small amount of light candles afforded.

The food was delicious, although it was different, without the usual meat and potato fare. Lizzie enjoyed the evening tremendously, eating too much as usual, promising herself that she would do much better at the next meal.

Their wedding gift was a Tupperware pitcher, something new, with a lid that sealed so you could shake the liquid inside without it leaking out. Lizzie thought it was a wonderful new invention to be able to mix a drink without having to stir it with a spoon. Iced tea mix would no longer settle on the bottom of a container because you could keep shaking it at intervals, and the sugar would always be mixed through. Before this, you ended up with watered-down iced tea at first, and then tea that was much too sweet when the pitcher was almost empty.

When the evening was over, Lizzie dashed through the rain and scrambled quickly into the buggy, slamming the side door shut with all her strength before wrapping the blue and green blanket securely across her lap. She watched Stephen's face as he frowned at the streams of icy water cascading down the window of the buggy.

"Still no let up," he murmured, more to himself than to her.

"No. It's been raining like this for …"

"All day," Stephen broke in.

He urged George forward, and they went flying along, homeward bound. Lizzie was glad to go home to their own little house, even if it was unfinished. As usual, they took the team down to her parents' farm, because there was no barn on their property yet. Stephen asked if she wanted to be dropped off at their house, but she shook her heard no, assuring him she could run up the hill through the rain as well as he could. They ran through the downpour together and arrived at the basement door, gasping for breath, completely soaked. Stephen turned the knob and unlocked the door, stepped inside, and stopped.

"What?" Lizzie squeaked.

Then she heard it. A decided splashing sound where Stephen stepped. Oh, no! Her heart escalated to her throat before banging way down to the pit of her stomach, spreading fear and anxiety through her. Water! Water everywhere! Her new furniture, the sofa, the recliner. Everything would be ruined, of this she was positive.

"Oh, Stephen!" she wailed, absolutely heartsick. "Where is all this water coming from?"

"Just be quiet!" Stephen almost shouted at her.

Lizzie was horrified. Water, cold rain water, spread across the entire floor, swirling beneath her new sofa and recliner, swishing along the table and new chairs, and now Stephen was yelling at her, clearly angry just because she squeaked one frightened little question.

It was pitch dark in the basement, but Lizzie knew she needed to find a pack of matches to light the gas lamp. Flashlights! That was the answer, but by the time she had sloshed over to the cupboard, Stephen had already found one, which by the sound of his muttering, wasn't cooperating.

"Doesn't that one work?" she managed, in a tiny voice.

There was no answer; only the sound of a flashlight being hurled against the unpainted cement block wall, accompanied by Stephen's frustrated accusation that she had lost all the flashlights.

That did it. Lizzie felt the anger course through her body, followed by a rush of adrenaline. She stopped in the middle of the wet basement, curled her hands into fists, and took a deep breath.

"I didn't touch your precious flashlight!" she yelled, "So don't go blaming me for everything that goes wrong!"

"There were two flashlights against the left cupboard wall. Now there's only one, and it doesn't work."

"I didn't use it!" Lizzie screeched.

There was only a resounding "Humph" from Stephen, and Lizzie became so angry she wished she had a flashlight to throw at him. All right, if that's how he was going to be, she'd just stand there with the water sloshing around her, slowly seeping between the leather layers of the soles of her Sunday shoes and soaking her feet with a miserable, cold wetness. She knew where the matches were, but she wasn't going to tell him. Let him figure it out.

Which, of course, he did. He rummaged around in a few drawers before sloshing over to the table and lowering the gas lamp that hung above it. Striking two matches, he heated the mantles until they ignited. Brilliant yellow light illuminated the entire basement as he carefully hung the lamp on the hook suspended from the ceiling joist.

Lizzie looked around very slowly, hardly daring to look at Stephen, knowing he was angry. A significant amount of water covered almost the entire floor. Water seemed to still be entering the basement through the east wall, where rain continued to pelt against the house. Lizzie felt panic rising in her throat. They couldn't even begin to sop up the water with towels and buckets. They'd be working the entire night.

"Stephen, what are we going to do?" Lizzie asked, wringing her hands in despair.

"Open the drain, for one thing," he said shortly, grabbing the broom and flipping it upside down as he searched for the drain opening.

Oh, that was it! They had a drain! Of course! All the water would run down the drain pipe, out into the yard and down the hill. Why hadn't she thought of that before? Why, of course. They would have a clean, dry basement in no time.

She almost cried when Stephen bent down and pulled at the top of the drain, and she heard a distinct gurgling sound as water began to flow down the new pipe. She watched in awe as a little whirlpool of water formed above it, the water continuing its spiral down this wonderful little outlet. Never had there been a sweeter sight in her entire life. Her new furniture wouldn't be ruined after all.

"Oh, Stephen, it's going down!" she breathed happily.

"Yeah, but more is coming in along that back wall, so don't get too excited.

"You mean ... you mean, it's still coming in?"

"Of course. As long as it continues to rain like this, it'll come down through those offset blocks. There's no spouting on the house, remember?"

Lizzie nodded miserably.

"You can start sweeping some of the water toward the drain awhile. I'll set up the things we can lift out of the water."

He started picking up the new kitchen chairs and placing them upside down on the table top, while Lizzie reached for the broom and began sweeping water towards the drain from the farthest corner. The water kept up its swirl down the lovely little drain. They didn't speak, just worked silently, each one doing what had to be done at the moment. Lizzie swept as if her very life depended on how much water went down that drain. When she reached the bedroom, she couldn't stop the wail that threatened to turn into a torrent of genuine little girl tears.

"My bedroom suit! My new bedspread!" she wailed. "Stephen, I mean it, everything will be ruined!" she cried.

"Not if we get it dried out as fast as we possibly can," Stephen answered, "The only problem is the water is still coming in."

"How … long do you think it will keep raining?" Lizzie asked, her mouth dry with anxiety.

"How would I know?" Stephen answered brusquely.

That did it. Lizzie began crying in earnest. She stopped trying to be brave and grown up, resorting to the heartsick despair she felt so keenly. She wanted to run to her old bedroom upstairs in her parents' farmhouse, crawl safely into her own bed way off the ground, and listen to the rain drumming on the attic roof. She would be dry and secure, and

Dat would take care of everything. She shouldn't have married so soon, she thought sadly. Then she felt so horrible for having that thought and she started crying harder than ever.

Perhaps this was what the preacher meant at their wedding when he said they would experience the joys of sunshiny days as well as the trials of rainy days. She supposed you put this experience smack dab in the category of trials and rainy days, for sure. The same preacher had also spoken at length about the trials in their lives producing fruit; in other words, making better people out of all of us. Lizzie couldn't see how this was possible. How was she ever supposed to like Stephen again? He was mean to her.

That was the thing about being married to someone. What if you could hardly stand them when they didn't act right? It was all so scary. How in the world did that preacher figure any good could come out of a mess like this? She doubted if even God could find the good in this situation.

Tears running down her face, and sniffling and coughing like a little girl, she kept sweeping water toward the drain. She made absolutely sure Stephen heard her crying, so he would feel sorry for her and feel bad that he had made her cry so soon into their marriage. She blew her nose loudly, sighed, looked in his direction, and sighed louder.

He kept on moving furniture out of the water, never stopping to glance in her direction. Bringing pieces of lumber down from upstairs, he set the sofa and recliner up and out of the water, which, Lizzie admitted to herself, was a wonderful idea.

"You'll have to help me with the dresser, Lizzie," he said, stopping to look at her.

"I'm still crying. Wait," she answered, finding the perfect opportunity to let him understand that she was, after all, completely heartbroken. Stephen's shoulders sagged, and he made a sound between a snort and a sigh. Mostly a snort. Lizzie blew her nose loudly again, then stepped over to receive her instructions.

"Now when I lift this end of the dresser, you slide that piece of two-by-four under it. Be careful."

Oh, it was a great idea, it really was, setting her precious furniture on two-by-fours. The things that were on casters—the hutch cupboard, the table, and the light stand—could all sit in the water without serious damage, so Lizzie began to feel better. Much better, in fact.

The rugs were soaked, so there was nothing to do except roll them up and place them close to the drain. Stephen put more wood in the stove, building a roaring fire, and soon Lizzie noticed dry spots on the new concrete floor.

Glancing at the kitchen clock, she saw it was almost midnight, and suddenly she felt very, very tired, actually on the verge of collapse. Her arms hurt from all the sweeping, which was why she was tired, she decided. She wondered vaguely if Stephen was tired, too, and fervently hoped so.

The following morning they were awakened by brilliant sunshine slanting through the east window of their basement home. Lizzie sat bolt upright and said quite loudly, "The sun is shining!"

"It usually does," Stephen said dryly from the depth of his pillow.

"Not when there's a rainstorm!" she said happily.

Oh, she could not believe their good fortune as she tiptoed around the basement in her bare feet, evaluating their situation. A small amount of water was still seeping through the block wall, but only in a few places, and not very much at that. The soaked rugs continued to leak water, but most of it ran down the lovely little drain.

They were saved! No furniture was ruined. All would be well, and Lizzie's joy knew no bounds.

"Oh, Stephen, I'm so glad it quit raining. Everything is drying out!" she trilled.

She made eggs and toast, heating the canned sausage Mam had given them with the remainder of their canned goods. She would have liked to make pancakes, but she didn't know how, and besides, she had no pancake syrup. She would have to remember to buy some when she went to town with Mam.

They ate and talked, Stephen saying they'd need to plan a few frolics on Saturdays to work on the house, since this basement was not the ideal place for new furniture. They needed to finish construction as soon as possible. Lizzie clasped her hands together with sheer happiness, hearing Stephen talk like that. Finally, he was going to hurry! Soon she would be living in a new house!

It was amazing how easily and completely she could forgive Stephen for being so short with her last evening. She guessed that must be because she loved him, believing that if you didn't love someone you didn't get over things that easily.

A new thought struck her then, and she looked at Stephen when he wasn't looking at her. Maybe he had thought she was being a frightful, big baby last night, sweeping water and crying, but he wasn't mad at her this morning, at least not that she could see.

"Were you mad at me last night?" she blurted out in her forthright manner.

"Not really. You burned this toast."

"What do you mean, 'not really'? Were you sort of?"

"Hmm-mm."

"Yes, you were."

There was no answer.

See, that was the thing about Stephen that irritated her. You couldn't get to first base about how he felt. She had always shared all her feelings with Emma and Mandy. Everything. But with Stephen....

Well, the sun was shining, the basement was partially dry, and life was definitely better than last evening. They had gotten through a very big trial in life, in Lizzie's opinion. They had come through quite well, considering Stephen only threw one flashlight, not both of them, and she had cried only once. Well, the crying had gone on for quite some time, but it wouldn't have if Stephen had been kinder and put his arms around her and pitied her the way she thought he should have.

She guessed that was how most men were. She was sure Stephen thought she had been terribly childish; that's why he chose to ignore her. So really, he had something to get over, too. Perhaps he could hardly stand her this morning.

That was a new thought, so she vowed to do better and never cry again. She bet most men didn't like it when their wives cried, especially when the tears were produced by a situation they had no control over. It wasn't Stephen's fault they had a rainstorm. Yes, she would figure this out and learn by her mistakes, becoming a better wife as time went on.

When Stephen got a clean, new tea towel and asked if she wanted him to dry dishes for her, she smiled at him genuinely and was very grateful. He was a good husband in so many ways, so what did it matter if he didn't tell her all his feelings? Putting up with her crying and drying dishes for her was a lot.

And when he said he wasn't going visiting anymore, that he was thoroughly tired of it, that they had plenty of wedding gifts, and that he would rather stay at home with her, she agreed heartily. That was fine. Perhaps the rainstorm had come so they would agree on this one thing and learn to accept each other in the process. Maybe that preacher knew what he was talking about after all.

Chapter 15

THAT SPRING, THE GLAD DAY ARRIVED WHEN the house was finished. Mandy and Mam helped Lizzie clean the new rooms so they were ready for the moving day they had set for Saturday. Stephen's whole family would come to help, as well as Joshua and Emma.

For a small house, their floor plan was very wise, Lizzie thought. The kitchen was in a part by itself, although the dining room and living room were all open, laid out in a kind of L shape. That meant Lizzie could set up her table with all the leaves in it if she chose to have lots of company for a meal.

She loved her new kitchen cupboards, stained to a medium walnut shade. She had plenty of cupboard space, plus a small pantry with deep shelves that held an amazing amount of things. The refrigerator sat along the opposite wall by the window, and the table and chairs were placed in the middle of the dining area near the back door that faced the east.

The linoleum was a shade of brown with a small brick design. The laundry room had hardwood flooring, with an open stairway going to the upstairs. The living room was small, but it flowed into the dining area, with only the line where the hardwood flooring stopped, and the brick brown linoleum started, marking where one room began and the other ended.

There was a small hallway off the dining area, where, on the left, the basement door opened to the stairs going down, and on the right, another door led to the bathroom.

Lizzie was very proud of her bathroom with its long vanity attached to a tall cupboard built into the corner. She had so much space for towels, washcloths, sheets, pillowcases, and anything else she chose to store there. It was really wonderful cupboard space, a part of the house that she loved the most, she thought, smoothing the towels properly as she placed them one by one into the tall shelves. She put the sheets there on the top shelves, all folded evenly. In her opinion, it looked exactly like a picture in the Sears' catalog.

At the end of this small hallway, a door led to their bedroom, a nice-sized one with less expensive linoleum in a shade of white with a small stone design. The bedspread was blue, but she hadn't made curtains for the windows yet, so it wouldn't seem finished until that was done. There was a second bedroom adjoining their room. Stephen had lots of things to put in this room, like guns, a gun cabinet, a bow and arrow, strange looking boots, gun cleaning kits, and a spare desk.

One thing bothered Lizzie, although she decided not to make a fuss to Stephen about it. It was the fact that no door joined these two rooms, which meant that any nice summer breeze wouldn't flow from one room to the next. A door between the rooms would take care of that.

But today was moving day, and there was so much to be happy about. She couldn't imagine making a big issue about the lack of one door.

Stephen's parents arrived early, eager to help carry the new furniture up from the basement. His mother brought more sheet sets, towels, and a brand new comforter made with purple and blue flannel and knotted with blue yarn. It was very pretty and of a medium weight that would be perfect for their bed. The wood stove in the living room was not very far away, so their bedroom probably wouldn't become too cold.

She didn't need to worry about that now, however, because spring was here and promised to bring beautiful sunshine and warm breezes nearly every day.

Joshua and Emma arrived. It was always a happy event when they traveled the 45 miles from their own farm in Allen County.

John and Mandy came up the hill with their black horse, the twins sound asleep in their little car seats in the back seat of the buggy. Mandy had made cookies for their coffee break, and Mam soon had the coffee ready, bringing it up the hill from the farmhouse below.

Lizzie would never forget this whole day. Everything was taken care of, down to the last detail. The curtains were all hung, the bathroom fixtures were in place, and even the canister set Mandy had given her was lined up on the counter top and filled with flour, sugar, oatmeal, and tea.

The canisters were made of glass, not ceramic, with the words "sugar," "flour," "coffee," and "tea" labeled across their fronts in brown, fat letters. It was an unusual canister set, Lizzie knew. No one else had one exactly like it, so she felt very classy and modern.

After everyone had gone home, wishing them the best, Lizzie's heart was filled to overflowing. How blessed she and Stephen were! They had so many caring relatives, so much love to absorb and be thankful for. She felt as if her whole life had built up to this moment. She was settled in a new house with everything the way she wanted, and Stephen was her husband. She was living a dream come true.

Before long, however, Lizzie was finished making curtains, cleaning the basement, baking Stephen's favorite chocolate cake, and sewing a few items of clothing, and she became very, very bored.

She wanted a lawn. That was the thing. She

wanted a bulldozer to come level the mounds of topsoil that were lined up on the south side of the house so they could rake them evenly and then sow grass, plant shrubs, and make flower beds and a garden. Lizzie had nothing to do.

Stephen told her they could not have a lawn that summer, because he was laying all the white bricks himself. There was no use putting a lawn in when he would just ruin it by trampling the grass while laying brick. Lizzie nodded, understandingly. She really did. But inside she saw no sense in it. Couldn't he lay brick by staying close to the house where the flower beds would be?

One evening, after she had literally been sitting in the recliner twiddling her thumbs, she opened the subject of having a lawn once again.

Stephen sighed, his eyes narrowing, and he laid down his fork.

"Lizzie, you just don't get it. How can I push a wheelbarrow across the newly seeded lawn? Or drag a water hose across it? Or set up the scaffolding? It simply won't work. Besides, it's too late in the season. The sun will be too hot, and we'd have to water constantly if we seeded now." Picking up his fork, he resumed eating his mashed potatoes and hamburger gravy.

Lizzie didn't say anything and only watched him eat, thinking he had an awfully big mouthful of food and that she didn't like him very much.

That was the trouble with having a husband. He was the one who made the decisions; not you.

What if you knew better? What if that lawn could be seeded right now?

Stephen took a sip of water, then tipped back his chair and looked at her.

"Besides, we can't afford to pay someone to spread the topsoil, and the best time to seed a lawn is late August or September. Not the beginning of summer.

"How do you know?"

"I asked."

"Who did you ask?"

"A guy that was planting shrubs at the house we're building."

"Oh."

Well, there wasn't much Lizzie could say to that since he had asked the landscaping fellow. He probably knew what he was talking about.

She sighed.

"But, Stephen, I'm terribly bored. I have nothing to do. Not one thing. If I had a lawn and flower beds and a garden, I'd be busy all summer long."

"Lizzie, you have to give up on having a lawn this summer. You'd make it a lot easier on yourself if you would."

"I should get a job," she said glumly.

"Why don't you?"

"I hate to think of grading eggs again."

"It would give you something to do, and we could save money and buy all kinds of nice shrubs this fall."

That did it. If there was anything Lizzie loved

more than a nice house it was a beautiful lawn. She would get a job, even if it meant going back to grading eggs.

The following morning she marched resolutely down the hill to the phone shanty they shared with Mam and Dat. She dialed Darwin Myers' number and waited anxiously till his wife answered the phone. Yes, they would be glad to have her work part-time, they really would. Yes, they could come pick her up, although Mrs. Myers was almost sure Lizzie could make arrangements with Fred Martin's wife, Dorothea, who had just started working there the week before.

Lizzie hurried in to the farmhouse to tell Mam, who was busily planting a few late purple and white striped petunias in her flower bed by the sidewalk.

"Good for you, Lizzie!" she commented when Lizzie told her she was going back to work. "That's a good idea. You know in Proverbs there's a chapter that speaks of a woman who is an honor to her husband by making things and selling them in the marketplace. Stephen will be glad if you help with the income."

Lizzie nodded happily.

"Yes, he will. He's the one who suggested it to me."

"Well, I'm glad. Idle time is the devil's time, Lizzie."

Lizzie's eyes narrowed, not sure how she should take that comment from Mam.

"You mean, if I have nothing to do, it's the devil's fault?" she asked suspiciously.

Mam laughed.

"No, no, no. I mean, to sit around doing nothing is not good for our minds. It's a time when, being human, we tend to think of ourselves, have dissatisfied thoughts, or whatever."

"Hmm, maybe that's why I become miserable because Stephen isn't finished with his brick-laying and we can't have a yard. Mam, you know how happy I'd be if I could mow lawn."

"Knowing you, Lizzie, you'll mow lawn three times a week with the mower set much too short."

Lizzie laughed. "Probably."

Mam bent to her task, and Lizzie decided to go home.

Dat and Jason were at work and the twins in school, so there was no one to talk to other than Mam, and she was, by all appearances, terribly busy planting her petunias.

"Do you need help?" she volunteered.

"Now Lizzie, you know I like to plant my own petunias. Did you see these 'cheraniums'? These new pink ones? Aren't they the prettiest color? I found them at the new greenhouse in town. They were a bit too expensive, but I love my 'cheraniums.'"

Lizzie nodded, knowing Mam's flower beds well. A complete mixture of colors, every petunia and geranium she could find for miles around, planted in a profusion of brilliant hues. Mam spent hours with a wheelbarrow, a bag of peat moss, and a bucket of water, planting flowers until her face became almost as red as her geraniums.

So Lizzie began a routine of working for the Myers three days a week, standing at the egg-grading machine sorting eggs. Since she had worked there before, the Myers had built a new chicken house, installed an updated grader, and hired more people.

The second week, Lizzie thought she saw a new and different car parked in the parking lot. It was a small black car with blue stripes along the side.

"I wonder if someone new started," she said to Dorothea, who picked her up in the morning.

"Looks like it."

Sure enough, when Lizzie walked into the egg-grading room, a new girl stood by the egg-grader, looking a bit uncertain. Lizzie felt suddenly a bit shy, mostly because this new woman was very pretty. Her dark hair was cut neatly and swung in glossy smoothness down her back. Her eyes were brown, and her mouth looked different than any Lizzie had ever seen, maybe because her teeth were perfectly straight and white. She wore a beautiful blue sweater with a navy blue skirt, and looked quite English. She seemed to be a woman of the world and very sure of herself, except on this first day at a new job, when everyone felt a bit ill at ease.

That bit of uncertainty helped Lizzie to move toward her.

"Hi, I'm Lizzie," she said.

"Hi! I'm Julie Morton. It's nice to meet you. I guess we may as well learn to know each other, as close as we'll be working together."

Lizzie laughed, Julie smiled, and a friendship sparked that instant.

At lunchtime, Lizzie was amazed to discover that Julie had just gotten married in a long white gown and veil with all of the English wedding traditions at her parents' home, even though her parents were members of the German Baptist group, or River Brethren, as they were commonly called in this immediate area.

Her parents were plain! How fascinating. Her mother wore a large white covering, and her father cut his hair and beard almost like Dat. As Julie talked about their way of life, Lizzie was reminded that there are lots of different denominations, different groups of plain people who were, really, much the same, with only a few differences. Although Julie's parents dressed plainly, they drove black cars and trucks and had electricity and other modern conveniences that Lizzie was not allowed to have. Yet they had basically the same views and values as the Amish.

The lunch hour flew by, and they both gasped to realize they had already talked five minutes past the allotted time. They hurried back to work, still smiling as they reclaimed their positions at the egg-grading machine.

Throughout the summer, their friendship deepened. Lizzie looked forward to her days with Julie. One day while they sat side by side eating lunch, Julie told Lizzie that she and her husband, Gary, had decided to give their lives to God and join the River Brethren. They would dress plain, as their parents did.

Lizzie blinked, surprised. She could see Julie was very serious.

"You mean you'll dress with a covering and a long dress? Completely different than now?"

Julie nodded soberly.

"But then... You'll be different? You won't laugh and talk the way you do now?"

Julie laughed. "Of course I will!"

Lizzie was hugely relieved. She had been afraid Julie would no longer be the same talkative, fun-loving person she was now when she started to dress plain.

At work that afternoon, Lizzie kept glancing sideways at Julie, at her beautiful dark hair and her pretty sweater, and wondered if she wouldn't turn out to be one huge disappointment, becoming so pious and holy that she would think that Lizzie no longer qualified to be her friend. It made Lizzie nervous, thinking about someone becoming a much, much better person, going from a carefree young English woman to being a good plain one. That evening she fretted about this to Stephen, telling him everything about Julie and her church.

"Why are they called River Brethren?" she concluded.

Stephen shrugged his shoulders, turning back to his *Outdoor Life* magazine.

"Stephen, you're not listening to me again."

"I'm listening."

"But what if I come to work and she's almost like, well, like an angel? She'll be all freshly baptized and good and pure, and her clothes will be so different, and I'll be ... well, the same sinner I always am."

"Lizzie!" Stephen scolded.

"I mean it. I did so many wrong things since I was baptized and gave my life to God, that sometimes I'm not sure if I did."

"What?" Stephen said absent-mindedly.

"Gave my life to God when I got baptized."

"Well, if it's as hard as you make it sound, we'd never make it." he said dryly.

Lizzie didn't know what he meant by that remark, and he soon laid his magazine aside, tilted back the recliner, and closed his eyes, after which Lizzie knew the discussion had ended then and there. That's how Stephen was. He didn't keep rambling on about nothing in particular, so she got up and sighed, knowing the conversation was over.

When Julie came back to work the following week, Lizzie was very nervous about her again. She tried to be polite and not stare at her or ask rude questions, but she studied Julie a lot when Julie wasn't looking at her.

She was still pretty, only in a subdued way. Her white covering covered most of her hair and all of her ears and tied snugly beneath her chin. Her dress had a cape over the shoulders and a belt around her waist and hung in folds almost to her shoes. She seemed sweet and old-fashioned, almost like she imagined the characters in the Laura Ingalls Wilder series of books looked. Thankfully, she was the same Julie, her smile coming quickly and easily. She seemed, like her clothes, a bit subdued and serious, but friendly and welcoming.

Lizzie had tried to comb her hair flatter than ever that morning, jerking her covering as far over her ears as it would go, feeling as if she would be more equal to Julie if she was well within her church's *ordnung*. It was just something she wanted to do to make herself feel better, since she definitely wanted to appear more pious herself. She didn't know whether Julie noticed her flat hair—she just hoped she did—and believed that Lizzie was with her on the road she had chosen to get to heaven someday. But the thing that really bothered Lizzie most was when Julie mentioned the fact that they would be farming her father-in-law's farm soon. Lizzie's eyes became big and round, and she swiveled her head instantly to stare at Julie.

"You mean milk cows?" she squeaked.

"Oh, yes. Gary is a real dairy farmer. He loves cows."

"Then ... then ... does that mean you will, too?"

"Oh, yes!" Julie said happily. "I'm looking forward to milking cows."

"Oh."

"Why, don't you like cows?"

Terribly afraid that she would fall way on behind, as far as being a good person, Lizzie assured Julie that yes, she liked cows, just not milking them. She thought Julie gave her an awfully funny look but had the good manners to let it go at that. Lizzie wondered how much sinning was involved in hating cows. She had never enjoyed milking cows at home with Dat, but maybe if Stephen became a dairy farmer she would learn to appreciate them. Although, if she was very honest with herself, she doubted that she would like Stephen very much if he wanted her to milk cows with him.

Chapter 16

Aʟʟ sᴜᴍᴍᴇʀ ʟᴏɴɢ, Sᴛᴇᴘʜᴇɴ ᴄᴀᴍᴇ ʜᴏᴍᴇ from working with Dat and Jason, ate his supper, and then went outside and laid the white brick with brown mortar around the base of their house. He enjoyed his work very much. In fact, he told Lizzie they should have planned to brick the whole house. Lizzie didn't say anything, but she was extremely glad he hadn't thought of that, thinking how frightfully ugly that would look. Like a prison, or something. But, since Stephen hadn't planned for that, there was no use saying exactly what she thought.

All summer long the weeds grew around the house and on the piles of topsoil heaped beside it. There wasn't a thing Lizzie could do about it, as long as Stephen meticulously laid his bricks, one by one, in perfect succession. Fortunately, since starting her work at the egg-grading room, she was no longer bored, so the days flew by.

One evening after Stephen had laid the very last brick, Lizzie helped him sort the few remaining ones, rinse the wheelbarrow well with the green rubber hose, and stack the few leftover bags of brown mortar. Then she went to the house to make a pitcher of lemonade. The sun was beginning its descent, dipping below the mountain, and a small flock of blackbirds fussed and twittered their way across the evening sky, the way blackbirds did when they started to sense the end of summer.

Stephen watched their flight, drank his lemonade, and said nothing. Lizzie clasped her hands around her knees, pulling her skirt down till only her bare toes were visible, and sighed happily.

"Oh, Stephen, I'm so glad those bricks are finally finished," she said.

"I'm not."

"Why not?"

"I enjoy laying brick."

"I know, but… weren't you even, not even once, a bit impatient to have the job done?"

Lizzie was incredulous, watching Stephen with narrowed eyes as he shook his head back and forth.

"Really? You were never in a hurry?" she asked.

"No use hurrying if the best time to seed a lawn is in September. That's another whole month."

"You mean you're not going to get started on the lawn next week?" Lizzie asked, trying to keep the desperation from her voice.

"No."

"Well… well… well… what ARE you going to

do in the evening?" she asked, her heart sinking.

"I don't know. Just relax."

"But ... why would you relax, when ... ?"

"Lizzie, there's more to life than hurrying to finish everything as fast as you can. What would you suggest that I do?"

"Well, nothing. I mean, if you don't want to."

"We only have enough money to have this topsoil spread by an excavating company; then our loan is completely used up. I'd love to have a new bow. A compound bow. Archery season comes in October, so I thought maybe I could do a few jobs in the evening, save the money, and buy a new bow."

Lizzie stared off across the hills of topsoil, trying so hard to say the right thing, but she imagined Stephen working in the evening and not having her precious yard put in until spring.

"You mean ...? Stephen! Surely not!" she wailed, losing all her premeditated composure.

She wanted a new lawn, shrubs, and flower beds so badly, especially now that they seemed so close, and he'd go prancing off, working for someone else to buy a bow! Just for himself!

"What?" Stephen asked, his head swirling in her direction, staring at her in disbelief.

"You wouldn't put in the lawn?" Lizzie said quite forcefully, her eyebrows lowered as she stared back at him.

"Yes, I would. How long does it take to put in a lawn? One day? A few evenings? We have a whole month before September."

"Oh."

Lizzie's relief knew no bounds and was followed by a rush of love for Stephen, and the fact that he would not go archery-hunting until the lawn was seeded. Now that was so nice of him, she thought, slipping her arm through his and laying her head on his shoulder.

Suddenly she remembered the Mennonite produce farmer, Robert Weaver, who had asked if there was anyone available to help pick tomatoes. Mam had told him her girls were no longer at home, and she wasn't sure who would be available to help. Tomato-picking was a good thing. Lizzie and her sisters had picked tomatoes for a farmer when she was only 15 years old, and they had made a substantial amount of money for Mam. Why couldn't they do that now? She and Stephen?

"Stephen, I know! We can pick tomatoes!" she said, beaming.

"Pick tomatoes? I guess not," Stephen snorted.

"I'm serious, I really am. You can make 20 dollars in a hurry picking tomatoes, and it's enjoyable work. I mean, as long as your back doesn't begin to hurt."

"A bow costs a lot more than 20 dollars, Lizzie."

"How much more?"

"More like 200."

"Really? Well, we could work about 10 evenings, and that would do it," Lizzie chirped, undaunted.

The thing about this whole bow business was the fact that if she wasn't nice about Stephen spending money for that bow, then perhaps he would become all strict and proper, deciding not to spend money for shrubs and mulch and other unnecessary but nice things she dreamed about.

All her life, Lizzie had admired neat lawns, closely trimmed shrubs, and meticulously cared for flower beds, always determining how she could achieve that look of perfection in her own yard. Even when she was at home on the farm, she mowed grass constantly. She cut away at the edges of the flower beds to make precisely straight borders until Mam had yelled at her from the porch, telling her to go store that hatchet before she hacked the entire yard away.

It made her nervous to think of wanting something so badly, to have it so nearly within reach, and yet to know that Stephen may not want to plant expensive shrubs. The new house was there now, and finished on the outside, anyway. All she needed to achieve her dream of a beautiful little home was a seeded lawn and shrubs.

"We could try it," Stephen said slowly.

So the following week when Stephen got home from work, Lizzie had supper ready and waiting so they could quickly eat. Then Stephen hitched up George, the horse, while Lizzie hurriedly washed dishes, and they were off. George was feeling frisky, and the two miles passed in a blur before they pulled up to the hitching rack on the Robert Weaver farm. Stephen hopped down and went to find Robert while Lizzie waited, watching the tomato-pickers bent over as they worked in the flat field.

It was a pretty sight, the sun beginning to take on its evening glow, the colorful prints of the Mennonite girls' brightly colored dresses brilliantly lighted against the backdrop of green tomato plants dotted with black plastic hampers filled with bright red tomatoes. She wished she could take a picture, but Amish people don't believe in having cameras, so she knew she couldn't and that was all right.

Stephen returned with Mr. Weaver, tied George to the hitching rack, and then they were off across the drive and down the lane leading to the tomato plants. Lizzie had to walk fast to keep up with Stephen. Robert had shown him where they could start picking, which proved to be farther away than it had appeared at first.

There was a stack of black plastic hampers turned upside down at the rows where they would begin. Eager to show Stephen what an accomplished tomato-picker she was, she stepped right up to the hampers and easily pulled several from the tall stack. She walked along, scattering a few ahead of them. She turned to find Stephen with his hat pushed back, scratching his head in bewilderment.

"Lizzie, it's going to take all evening to fill 10 baskets, and that's two dollars and fifty cents. This is not the smartest thing we've ever done."

Bending to the task, Lizzie lifted the dying tomato vines to find an absolute trove of large ripe tomatoes all piled in one heap.

"Look, Stephen. This is no problem. Watch. How long does it take to fill a hamper when there are so many of these huge red tomatoes on top of each other?"

She began pulling at the tomatoes, remembering how easily they were removed from the stalk, and slamming them into the bin as fast as she could. She pulled tomatoes, showing off for Stephen and going much faster than what was absolutely necessary.

Stephen watched, then grabbed a hamper.

"I'd rather be building pole barns," he grumbled, but he soon began throwing tomatoes into the hamper, keeping up with Lizzie.

She said nothing, grimly determined to pick as many tomatoes as she possibly could. The sun slid down, the air began to cool a bit, and still they kept picking tomatoes. Lizzie's back hurt horribly, but she was determined Stephen wouldn't know, as he showed no signs of slowing.

They were both on their tenth basket now, so Lizzie figured at 25 cents a basket, they would have five dollars for 20 baskets. That was far from 20 dollars, though, and her back could not stand one more basket before she would collapse into a heap in the tomato stalks. Straightening up, she rubbed her back with both hands, grimacing as she did so.

"Doesn't your back hurt?" she asked, watching intently as Stephen kept on picking, whistling under his breath.

"Hmm-mm."

"Not one bit?"

"Hmm-mm."

No use showing her weakness now, she thought grimly. I can't stand bending over picking things too long at a time, but he's not going to find out. This was my idea. Groaning inwardly, she bent over and began her eleventh basket, glancing over her shoulder to see how far away the sun was from dropping behind the mountain. Pretty far.

"Stephen, what time is it?" she asked.

He straightened, pulled his watch from his pocket and said, "Six-thirty."

"Is that all?"

"What do you mean, is that all? If we're going to make 20 dollars, we still have a long way to go."

Lizzie nodded, bent her back, and picked tomatoes as if a mad bull would attack her if she didn't keep up with Stephen. Now the backs of her legs hurt miserably, a dull ache that went clear down to her ankles. But on she toiled, her only source of energy derived from her stubborn will and determination to prove to Stephen that she could pick tomatoes as fast or faster than he could.

Lizzie kept going, trying to think of any subject to take her mind off the pain in her back, but nothing worked for very long. She thought of shrubs, lawns, flowers, the porch Stephen wanted to build, but nothing made her feel better. She thought of the way they tortured prisoners during wars to get them to talk about secrets they needed to know in order to win a battle. Tomato-picking could work as torture. She wondered if anyone had ever thought of that before. It would be a very good idea. Lizzie decided she would tell anyone just about anything to get out of this torturous backache. She would even tell Stephen her back hurt, she finally admitted.

"Stephen!" she blurted out.

"What?"

"My back hurts. Let's quit."

Stephen straightened and looked quizzically at her face. It bore the pain of the past hour, with her eyebrows poking straight up in the middle, her eyes resembling a coon hound's, sad and begging for pity. He tried desperately to keep a straight face, certainly not wanting to laugh at his wife if she was suffering. But the suffering was only half as bad as she portrayed it, of this he was positive.

In the short time they had been married, he had learned to know her quite well. She preyed on his pity, which really was all right, actually a bit endearing, except for now. Whose idea had this been, anyway?

"How many baskets did we pick?" he asked.

"Don't worry about that, Stephen. Don't you care one tiny bit about my back? I'm going to ruin it for the rest of my life, I mean it."

"Lizzie, this was your idea."

Suddenly her face turned beet red and she leaned forward, clenching her fists. "Stop saying that, Stephen!" she yelled. "You didn't have to come with me. It's your fault, too!"

He hurriedly bent his back, picking tomatoes so she couldn't see him laughing. His shoulders shook, and he sputtered to keep from laughing out loud, knowing her anger would only increase if she saw that he thought it was funny.

"Why don't you say something?" she asked, still angry.

"Oh, go pick tomatoes, Lizzie. You'll be all right," he managed, behind the huge grin on his face, which by now he had turned away.

By the time the sun actually, finally, slid behind the mountain, casting a spell of shadows across the abundant field of tomatoes, Lizzie was seriously afraid she would not be able to find enough strength to return home. She would probably need to spend the remainder of the night in the tomato patch.

Stephen rubbed his grimy hands together.

"That was fun! We made 25 dollars! A good start. If we return tomorrow evening, that will be 50. A fourth of what I'll need. Probably not even that much."

Lizzie hobbled between the rows, rubbing her lower back and glaring at her husband.

"I'm not coming back," she said shortly.

"Really?"

"No."

"Ach, come on, Lizzie. Be a sport. Till tomorrow evening you'll be used to it."

Lizzie was going to answer, she really was, but nothing would come out of her mouth. For one thing, she was almost crying, and for another, if she didn't answer, then maybe he'd worry about why she didn't and start to say things husbands should say. Things like she did so well, and he appreciated her help, and he loved her very much, and he never saw anyone pick tomatoes as fast as she did. Things that would make her want to help him save money to buy his archery supplies.

They finished up in the field. After they were paid, Stephen untied the horse and they headed home. It felt very good to sit beside him in the buggy and pity herself, but it bothered her that he was whistling low under his breath, intently looking out the side door for deer. They wound their way up the hill beside the creek and through the woods until they came to a halt on the main road. George chomped impatiently on his bit as they waited for a few cars to pass.

It was a lovely evening, the last glow of light making everything look prettier than it actually was. Farmhouses and barns that weren't perfect because of a rusted roof, faded siding, or sagging shutters suddenly appeared almost brand new and beautiful in the fading half light of a summer evening. Cows grazing in the pasture after milking seemed much cleaner, and the pasture itself appeared even and dark green with no thistles or cow dung in it. It was amazing. Without thinking, she told Stephen this, and he turned to look at her, slid an arm around her, and held her tightly against his side. Lizzie was startled, then grinned smugly to herself.

Ah-hah! He DID appreciate her. He just wouldn't tell her in so many words the way her family did at home. Snuggling against him, she already looked forward to another evening of picking tomatoes, backache or not.

So during the course of a few weeks, Stephen and Lizzie made 184 dollars. Lizzie's back actually became used to the work, and she learned how happy you could become by doing something unselfish for your husband. Stephen even asked her to go along to the archery shop, but she declined, knowing he would enjoy it more without her waiting impatiently by his side.

Then, one glorious week in August, the excavator spread the topsoil. They let it settle for a few weeks, then bought grass seed and fertilizer. Stephen brought bales of straw from his father's farm. Their friends, Dan and Leah Miller, offered to help them with their lawn since they had seeded their own yard the year before.

The evening Stephen and Lizzie decided to seed the lawn turned into a fun-filled, festive evening. First, everyone raked the soil until it was fine and smooth, removing small rocks and leveling uneven hills of dirt. Dat and Jason arrived with their own rakes, Mam brought homemade cinnamon rolls, and they all worked on the new lawn, moving along the front of the house, down the opposite side of the driveway, and all along the sides and back of the house.

Then, while everyone else rested, Dan and Stephen spread the fertilizer and seeds, raked lightly again, and spread straw to absorb the moisture and protect the tiny little seeds. Lizzie washed her hands well, made coffee, mixed iced tea, and then served a good snack. They all sat around the table, enjoying each other's company and Mam's delicious cinnamon rolls.

No one knew, though, quite how happy Lizzie actually was. All those weeks of anticipation and waiting until Stephen was ready to seed the lawn had been very hard for her. She wanted things done right away without waiting four weeks. But now here they were on a warm, balmy evening with their very own lawn properly seeded. Lizzie was quite confident she would have a beautiful lawn by the next spring.

She chewed happily, smiling at Leah, who was a petite, tiny woman, about eight years older than Lizzie. She was indeed a good friend, giving Lizzie advice about different things, including how to get along with your husband, which Lizzie really appreciated. Lizzie was a bit dubious about being the willing servant that Leah talked about, but it was something to think upon, especially the part about never grumbling or nagging, which was very hard for her.

What other way was there if you wanted something done? Especially if you wanted it done now and not two months later? Oh, well, tonight nothing mattered except the friendship of these two kind and helpful people, Dat and Mam and Jason, and the fact that, finally, at long last, they had a lawn. Now for the shrubs.

Chapter 17

LIZZIE WAS ENJOYING A DISH OF STRAWBERRY ice cream while sitting at a picnic table in the park with her friend, Julie, who she worked with while grading eggs. Suddenly, the ice cream tasted like Pepto-Bismol and the succulent strawberries took on a shiny, grainy quality that turned her stomach. Waves of nausea rippled up her throat, and she looked over at Julie, a bit wild-eyed.

"I don't feel one bit well," Lizzie said shakily.

Julie raised an eyebrow.

"We're not expecting a baby, are we?"

"No," Lizzie said firmly. "It has to be a bug."

"Oh, but Lizzie, some bugs turn into a serious malady called pregnancy."

"I know, Mam told me that."

Lizzie was a bit miffed, sitting there feeling so terribly sick and miserable, the ice cream melting in it's Styrofoam dish and sliding farther and farther down her lap as she held it in her nerveless fingers.

Julie didn't have to talk to her in those condescending tones, as if she was only 12 years old.

The ride home was pure torture. Lizzie was humiliated beyond words when the movement of the car made her so dizzy that the strawberry ice cream churned in her stomach. She had no choice but to ask Julie to please pull over and stop as soon as she could. When the car came to a stop, Lizzie opened the door, lurched into the deep weeds at the side of the road, and threw up the strawberry ice cream.

"Oh, dear, I am so embarrassed," she said, as she climbed back into the car.

"It's all right, Lizzie. There's a bug going around."

Lizzie glared at her friend, and they both burst out laughing.

Julie was right. Lizzie and Stephen were ecstatic to find out they would be parents. Stephen smiled everywhere he went—to work, to church, to visit his parents—which only increased Lizzie's own anticipation.

Mam smiled and nodded when Lizzie told her the news. They discussed babies, mother, hospitals, doctors, buying baby clothes, just everything. Mam told her in a serious sort of way that having a baby wasn't easy.

Lizzie took this to heart, although she told Stephen she could handle her pregnancy just fine. She was tough. She could work as hard as he did, well, almost, and she was healthy, robust, and certainly not weak or skinny.

The weight gain began then, which was a constant source of frustration for Lizzie. The doctor told her 25 to 30 pounds was ideal, and she was determined to stay within those boundaries. At first, it was easy. Foods that were ordinarily delicious turned into vile, unappetizing concoctions that propelled her in the direction of the bathroom, and she threw up almost anything she ate.

Saltines and ginger ale. Pepsi. Ginger tea. Dry toast. Pretzels. It all came back up. Just when she thought she must surely die, unfairly, at a young age, she noticed that the smell of vegetable soup was no longer quite as nauseating. She could eat cheese sandwiches with mustard, which perked her up considerably.

After her nausea passed, her appetite came roaring back. She wanted to eat everything she saw, from the time she got up until she went to bed. She baked whoopie pies, wrapped them individually in plastic wrap, and kept eating them just about all day.

The thing about whoopie pies is that they stick to the plastic wrap in chocolaty layers, and when you pull the wrap away, the part underneath is so soft and good and so close to the creamy white frosting that you take one big bite after another, and before you know it, it's all gone and you want another one.

Lizzie faithfully swallowed her prenatal vitamins, ate healthy foods—orange juice, peas, tomatoes, peaches, and corn—as well as whoopie pies. She went to visit her doctor regularly and immensely enjoyed all the attention she received. Emma and Mandy were overjoyed that Lizzie and Stephen would soon be parents. So much joy, Lizzie thought, as she headed to the hospital with Stephen the night her labor started. *I just can't wait for this baby.*

Hours later, Lizzie was startled by a strange sound in the hallway, waking instantly when she realized where she was and why she was not at home in the little house on top of the hill. She and Stephen were parents now. She had given birth to a little girl the morning before at the hospital in Cedar Falls.

The baby, her baby, weighed seven pounds and one ounce, a perfect miracle, with a deeply tanned complexion, almost as if she had been lying in the sun before she was born. Her eyes were blue, her nose was only a little bump—not really a nose yet— and her mouth was small and perfect. Lizzie was thrilled and very, very scared of this little human being that she was suddenly responsible for forever.

They hadn't decided on a name. Lizzie had informed Stephen quite early that if the baby was a girl, she would name her Laura for Laura Ingalls Wilder, the heroine of Lizzie's life. Stephen didn't say no or yes. He just smiled and didn't make a comment at all, but Lizzie figured his smile must have meant something like an approval, so she went right on thinking about a baby girl named Laura.

She felt a tiny bit guilty about that fancy name. Amish people were encouraged to give their babies plain names like Sarah, Barbara, Anna, and Rebecca, old Bible names that the Amish had used for generations. The thing was, if you really wanted to know which Sarah or Barbara someone was speaking of, you had to add her grandfather's name and her father's name to identify her. You couldn't just say Barbara Zook or Anna Stoltzfus. You had to say, "She is one of Dan's Sammie's girls." It was quite frustrating.

Take her own name, for instance. Lizzie Glick. Her dad's name was Melvin. But which Melvin Glick? There were lots of Melvin Glicks in the large Amish community surrounding them. So you had to say Doddy Glick's name, and then Dat's, before people knew who she was.

Besides, she liked something different, something pretty. Like Laura. It was old-fashioned, for English people, anyway, and it had a nice sound, especially when she added the middle name, Anne.

So here she was, waking up in this strange place, her heart sinking when she thought of the previous night. She had been so very tired, wanting to sleep so desperately, but they kept bringing Laura in, saying it was time for her to eat. But no matter how much the kind nurses tried to help, or in what position she held Laura, she refused to nurse for longer that a few tense seconds. The whole night had been a complete disaster. Lizzie fought tears of despair, she was so upset about the ordeal of trying to breast-feed her baby, who, apparently, was absolutely clueless as to what was required of her.

Lizzie sighed and smoothed the blanket a bit self-consciously as a very large nurse opened the door with her foot and bustled efficiently about the room. She checked Lizzie's blood pressure, took her temperature, poked and prodded her, and asked questions fast and furious like a game of ping-pong. Lizzie was having trouble keeping up with the ball.

"Time for your shower!" the nurse chirped. "Breakfast at eight!" Lizzie groaned, thinking about getting out of bed, but soon realizing that she had absolutely no choice whatsoever, without even a minute of reluctance. Her sheets were pulled back, a pair of very large solid arms were extended toward her, and she was propelled out of bed, her head spinning, the room seeming to tilt permanently to the left. She shuffled to the shower, depending on this solid pillar of strength beside her.

Lizzie had to admit that the soothing hot water and soap, and having her hair washed squeaky clean, were great spirit-boosters, for sure. Her breakfast tray did not stir her appetite at all. In fact, the smells assaulting her from beneath the brown plastic covers made her feel nauseous. She sat in her bed, her back propped against pillows, and wished with all her heart she could figure out why she felt so alone and insecure. She tried to swallow the lump in her throat.

Surely something was wrong with her. Wasn't this supposed to be a time of great love and joy?

She had often looked longingly at pictures in magazines of a wife holding a sweet, perfect, newborn baby. The father always had his arm around both of them, looking so happy because he simply adored his beautiful wife and baby. That was what she had always imagined, the perfect moment from which they would live happily ever after.

Mam had told her once, in her wise way, that having a baby was more than just a soft woolly blanket and cute baby clothes. Lizzie had blinked her eyes a few times and watched Mam suspiciously for awhile after she said that, trying to gauge her level of seriousness. As far as she could tell, Mam was pretty serious. Oh, well, she had thought then. Having a baby was something she was quite certain she could handle. Weren't there thousands and thousands of babies born in the United States every day? It couldn't be that bad.

But, now, sitting alone in the green, sterile environment of her hospital room, her head back against the white pillows, she closed her eyes and tried desperately to fight back the feeling of dread as she thought of the nurse bringing baby Laura to be breast-fed. The whole thing was so devastating. Laura simply would not nurse right. Lizzie sighed, casting a sideways glance at her roommate, Dorie, who was serenely eating great forkfuls of scrambled eggs. Lizzie watched her and wished she could pull the curtain between them.

Chewing happily, Dori swallowed, and then trilled joyfully. "Good morning!" Lizzie quickly gathered her trembling mouth into a quivering smile and answered, "Good morning!"

"Did you sleep well?" Dori asked, spearing a piece of bacon with gusto.

"Not really. Well, only when they didn't bring my baby in."

"Yes, she was a bit fussy, wasn't she? Oh, well, the first few days won't really determine how she'll be once you get her home."

Lizzie nodded gratefully, her eyebrows held high, the lump in her throat swelling to gigantic proportions when Dorie spoke so kindly.

Why in the world did she always feel like crying? This was awful. Perhaps she would become mentally ill now. Biting her lip and struggling to regain her composure, she squeaked, "Is that what they say?"

"Oh, yes!"

Lizzie nodded, a ray of hope beginning to dissolve the lump in her throat. Yes, she would be fine, she really would. She could handle this.

"Aren't you eating?" Dorie asked, concern in her voice.

"I'm not hungry."

"But you should eat. It'll give you strength."

Lizzie nodded, biting her lip. She felt like crying all over again but was saved from another battle with her emotions by two nurses bringing in the babies.

"Time for the little ones' breakfast!" they announced happily.

Lizzie's heart took a complete nosedive, down, down, until her stomach actually hurt from the dread and fear of another despairing episode of trying to feed her baby. But the sight of little Laura made her temporarily forget her fear, as she pushed the white flannel blanket aside and gazed at the small brown face beneath it.

She was so cute, except her forehead was too high, creating the impression that her eyes, nose, and mouth were all one little package, farther down on her face than it should be. Holding the blanket away, Lizzie closely examined the amount of hair Laura had. She had enough not to look bald and ugly like some babies, but not so much that she would need it to be brushed immediately. Yes, she was indeed a cute baby girl, exactly what Lizzie had always dreamed of.

Then, to her amazement, the nurses both left. Just like that, with no warning, they both walked out the door, leaving Lizzie to fend for herself. She felt very much like she was afloat in the middle of nowhere, on a boat with no oars or engine or much sense of direction. She sat bolt upright, clutching Laura as she watched the girl beside her expertly position her little red-haired boy, lean back, and smile. The baby began nursing, as if he knew exactly what he was supposed to do, and went about his business.

Oh, dear, Laura thought wildly, as she cradled little Laura, who promptly threw her head back and began screaming and crying in earnest. No matter which way she held Laura, her response was the same—screaming until beads of perspiration formed along Lizzie's forehead. She was quite seriously afraid she might faint away, letting her baby fall in the process.

Desperately, she kept trying, with Laura consistently refusing, until they were both in no shape to resume breast-feeding. Lizzie glanced around wildly, afraid her baby's constant crying would upset Dorie and her little boy.

"I'm sorry," she offered contritely.

"It's O.K. We're fine."

Maybe she should sit on a chair. Gingerly, she laid Laura crosswise in the middle of the high, narrow hospital bed, and then slid out. Better go to the bathroom first, she thought nervously, as she headed in that direction, quickly glancing at Laura who was still crying at the top of her lungs.

When she emerged from the bathroom, a nurse was bending over the baby, crooning, but as Lizzie approached, she gave her a disapproving glare.

"Never, ever, leave your baby lying alone across a bed. Do you want her to fall and break her head? Fracture her skull?"

Lizzie was shocked, her eyes opening wide as she tried to fathom why the nurse was speaking to her in this way.

"But...I...I..." she stammered, trying to maintain a bit of composure.

"No. There are no excuses. You cannot leave a crying baby in the middle of a bed."

Lizzie bent her head to hide the onslaught of tears, bit down hard on her lip, and shuffled weakly to the chair.

"Have you fed her?" she asked.

"No," Lizzie answered in total and absolute defeat. "I can't get her to nurse."

"I'll take her to the nursery and give her some formula," the nurse announced, whisking the crying baby out the door.

Lizzie sagged weakly in her chair. She never, ever wanted another baby. Why had she ever wanted one in the first place? That nurse should be fired immediately before she hurt more young mothers' feelings. There was absolutely no way her baby could have fallen off that bed when she was in the bathroom for only two minutes.

She lifted her head when Dorie turned and clucked her tongue.

"That wasn't nice," she said softly.

Lizzie shrugged her shoulders, unable to speak, then sat back and thought more sad thoughts. Stephen should have stayed here, and Mam should come for a visit right now.

"What time are visiting hours?" she asked.

Dorie held her little boy over one shoulder, softly patting his little back, and was rewarded with a perfect little burp.

"There you go, my little man. Visiting hours? I think from four to eight."

Lizzie became sad, then, really sad. So sad, in fact, that she stared out the window at the gray

November sky and truly wished she didn't have a baby. Why didn't anyone send her flowers? All the bright, colorful bouquets on the wide green windowsill were her roommate's, not hers. No one thought of her down here in Cedar Falls at the hospital, and likely no one would send her flowers anyway. English people were nicer than Amish people. A beautiful flower arrangement was very, very necessary right now.

So what would happen if they gave Laura formula? She would drink it nicely from a bottle, then go right off to sleep, but what about the next time Lizzie tried to feed her? There had to be a next time. Lizzie heaved herself out of the chair, climbed back into her high, narrow bed, pulled the snowy white sheets over her shoulders, turned her back to Dorie, the perfectly successful mother with all that calm serenity shining from her face, and closed her eyes and cried. Great big, gulping, quiet sobs, with a steady river of tears that ran out of the corners of her eyes, across the bridge of her nose, and onto a puddle on her clean white pillows.

The truth was, she had never felt quite so frightened or quite so alone in all her life. This baby was such an enormous responsibility, something so scary and so defeating. She wasn't a fit mother. That was it. That was the whole thing. She remembered the times when other girls always wanted to hold babies in church, and she had never really wanted to. Not at all. She tried to like babies, often, but they grabbed your covering strings and threw up a thick white substance that smelled like sour milk, scratched your face with their tiny white fingernails, and were just not pleasant to hold.

Now here she was with a baby of her own, and what was she supposed to do with it? She hardly wanted it very much right now, if she was honest. She wished Mam was here. She had to find out right now if she was normal or not. She couldn't believe for one moment that any young mother had ever felt this way before.

You were supposed to be absolutely enamored, so much in love with your baby so that all you wanted to do was hold and cuddle her constantly. Yet here she was, relieved to find the nurses taking her back to the nursery to give her a bottle of formula.

Just when she thought she was stuck in this deep dark moment of panic, the door swung open again. A nurse, dressed in the usual white uniform, stepped in, shaking a bottle of liquid and smiling as she turned to look behind her.

"Someone's getting flowers!" she announced.

Lizzie rolled over and dragged the sleeve of her hospital gown across her eyes, trying desperately to conceal the fact that she had been crying.

"Stephen and Lizzie!" The florist's delivery person read from the card that was attached to a beautiful flower arrangement, looking at Dorie and Lizzie expectantly.

"That's me." Lizzie managed to say a bit shakily.

"You! Good for you! They're gorgeous!"

The nurse rolled over a tray on wheels, set the

flowers carefully on top, and the delivery person left with no more fuss.

Lizzie was amazed! She had never received flowers from a real florist before. Mam said they were terribly expensive. Slowly, almost in awe, she took the envelope from the plastic holder that was stuck into the potting soil and extracted a pink card that said, "Congratulations! Dad and Mom Glick."

How lovely! That was so thoughtful of Mam. It was the most beautiful bouquet Lizzie had ever hoped to see. Real greenery—little ferns, a palm tree, and other real plants which she could pot into larger separate containers when she got home—filled the base of the pretty ceramic pot. Pink and white carnations topped the colorful, perfectly aligned bouquet. A huge pink bow was attached to one side, making Lizzie very happy that she had a little girl.

Then, because Mam had been so kind to think of her and Laura, she began to cry again. There was not a single thing she could do to stop, so she kept crying. She just sat in the middle of the hospital bed and squeezed her eyes shut while tears ran from behind both lids, like a pot of potatoes boiling over when there was no one around to turn down the burner.

"What?" Lizzie's eyes flew open as the nurse stopped at her bed and clucked her tongue.

"Tsk! Tsk! Crying, are we? Baby blues?"

Lizzie nodded miserably as the nurse brought a box of Kleenex, perched on the side of the bed, and tilted in, putting both arms around her in a soft, motherly hug. Lizzie leaned against the softness of her clean, white uniform and inhaled the smell of soap and something that smelled like Mam's ironing. That made her cry some more, the memory of Mam ironing, standing in the old kitchen running the gas iron back and forth, back and forth, singing softly.

"There, there, honey. It happens. It happens all the time. Is this your first one?"

Lizzie nodded, sniffing, dabbing her eyes.

"You'll be fine. Is she doing all right for you?"

Lizzie shook her head back and forth. "She won't nurse. They took her back to the nursery and gave her formula."

"Let me go get her for you."

With that, the nurse was off through the doorway, and Lizzie cried fresh tears because the bouquet of flowers was so pretty, and the nurse had given her a hug, and she was so kind, and just maybe she wasn't abnormal after all, crying like this.

When the nurse returned, Lizzie's tears stopped momentarily, as the kindhearted woman made quite a fuss over Laura's complexion, her perfectly shaped face, and how fortunate she and Stephen were to have a darling little girl. Lizzie felt deeply ashamed then, chiding herself seriously for being such a big baby as she set about the task of trying to feed a very upset newborn girl. In the end, the nurse was perplexed, the baby screamed, and Lizzie was soaked with perspiration from all the effort of trying to get

Laura to nurse.

That evening Mam and Dat came to visit, bringing Stephen. Lizzie's world seemed to turn right side up again with him by her side, gazing at her as if she truly was a wonder. Dat said he picked out Laura in the nursery. He didn't even look at the name tag on the little crib to know which she was.

"She's as dark as Stephen," he crowed, so proud of his granddaughter. Mam just kept holding the baby and laughing and laughing. Mam was like that when she saw newborns for the first time. She laughed. A lot, actually. Then she would talk to them, cooing and fussing and giving them funny names, pursing her lips in the most serious manner. While Mam was there, Lizzie did not feel afraid, depending on her to guide her through this bewildering maze of being a mother to a newborn.

"Oh, she doesn't like your milk," she said matter-of-factly when Lizzie explained this huge obstacle called breast-feeding. "Nothing wrong with the bottle. I'll get you some formula on the way home and don't worry about it."

But Lizzie did. She wanted the best for her baby, and mother's milk was the best. Mam didn't think it was a big deal, but Lizzie did. She felt like a failure and wished some miracle would occur so her baby would quit screaming when she tried to nurse. She looked forward to going home tomorrow, learning if she could handle one tiny, dark, complicated, screaming baby named Laura.

After they were settled in at home, Lizzie felt

much, much better. This whole thing of having a baby to care for seemed so possible now, with Stephen helping her and Mam just down the hill from the little house.

Chapter 18

"BUT LIZZIE, JOSHUA, AND EMMA ARE LOOKING for us," Mam protested, looking troubled as she gazed at her daughter.

"But, Mam. I feel so alone with my baby. I wish you wouldn't go."

"Stephen is here. You'll do fine. There's nothing to it. Just make sure the formula is not too hot when you put it in her bottle."

It was Saturday afternoon, and Mam had come up the hill to say they were going to Allen County to church services at Joshua and Emma's house. Mam knew Lizzie would be all right, although she wished she could put a stop to her fits of crying. When Mam said that, Lizzie said nothing, only nodded her head in acceptance, and Mam hurried down the hill to prepare for their weekend in Allen County.

The truth was, Lizzie thought Mam was not doing her duty. She should stay right here with her and Stephen. Joshua and Emma could have church without them. But, no, off they went, just like that. It made Lizzie mad. Then she felt guilty for becoming angry. Then she started crying again. This was the third day of mostly crying, and Lizzie felt absolutely at the end of her rope. She had given up even trying to be happy. There was no use. She shuffled around and heated formula, sterilized bottles and pacifiers, cried, and listened to Laura scream.

Stephen came home and tried to help, hanging his clothes on their proper hooks, making small talk, trying to hold Laura on the rare occasions when she didn't cry, and, in general, struggling to keep his small family afloat. Lizzie sat on the sofa and cried as Stephen came in and leaned against the wood stove, his arms crossed in front of him as he watched Lizzie, softly sniffling on the couch with Laura beside her.

"Now what's wrong?" he said, kindly.

"Mam was here. They're going to Allen County to Joshua and Emma's for church services."

"But ... what's wrong with that?"

"They don't have to go, Stephen. They could stay here with us," Lizzie's voice caught on a fresh sob.

"Lizzie, we can be alone. You're going to have to get ahold of yourself and stop being so terrified."

"I'm...I'm not. It's just that she...she cries so much."

"But Mam said some babies do."

"I know, but when she cries all the time, I feel like I'm a horrible failure. What am I doing wrong? Why does she cry?"

Stephen laughed, running his hands through his hair.

"She's quiet now."

Crossing the room, he sat beside Lizzie and pulled her against him, holding her gently.

"You're not a failure. You're doing the best that you can. Maybe she's just a grouchy baby and that's simply how she's going to be."

Lizzie sat up and looked at Stephen.

"You mean, you think I'm doing the best I can?"

"Of course. You're doing a great job. She takes the bottle well, she's clean and dry and warm, and sometimes she sleeps and sometimes she cries, just like babies do."

Lizzie looked at Stephen, then dubiously down at Laura who was wide awake, looking around with her small bright eyes.

Lizzie laughed, then sagged against the back of the couch.

"I wish I could take a pill to quit this awful crying and sense of helplessness. I feel like a boat that weathered one storm, and before it's really recovered, another storm starts battering it."

"You're probably overtired, and once you sleep more regularly, you'll feel happier."

Lizzie sighed, then resolved to try harder. Stephen always had a lot of common sense when he spoke about matters like this. She would try and get her rest and see if that stopped the crying.

But now, when she did lie down at night, or during the day, she was so tense and nervous about having a new baby that she couldn't sleep anyway, or not for a long time. She had never known that a person could get so tired and still go on living. She doubted very much that she would ever fully recover. In fact, she believed she would always shuffle around like an old lady and never truly feel strong and laugh for real.

But she and Stephen did survive the weekend without Mam, although Lizzie struggled every hour, trying mightily not to resort to endless unexplained tears. It was like a summer rainstorm that showed up at the most unexpected moments. Dark clouds threatened to overtake her sense of stability, the well-being and genuine happiness she was accustomed to feeling most of her life.

The worst part came after Laura finally settled down for the night, tucked into the small wooden crib in the corner of their bedroom, covered cozily with soft pink and white blankets. Lizzie lined up her bottles in the kitchen on the counter top and placed a small saucepan on the stove, ready to heat the formula during the night. Then Lizzie would climb into bed, feeling as if she would melt into the mattress and never be able to get up again. She was so tired, but there she would lie, her eyes open wide, staring at the ceiling. Meanwhile, every snuffle, breath, and whimper from the crib seemed to be amplified 10 times.

She was completely overwhelmed with the responsibility of caring for this tiny, pink human being, who depended on her for her every need. Lizzie was worn out with diapering, bathing, feeding, burping, and deciphering what Laura wanted every time she opened her sturdy little mouth and yelled, which, in Lizzie's opinion was far, far too often. Lizzie was sure she was doing something wrong.

So, much like she had done when she was four years old and had gotten Snowball, the kitten, Lizzie lay and worried about her baby. Sometimes babies spit up and choked, or simply died in their cribs. What if that happened to Laura? Or what if Laura cried and cried and cried, and nothing, not one thing Lizzie tried, would stop her?

Lizzie tried to pray, to ask God to help her, she really did, but that only brought more tears. She only felt more pitiful. Probably God was very kind to young, scared, first-time mothers, so she cried because God was so loving. Stephen's breathing, slow and steady, was a source of comfort for a reason she couldn't explain. Probably because he was a rock-solid human being that could help if everything spun out of control, even if she still had to go down the hill for Mam's advice.

On Monday morning, Stephen's sister, Mary, arrived with his mother while Lizzie was sweeping the kitchen floor. They tied their small black horse to the hitching rack and breezed into the house, bringing a whole new world of optimism with them.

First of all, Stephen's mother, Annie, grabbed the

broom from Lizzie and, in her forthright manner, told her to go sit down. Young mothers should not be sweeping their kitchen when the baby was only a few days old, she said, clucking her tongue while Lizzie sat down, bewildered. No one had told her that, so she smiled to herself and figured it wouldn't hurt to listen to her mother-in-law.

"Where is she?" Annie asked, looking around for a crib in the living room.

"She's sleeping in her crib," Lizzie answered.

"In the bedroom?"

"Yes."

"Oh, you don't want her in there. You should have a small crib out here, so she's with you during the day."

Bustling into the bedroom, she came out with Laura, clucking and exclaiming about her complexion.

"Lizzie, she's really cute!" she said, beaming happily.

Mary smiled, talking to the baby. Lizzie sat back against the cushions, a real bubble of happiness beginning to well up inside. She was thrilled that they made such a fuss about her baby. Knowing that Mary would stay with them the whole week made everything seem more secure and possible. Actually, there was hardly a reason for her to cry at all. Stephen's mother continued to fuss and ask questions, and Lizzie completely forgot about herself, or how she felt, as Mary gathered the laundry and tidied the house.

"You know, you need to keep babies very warm," Annie chided, as she wrapped the soft, white, thermal, knit blanket securely around Laura again. "They don't stay warm on their own, the way we do. Maybe that's part of the reason she's fussy. Maybe she's not warm enough. Mary, check the fire. See if there's more wood."

While Mary did the laundry in the basement, Annie made coffee and put away the things she had brought, including shoofly pie and some of the fresh sausage from the hogs they had just butchered. Lizzie felt very cozy, knowing that having a baby was a special event, especially since Laura was Annie's oldest son Stephen's baby.

That day, Lizzie had her first, deeply restful nap since Laura was born. Mary kept Laura in the living room with her while Lizzie slept. Lizzie awoke feeling so refreshed and happy, she couldn't believe it.

Mary was holding Laura, who was sucking peacefully on her pacifier, her eyes wide open, when Lizzie walked into the living room. Lizzie was surprised to feel a genuine rush of affection for her little bundle in Mary's arms. Reaching for her, she bent to kiss the soft little forehead, and held her tightly against herself. Suddenly she realized that she was perfectly normal, and she genuinely liked her baby. What was so bad if she cried? All babies cried.

Mary proved to be a good *maud*, cheerfully going about her duties, laughing about everything, which was like a good spring breeze to Lizzie's battered emotions. Mary did laundry, cleaned, baked cookies, ran errands, folded clothes and put them away, anything Lizzie asked of her. Lizzie felt quite queenly, sitting on the recliner asking her maid to do things for her.

When Stephen returned from work in the evening, Mary had supper ready for them. Lizzie's appetite returned with full force. It seemed as if Laura knew exactly the time they sat down for supper, and she would begin crying from her little crib.

But now, that was all right. Lizzie knew it was something she could handle quite well, in fact. Laura was either hungry or had to be burped or just wanted to be held for a while, which made Lizzie feel very capable and very motherly. Mary thought she cried an awful lot and was most certainly a grouchy baby. One day she peered in over the sides of the small porta-crib in the living room, lifted the blankets, and said, "She even looks grouchy when she sleeps!"

Lizzie looked over Mary's shoulder to see why she said that. Indeed, Laura's eyebrows were drawn down in an expression of displeasure, her little mouth puckered into a pout. Mary giggled and Lizzie laughed softly.

The glad day arrived when Emma came from Allen County, and Mandy came all the way to the farm in her horse and buggy. Lizzie wore her best everyday dress and bib apron, taking special care in the way she combed her hair and put on her Sunday covering. She felt very thin and pretty that morning, weighing less than she weighed on the day she became Stephen's wife. She was so excited to see her sisters. Her cheeks were flushed and her eyes finally looked the way they were supposed to, now that all the crying had stopped.

Mary had baked chocolate chip bars, and the coffee was hot, waiting on the back of the gas stove. She bustled about the kitchen, tidying the counter top, while Lizzie watched from her position on the recliner. It was almost uncanny the way Mary resembled Stephen, with the same dark, nut-brown complexion, sun-streaked, dark brown hair, and large heavily-lashed eyes. Today, Mary wore a pale-colored dress which made her appear even tanner. She was thin as a reed and ate more than Lizzie did, which only assured Lizzie that there was a difference in people's metabolisms. Some people just burned calories faster and more fully than others.

"Here they come!" Mary said, from her vantage point at the kitchen window.

"Do they?" Lizzie asked, jumping up, rushing to the window. Sure enough, Mam, Emma, Mandy, Susan, and KatieAnn all came walking up the hill, along the little pathway worn down through the grassy field.

Mam was carrying one of the twins and Mandy the other. Emma carried her baby while KatieAnn held on to Mark's hand. Lizzie watched and fairly skipped to the back door to open it for them, exclaiming in delight that they had all come together for a long anticipated visit.

Emma cried as she hugged and hugged Lizzie,

but that was all right. Emma always cried when a baby was born to someone else. She thought, as did Joshua, that babies were the greatest blessing there ever was, and they had always wanted a large family. Mandy laughed and looked at Lizzie and told her she looked very skinny—for her—and her face looked nice, and did she have on a new covering?

Lizzie cried with Emma—only a little bit—then laughed with Mandy while Mam stood by and wiped her tears. Her nose became red the way it always did when she cried. KatieAnn and Susan took off the children's coats and laid them on the bed in Lizzie's bedroom, knowing their mother and older sisters would be incapable of thinking about normal things for the next five minutes, at least.

Then Lizzie walked over to the small, wooden porta-crib and held Laura out for her sisters to see. She had put her in the prettiest sleeper she owned, a pink and white one with two small appliquéd hearts on the shoulder, and wrapped her well in a pink blanket.

"Oh, oh, oh, my goodness!" Emma exclaimed, fluttering her hands, clearly beside herself. "Lizzie!"

Mandy, in her self-contained, quiet way, said quite firmly, "Lizzie, she's the cutest baby I've ever seen!"

Then Mam's nose became even redder, and she laughed and cried at the exact same time. Lizzie had never felt quite so important to her Mam and sisters as she did at that moment. Not even on the day she got married.

They all took turns holding Laura, while Katie-Ann and Susan entertained the other children with Mary's help. Everyone chattered and exclaimed and talked all at once, and no one truly listened much to what other persons were saying. After the initial frenzy of seeing the baby and saying the most important things had died down, they had coffee around the kitchen table, savoring the chocolate chip bars, and talking at a much more normal volume and speed.

Mandy's twins were walking now and beginning to say whole sentences. They looked just like two little girls exactly the same age, except they were different in every way. One was dark-haired and dark-eyed while the other had blond hair and blue eyes. John and Mandy had been blessed with another little girl, named Sadie, who was nine-months-old and as blond and blue-eyed as the one twin. Mandy was a very busy young mother, very capable and sure of herself, now with three little girls. Joshua and Emma had a third baby, too, a little boy named, Isaac.

They listened sympathetically as Lizzie recounted the horrors of her hospital stay, her baby's crying, her own helplessness, the mean nurse, and her roommate who successfully nursed her red-haired baby boy.

"But, Lizzie, I don't even know what you mean. I have never once in my life felt that way," Mandy said.

"Not even with the twins?" Lizzie asked, incredulous.

"Never."

"Me either," Emma chimed in.

"Well, why? Why would I be the one to have those awful blues?" Lizzie asked, becoming anxious all over again, her eyebrows raised in bewilderment.

"You were always like that, Lizzie. Always." Mam chimed in.

"I didn't cry about stuff, Mam."

"No, but you think ahead too much. You worry about things, not taking it a day at a time. Remember how you acted about Snowball, the kitten?"

"I did think about that, really I did, Mam."

"Well, if you'd relax and quit thinking about situations that could happen, but very likely never will, you'd be much better off," Mam said wisely.

"But you can't help the way you are," Lizzie answered, a bit miffed.

"You can learn from this, though, Lizzie," Mam assured her.

"Well, I won't have to worry, because I don't plan to have another baby. Not ever."

Lizzie said this quite forcefully, much to Emma's consternation. Mandy was aghast. Mam's nostrils got bigger, and her eyes snapped behind her glasses. No one said anything for awhile.

"Lizzie, you wouldn't do that," Mandy said finally.

"Not just one," Emma said kindly.

"Do you have to have a whole pile of babies?" Lizzie asked. "Does it say anything in the Bible about how many babies you should have?"

Mam shook her head back and forth slowly, swallowing a mouth full of coffee. She raised her hands in the air and brought them back down on her lap, the way she did when she laughed.

"I don't know, Lizzie. I just know that babies are a blessing, and 'blessed is the man who has his quiver full,'—meaning children are the arrows—which is a verse in Proverbs. There's no real law about how many babies each individual family should have, but among the Amish, especially, we're expected to have children."

"Why?"

Emma and Mandy looked at each other in their superior, "that poor thing," kind of way, which made Lizzy cross her arms and stare at them rebelliously.

"Tell me why one baby isn't enough."

"Lizzie, just wait. You'll want more children as Laura becomes older."

"No, I won't."

"What about Stephen?" Emma asked gently.

"He didn't say anything about having more children," Lizzie snapped.

"Lizzie, there's another verse in the Bible about women reaching salvation through childbearing," Mam said flatly.

"I thought our salvation is through Jesus on the cross. You know, grace, and that we can't earn it," Lizzie countered.

Then Mandy, in that wise, prophetic way she always had, said Lizzie probably didn't need to think about more babies now. And then Mandy went on, "Did you know that the other day we had a cow with a twisted stomach, and the vet could do nothing, not one thing, and the cow died?" They all returned to the living room, the subject changed to much safer ground. Lizzie's happiness was restored as she thought about a dead cow instead of having more babies.

"Wasn't that quite a loss?" Lizzie asked.

"Not really. She was not a good milker, and we're butchering her, so we'll have ground beef you can buy from us for a good price," Mandy answered.

"Oh, goody! Then I can make meat loaf and barbecue sandwiches and vegetable soup and lots of good things for Stephen's supper," Lizzie said, smiling.

The rest of the day passed in a happy glow, with good advice from Mam about being careful not to give Baby Laura more than two ounces of formula before burping her. She also told Lizzie to hold Laura's head up when she gave her a bottle, although Lizzie still felt inferior watching Emma and Mandy peacefully nursing their babies, relaxed and at ease with the whole deal. Oh, well, sometimes life just was that way, and you had to do the best you could, even if it meant giving your baby formula from a bottle.

Chapter 19

IN SPITE OF ALL OF LIZZIE'S INSECURITIES AND her lack of expertise when it came to babies, Laura thrived and grew, although crying lustily much of the time. Lizzie switched to a different formula, but with no success. One evening Stephen's mother, Annie, persuaded Laura to try goat's milk, which was natural and she thought as close to mother's milk as nature could provide. Laura drank well, cried just the same, and smelled exactly like a baby goat. Lizzie switched to a soy-based formula, and Laura smelled exactly like a little soybean.

But they continued on with the soybean formula, simply because her crying bouts were fewer, her nights were better, and she seemed more relaxed. That, in turn, made Lizzie feel better and calmer about babies in general.

The winter was a harsh one, with many snow-storms and temperatures hovering around zero degrees many days. The township plows, with their bleary-eyed drivers, did their best, but still some of the less traveled roads remained closed for days with snowdrifts making the roads impassable. Still the snow fell and the wind blew great walls of it to distant places, blowing anything shut that bore even the semblance of a dip. Lizzie loved the snow and the excitement of seeing cars slip and slide, revving their engines as they tried repeatedly to make their way to the top of the small, steep incline below their house.

On one of those days after yet another snowfall, when the weather turned bitterly cold and a strong, steady, forceful wind began to blow during the night, Lizzie was awakened by the tingling of her nose. She lay shivering beneath the heavy comforter, listening intently to the steady whine of the wind, ever increasing outside the window.

That morning, Stephen got up a bit earlier to make sure there was plenty of wood in the box beside the stove in the living room. He had a good strong fire going by the time Lizzie got up to make breakfast and pack his lunch.

"I'm glad I have work inside today," he said.

"Won't you have a problem getting to your job?" Lizzie asked worriedly, knowing their weekly paycheck had been decreasing during most of the winter months because of the weather, but their mortgage payment was due on the same date every month.

"I don't think so, not with Jerry," he replied, grinning. "He's not afraid of anything with that four-wheel drive."

"Just be careful," Lizzie said.

"I want you to be careful, too," Stephen said seriously. "Don't let the woodstove get too hot in this wind. Sometimes I don't really trust the chimney. I don't think it's built well enough with just the flue liner and chimney block."

"Doesn't everybody build their chimney that way?" Lizzie asked.

"Pretty much. But I'd still feel more comfortable if we had built a better one."

Lizzie tried to heed Stephen's advice, but the house would not warm up sufficiently. Laura's little hands were cold, and shivers went up and down Lizzie's spine as she sat at the sewing machine. She stopped treadling just to listen to the wind as it wailed and howled around the little house, rattling anything that wasn't securely nailed down. She felt thankful for their good sturdy home, covered with bricks, white or not. They kept out the cold, increased the strength of the little structure, and helped her feel safer.

She added a few pieces of wood to the stove and opened the draft in the back, telling herself there was no sense in being chilly all day, especially with Laura shivering. She returned to the sewing machine, quickly becoming engrossed in putting in a difficult sleeve, and forgot about the draft in the back of the woodstove.

Suddenly she felt quite warm, so she stopped sewing and went to check the fire. She was alarmed to find the stove radiating much more heat than usual. She quickly turned the knob to shut down the draft and was rewarded with an instant crackling sound as the wood lost the draft that had caused it to overheat. Anxiously Lizzie put her hand close to the stovepipe. It didn't feel red hot. Everything would be all right, she thought, hurriedly returning to her sewing while Laura slept.

The wind increased its fury, whining and making the snow swirl in great expanses across the countryside. Lizzie could hardly understand how Stephen could get to work on a day like this. But she shrugged off her concern, knowing he would be safe as long as his crew worked on the interior part of the new building.

She resumed sewing, then stopped to listen. What was that noise? A bumping sound seemed to be coming from upstairs. Bump! There it was again. It sounded like someone dropping a stone or a brick on the floor.

Hurriedly she left the sewing machine and stood, barely daring to breathe, at the open stairway listening. Bump! Another one! What if someone was up there, trying to lure her upstairs so he could grab her as she opened the door?

Now she heard another sound, only a bit lighter, like popping. Pop! Pop! Oh, dear! Lizzie looked left and right frantically before realizing there was only one thing to do. She had to charge up the stairs and see for herself what was making that unusual noise.

Quickly, she raced up the stairs, flung open the door, and peered inside. Nothing. The bed with its multicolored Sunshine and Shadow quilt stood against the opposite wall. The rugs lay straight beside the bed and in front of the dresser.

She dashed across the hallway, opened the door on the opposite side, and instantly knew there was something wrong when a wall of warm air hit her. It was much too hot in the room. Reaching out tentatively, she touched the wall surrounding the chimney and yanked back her hand when the drywall burned her fingers.

Pop!

Now she heard the sound quite clearly, coming from the chimney. The chimney was on fire, popping and crackling in its ferocity. Laura! Her baby! She was all alone and had to call the fire department with no telephone in the house. Dat's phone shanty at the bottom of the hill was farther away than their next-door neighbors, a young English couple named Lance and Alice Wingert, with three children. She wondered wildly if Alice was home and which direction she should go. She could not waste one moment. The chimney was burning, and perhaps their little house would be next.

Dashing down the stairs, she grabbed the heaviest homemade comforter in the bedroom, threw on her coat and scarf, rolled Laura in the comforter, hearing her cries of protest, and dashed outside, running a short distance from the house.

The cold and the wind hit her with unbelievable force as she turned to look at the top of the chimney. She began crying as the evil-looking flames leaped out and danced around the top of the chimney while black smoke pour out in thick plumes.

Oh, dear God, don't let our little house and all our stuff burn, she prayed, as she ran as best she could, carrying Laura in the heavy comforter. Never had the short distance between her house and the Wingerts' home seemed so far. She finally slipped between the shrubs by their back door. She tried not to pound madly, but knocked louder and more quickly than usual until Alice opened the door, peering out at Lizzie.

"The...the house! The chimney is burning! I need to call 911!" Lizzie burst out.

"Oh, my! Where? Your house! Come in! Hurry!"

She stood aside as Lizzie hurried past, then reached for the phone and dialed 911, those blessed three little numbers that meant help would be on the way soon. Alice spoke in a clear articulate voice, giving the operator the correct address and describing the house.

"You go back now, stand in your driveway, and direct the fire trucks," Alice ordered, taking control of the situation quickly. "I'll watch Laura."

"But...she doesn't have a bottle!" Lizzie said hopelessly.

"She has her pacifier. She'll be fine. Go!"

So Laura ran, sobs catching in her throat as she saw the bright orange flames still leaping from the chimney. She had never felt quite so helpless or so inadequate in all her life. What would Stephen say? That was the most terrible thought.

She stood, then, in the gently curving driveway in the bitter cold with the strong winds blowing her skirt around her legs. She watched the chimney burning, until she finally, blessedly, heard the wail of the fire siren. Even then, it seemed like a very long time before the huge red trucks, with all the white and gold lettering, the fancy silver grillwork, and the yellow whirling lights on top of their cabs, actually came into view.

Lizzie waved her arms, pointing, but it was a useless gesture, as they had likely spotted the burning chimney half a mile away, since the house sat on top of a hill.

"We can't get up the drive!"

The firefighter rushing past her explained this to her, as he held a large fire extinguisher with both arms. He was followed by another, and then another fireman. There was nothing left for her to do except follow as they dashed up the front porch steps and into the living room, already on their way upstairs before Lizzie entered the house.

She stood at the bottom of the stairs, breathing hard, hearing the sound of chopping, followed by the hiss of the fire extinguishers. More men came charging in through the front door and up the stairway, their heavy firefighting gear clanking as they went. Then there was nothing to do but wait. She listened anxiously to the firemen stomping about upstairs, talking in low tones, until she smelled a smoky sulfurous odor wafting down the stairway, swirling around the living room.

Lizzie coughed, barely able to contain her curiosity, wondering if her house would burn down after all the firemen did to stop the burning chimney. She bit down hard on a fingernail and watched anxiously up the stairway as a fireman came back down, looking as if he wanted to talk to her.

"Do you live here?" he asked kindly.

"Y...Yes," Lizzie answered uncertainly, not sure if he would scold her for letting the stove become overheated.

"Let me tell you, you are a very fortunate young lady. The chimney block was so hot the rafters were beginning to burn behind the drywall. Five more minutes and your roof would have been aflame."

Lizzie watched him speak, her eyes wide, barely able to comprehend what he was saying.

Five more minutes!

What if she hadn't heard that sound? Or had not gone immediately for help? Or what if Alice had not been home? Oh, surely God had heard her prayers and had not let the house burn to the ground. Their very own house!

"You have a bit of a mess upstairs, but everything is replaceable. I suppose your husband isn't home?"

"No, he isn't. He'll be home around six."

"The fire in the stove will be out, so you'll have to find another source of heat until he returns. In this cold...Is there any way you can get ahold of him at work?"

Lizzie nodded, remembering the phone number stuck to the refrigerator door. After thanking the firemen, she ran over to the Wingerts, made the phone call to Stephen, and then ran back to the house with Laura still wrapped in the comforter. Already, the house was cool, so she turned the oven on and propped the door open, figuring that would help a small amount until Stephen arrived. Laura was screaming at the top of her lungs, protesting the great weight of the comforter wrapped around her, trying with all her mighty little strength to worm her way out of it.

Lizzie laughed, calm now and so relieved that the fire was extinguished. She wrapped Laura tightly, telling her she should be grateful for the warmth of the big comforter instead of complaining like that. Finally Stephen arrived. His face was pale; his eyes wide with alarm. Lizzie felt like crying when she caught sight of him climbing out of the truck, but she didn't.

"What in the world, Lizzie!" he burst out, as he came through the back door.

"It … it just … "

"Are you all right? What about Laura?" he asked, coming over to peer into the heavy comforter.

"Yes, we are both all right, Stephen. It was…was my fault, letting the stove get so hot."

"No, Lizzie, not entirely. I never did feel safe building that chimney cheaply like that. Now we'll do something different. I'll go to the lumber company in town today and ask them what to do."

Lizzie followed him upstairs to see the damage the firemen had made in order to extinguish the flames. There were huge, ragged holes chopped in the drywall, and when they peered into the wall, they could see the shiny blackness of the charred rafters. The entire room had a smoky, sulfurous smell, and the chimney still radiated some heat behind the battered drywall.

Stephen gave a low whistle as he laid his hand on the chimney block.

"That's scary, Lizzie. We came so close to losing everything."

Lizzie nodded soberly.

"But...you and Laura are all right, and that's what matters most."

Lizzie blinked back tears of gratitude as she hugged Stephen, thankful that he was not angry and that it had not been her fault. Well, at least not completely.

That evening Dat and Jason helped Stephen install a new stainless steel chimney. Stephen explained everything to Lizzie. He showed her the instructions, and how black soot, the buildup from burning green wood, couldn't accumulate on the sides of the chimney.

When the whole setup was complete, Lizzie could not believe how thankful she felt as the fire crackled and popped, and the heat spread throughout the cold house. Everything felt safe and secure, cozy and homey again. She was so grateful that they were here in their own little house with their possessions intact, and with the danger that had threatened to take everything extinguished.

That spring, after the harsh winter winds had slowed to a warm, gentle breeze and the melting snow ran in little rivulets into the spouting, splashing onto the ground and turning it into soft, spring mud, Stephen built a barn. The nice little building with brown siding matched the house and had a roof that wasn't straight, but was bent in the middle—a hip roof Stephen called it.

Lizzie loved the little barn. It completed the property, making it look much more like an Amish homestead and not just a house on top of a hill. Stephen built stables, one for George and one for an extra horse when company came, or in case they ever decided to buy a new horse, which Lizzie doubted would ever happen. Stephen thought one horse was enough. She would have loved to fill the barn with miniature ponies like Teeny and Tiny, the ponies Dat bought when Lizzie was little. But Stephen did not like ponies at all, saying they were stubborn little creatures, and why would she want a pony? If she wanted a pony, she could just walk down over the hill and drive her parents' ponies.

He would get a dog, he said. Lizzie said, no, she didn't like dogs. If she couldn't have ponies, then he couldn't have a dog. She didn't feel very virtuous after she stated that a bit too forcefully, but she figured it didn't hurt Stephen to hear it. Otherwise, he'd become too selfish and just walk all over her, and didn't the marriage books say the wife shouldn't be a doormat? Lizzie figured she was coming pretty close to being a doormat, not being allowed to have ponies. Stephen wanted to go and buy a dog that ran all over the neighborhood and dug in her flower beds and barked up an insane storm every time someone came for a visit. She didn't like dogs, and that was that.

She thought Stephen was being very quiet after she said that, so she kept watching him out of the corners of her eyes when he wasn't looking. Was he angry, or just thinking about buying a pony for her?

Probably that's what it was. He was planning a surprise for her, putting a cute pony in that extra stall when she least expected it. But when she asked him a question at bedtime and he didn't answer, she figured it didn't take that much thinking to decide to buy a pony. He was mad.

Oh, well, he'll get over it, she thought unhappily. We're not having a dog. In fact, she so desperately didn't want a dog that she didn't care if she was being virtuous or not. Dogs were annoying.

Chapter 20

Lizzie loved taking her baby to church. There was just something about it that made her feel quite capable, so much like a real mother who knew what she was doing, even if she didn't. Every two weeks, on Saturday evening, she would get out the little straw basket with a lid on it, called a *kaevly* in Pennsylvania Dutch. Stephen's mother had ordered it for her and had given it to her as a baby gift.

In this little basket, Lizzie put a neat stack of snowy white cloth diapers, smelling so fresh and clean, she loved to bury her nose into them and take a deep breath of the scented softness. On top of this stack of diapers, she folded a pair of rubber panties, the stretchable little outer garment that held the wetness against the diaper, a clean pair of white tights, and a clean T-shirt, just in case she might need them.

Beside that pile of baby necessities, she placed one little jar of baby food, usually fruit-flavored. Lizzie's favorite flavor was Tutti-Frutti. It tasted so good she probably ate half of it, licking the spoon while she fed Laura. She also had a small container of rice cereal with a tiny bit of sugar sprinkled on top, a small baby-sized spoon, and a bottle containing a wee bit of apple juice mixed with water. She also added bottles of soy formula, two extra bibs, and the best part, baby toys.

It was fun to pick out the cutest toys to put in her *kaevly*, because she felt classy when other mothers watched what she gave her baby to play with during church. A string of pink and white glass beads with small key chains attached and little plastic rings kept Laura entertained for awhile.

She picked out a dress for Laura the evening before, sometimes pink or navy blue, just whatever she felt like. Often she would match the color with her own, especially if she was wearing a pretty color, like burgundy or forest green.

She completed Laura's outfit with one of the little homemade bibs Lizzie had bought at the dry-goods store in Lampeter. The bibs were usually crocheted or surrounded by lace of the same color as the baby's dress. Oh, it was all so much fun and exciting to take your baby to church, that she wished they would have services every Sunday instead of only on alternating ones.

In the wintertime, she dressed Laura in a little pink sweater set with a pretty blanket to match. On top of that Lizzie pinned a little black, woolen shawl securely around her that was just like her own, except it was baby-sized, of course. On Laura's head, she placed a stiff little royal blue bonnet, just like her own, except baby-sized as well, and tied it securely under her chin.

She thought the shawl and bonnet were the cutest things she had ever seen, with Laura's little brown face peering out from the dark shades of fabric. So cute, in fact, that she squeezed and squeezed her before putting her own shawl and bonnet on. She carefully held Laura beneath the folds of her shawl when they went outside to protect her from the cold. She carried the *kaevly* with the other hand and went down the steps to where Stephen was waiting with George and the buggy.

When they arrived at church, Mom or KatieAnn or Susan would come with their arms extended to take Laura. Lizzie felt so loved and important and so Amish and motherly. Stephen's mother would fuss over her, making Lizzie feel happy and cuddly and warm inside, secure in the fact that she belonged to a group of family and friends. A complete circle of contentment.

Sometimes Laura would have a genuine crying spell, when nothing seemed to pacify her. Lizzie would take her away from where the service was being held, often upstairs, and rock her or feed her or do whatever it took to get her to stop crying. Often a friend and her fussy baby joined her, and they talked about babies, their sleep patterns, how much they weighed, or whatever.

Church wasn't nearly as boring when you had a baby to take care of, especially when a minister droned on and on and wasn't very interesting. Then

Lizzie just up and took Laura upstairs, whether she was crying or not. People didn't know what was wrong with her baby, and really, they didn't need to know.

Sometimes she would put a package of cheese crackers in her *kaevly* and eat them while she fed Laura, because it got late and she became very hungry. The thing was, when they served lunch, she was never able to sit at the first women's table because they were seated according to their ages. So she had to wait with the younger women and girls till the older ones had eaten. It seemed as if that table of older women always took their time, drinking coffee and talking way too much.

On this fine spring morning, Stephen brushed and brushed George with careful attention, put the glossy black harness on his back, and then attached all the buckles and straps before putting the horse back in his stall. He went to the house to dress in his traditional white shirt, black broadfall pants, and black vest with hooks and eyes that closed down the front.

Humming under his breath, he opened the back door. He was amazed to find Lizzie hunched over the table with a small dish of water. She held a fine-toothed black comb, called a *shtrale*, in Dutch, and two tiny pieces of metal he remembered his mother using at home.

Lizzie did not look up when he entered, so he walked over to the table, peering down to see how she was faring.

"Bobbies?" he asked.

His wife nodded grimly, intent on parting Laura's silky baby hair in the middle and creating a wet strand on each side of Laura's forehead. Lizzie intended to roll the tip of each strand upward and around a sliver of soft bendable metal. With that action, she would form a small roll of hair on each side of Laura's forehead, called bobbies. It was an old traditional way of keeping a baby's thin hair from hanging in her face without cutting it.

Stephen soon sensed that Lizzie was pretty close to panicking, so he walked quietly away, down the hallway and into the bedroom. Lizzie wet the *shtrale* once more in the tiny dish of water and pulled it through Laura's hair on the left side of her part. Carefully holding the small bendable piece of metal, Lizzie began rolling upward, just as Laura turned her head, leaving Lizzie holding the metal, but no hair. She glanced with apprehension at the clock. Only 15 more minutes and they would have to leave, no doubt about it.

"Hold still," she hissed, putting her fingers on each side of Laura's cheeks and pulling her face to the desired position.

Once more, Lizzie tried, rolling upward until the bobbie was at the right spot on the side of Laura's forehead. Sighing with relief, she patted Laura's cheek and said, "Good girl."

"Now hold still," she murmured, and began the other one. That was when Laura decided she had had enough. She clearly saw no sense in putting up with these atrocities. She pulled her little body into a cramped position and howled shrilly.

Instantly, Lizzie bent over her, whispering, "Shh-shh-shh."

But Laura was indignant now, and she was not about to be lulled into submission by anyone. She kept screaming, one bobbie firmly in place and the other pieces of hair becoming drier by the second. Scooping her up, Lizzie held her distraught baby. They would never make it to church on time. She felt like crying but knew that would only make matters worse. She had to get that other bobbie in place.

"Sh-sh, you'll be all right. I know, it's not nice. Sh-sh-sh," Lizzie kept saying, bouncing Laura up and down.

Finally, with only five minutes to go, Laura quieted enough for Lizzie to lay her back down on the table top. She gave her a bright little toy to play with, anything to get her mind off whatever Lizzie was doing to her hair. Swiftly, she wet the comb, raked it through her hair, adjusted the soft piece of metal, and began rolling, just as Laura twisted her little body to roll over.

"No, Laura! No!" Lizzie wailed. Laura promptly began crying again.

"Stephen!"

In the bedroom, Stephen jumped, then rushed to the door, adjusting his suspenders, alarmed at the panic in Lizzie's voice.

"Stephen, I can't make bobbies! She just turns her head! We'll be late for church!"

"It's not that bad, Lizzie. We still have a quarter of an hour."

"We don't! Remember last time? We left at eight-thirty and were last."

"We weren't last. Some of the youth were."

Lizzie turned her back without bothering to answer. They were the last ones to arrive, she knew that.

"Hold her still," she barked.

"How?"

Stephen looked helplessly at his screaming daughter, then at his upset wife, and wondered if this was the way things were going to be from now on.

"I have to make the other bobbie. Just hold her head on each side so she can't turn it. Sh-sh, Laura. It's not that bad!"

So Stephen bent down, his elbows on the table, his hands gently cradling Laura's head, while Lizzie concentrated on the bobbie. He wasn't prepared when Laura suddenly turned her head hard to the right, twisting her entire body.

"Stephen!" Lizzie shrieked.

It really irked him when Lizzie yelled at him like that. He was doing the best he could. But he said nothing.

"You have to hold her head firmly," she ordered, wetting the comb for what would be the twentieth time.

"Why don't you just stick her head in a vice?" Stephen asked sarcastically, as he bent to his task.

Lizzie shot him a withering glance but said nothing, returning to her task with desperation now.

Laura screamed, but Stephen held her head more firmly, murmuring to his daughter. Lizzie deftly rolled the hair and clipped it into place, standing back to view the two bobbies.

"They're crooked!"

Straightening up, Stephen picked up his wailing daughter and patted her back, soothing her over and over while glaring at Lizzie.

"You're not going to redo that bobbie," he said firmly.

"But they're not straight, Stephen. I have to."

"Give it up Lizzie. She looks fine to me. It's time to go!"

"I'm not ready."

Grimly, Lizzie scooped up the dish and comb, swiped the tabletop with a wet cloth, then reached for Laura as Stephen hurried to the bedroom to finish dressing. Lizzie's heart sank seriously when she looked at Laura's forehead. One bobbie was up higher and closer to the middle of her face while the other one hung to the side. Oh, it was so pathetic-looking. She couldn't take her baby to church with those bobbies.

Weighing her options, she decided that arriving at church late would create more of a stir than two bobbies that were not quite straight, so she put the bottles of formula in her *kaevly* and said nothing.

Stephen emerged from the bedroom looking as handsome as he always did in his Sunday suit, and Lizzie forgave him readily for not allowing her to fix Laura's bobbies.

"Is it chilly this morning?" she asked, hoping he had forgiven her for acting so hysterical.

"A little."

So Lizzie put the little black woolen shawl around Laura's shoulders, secured it with a pink safety pin, put the blue bonnet on her head, and tied it beneath her chin. She stood back to look at her, chuckling softly.

"Oh, Laura, you look so cute and so Amish with your bobbies!" she exclaimed, then swept her up into a tight hug.

Grabbing her *kaevly*, she went outside where Stephen had gone, put her *kaevly* into the *doch-veggley* or buggy, and climbed in, holding Laura firmly. Stephen gathered the leather reins, then reached up to George's neck and attached the neck rein, that part of the harness which held George's head up.

Lizzie always disliked neck reins. Always. They were the cruelest invention anyone had ever thought of. How would a person like to pull a load up a hill without being allowed to hunch over to pull? She always felt a small sense of rebellion every time Dat, and now Stephen, attached that thing. It was cruel, that's what.

As Stephen climbed quickly into the buggy beside her, George tossed his head, made a running leap, and was off down the curving driveway. Lizzie clutched Laura tightly, nervously hoping Stephen could handle George. She was not in a good mood after all the tension of the morning, and it only elevated her bad humor to start off like that.

"I guarantee one thing," she said dryly.

"What?"

"If you wouldn't attach that neck rein quite as tightly as you do, George would behave himself better as he starts off."

"That rein isn't tight. What do you mean?" Stephen asked, turning to look at her quite sharply.

Too sharply, in Lizzie's opinion, so she didn't answer.

Stephen tried again. "What do you mean 'that rein is tight'? He's running with the rein loose now."

Lizzie still didn't answer, only because it felt too good to see him trying to get her to talk. So he shrugged his shoulders, thinking he'd never understand women as long as he lived, at least not Lizzie, anyway. She could be a strange duck.

They drove on in silence, Laura relaxing against Lizzie after the traumatic morning she had just endured. Her eyelids fell heavily as she fought sleepiness, the way she always did when they went away in a buggy. Lizzie shifted her arm more comfortably, then sat back against the blue upholstered buggy seat, sighing as her shoulders slumped in relaxation.

What a morning it had been, she thought wryly.

She sincerely hoped this was not a harbinger of things to come. It wasn't right. Here it was Sunday, the Sabbath, the Lord's day, and she had already panicked, lost her temper twice, and was still coddling ill feelings toward her husband. She thought the devil sure didn't take Sundays off, the way he had made her carry on.

She glanced at Stephen, who appeared a bit worn and weary for so early in the morning. She wondered what he was thinking, but she was still a bit too miffed about that neck rein deal to ask him. That was the trouble with being married. If that harness were Lizzie's, she would have seriously lengthened the neck rein, but since it wasn't hers, she had no business speaking her mind. She should sit back and leave it entirely up to her husband's judgment, with absolutely no will of her own.

It was all so weird, strange, and stupid. Whoever heard of such a thing? She thought she had this all figured out when she was dating Stephen. Yet here she was, upset about that short neck rein, while he drove along, contently secure in the fact that he could drive with that rein exactly the way he wanted. He was the husband and she was the wife, and that meant he was the boss. She would have to figure out how to live with that.

She was just angry all over again. No one ever talked about the husband giving his life for his wife, as Christ gave himself for the church. To Lizzie's way of thinking, if Stephen loved her so that he gave himself for her, he would lengthen that rein because it bothered her. Then when he came to church and the men asked him why his horse's neck rein was so long, he should smile nicely and say his wife liked it that way, and that since it bothered her, it bothered him as well.

Then all the men would think what a good husband Stephen was and how fortunate Lizzie was to have him. Wasn't that the way the Bible said it should be? But no, here they went, racing down the road, Stephen secure in his kingly position and she wrestling with this huge mountain called submission.

Suddenly the whole thing was unbearable and, forgetting to pout, she said loudly, "Doesn't it bother you that George's head is held up so high?"

"Lizzie, would you get off it? The rein is loose. He's comfortable. It's the way he naturally holds his head."

"Oh, no, it isn't, Stephen."

"Lizzie, now stop. You're still upset about making those bobbies, and you can't give up that they're crooked, so you're taking it out on me. Now stop it."

That really made Lizzie see red, so much so, in fact, that she felt like crying. The nerve of him! How did he know?

"You … you … "

"You can sputter around all you want to. It's true."

"You're mean."

"I don't try to be."

"I'm just telling you the truth."

So Lizzie thought about the truth for the next mile or so, finally coming to the conclusion that he was probably right. That rein bothered her a lot more than usual because of her own frustration. Well, she wasn't going to let him know she thought he was right. That would for sure only make him feel more superior than ever.

But when the visiting minister spoke eloquently about the blessing a family receives by a quiet, well-spoken, godly mother staying in her rightful position, Lizzie bent her head and cried a few tears in her rose-colored handkerchief. It touched a part of her soul that wanted to be good, but which her own willful nature made extremely difficult.

Glancing around furtively, she looked to see if other women felt the same desire to be such a person. Rather a large amount had tears in their eyes, and a few were blowing their noses. Lizzie felt very righteous and good inside, feeling as if she actually was like that. Well, not really, but by the time they had a larger family, she would be a virtuous woman. After all, these things take time.

Chapter 21

Laura was outgrowing her little brown porta-crib. Lizzie's mind began churning, trying to figure out a way she could fit a big, normal-sized crib into their small bedroom. Any way she arranged the furniture in her mind, the room was still too crowded. So she decided she would approach Stephen about transforming the room where he kept his gun cabinet and desk into a really cute little nursery.

As she hung her Monday's washing on the line, she thought about it. When she ironed coverings she thought about it, and when she cleaned the basement she thought about it. In fact, that was all she could think about most of the day, becoming more and more excited as the day went on. She would make little gingham pink and white curtains and cover the bumper pad around the crib to match. Perhaps she could make a tiny comforter with pink and white flannel, knotting it with pink yarn. Or would white be better? Maybe white.

By the time Stephen came home from work, she had thought herself into quite a stew, her cheeks flushed, her eyes bright with anticipation, eagerly waiting to see if he was in the proper mood for her to ask such a huge favor.

Her heart fell as he climbed out of his co-worker's truck, his trousers covered with mud, his face dark and very, very tired. Even his hands and thermos were muddy. It didn't look too promising, she decided, so maybe the best thing was not to ask him at all this evening if he was tired and grouchy.

She waited nervously as he entered the basement, took off his shoes, and washed up at the sink, puttering around down there for far too long, she thought. When he finally did come upstairs, he did not have his usual smile of welcome.

"Long day?" Lizzie asked, too quickly and much too brightly.

"Yeah," he said brusquely.

So Lizzie kept quiet as she served the good supper she had prepared—mashed potatoes and beef gravy, peas and carrots, and macaroni and cheese, one of his favorite meals. Lizzie tried to keep the conversation light and happy until Stephen pushed back his chair and sighed, finally smiling at her. Instantly Lizzie dove straight into the subject, plying him with all kinds of questions about many different subjects pertaining to that particular room.

"But you know, Stephen, the biggest problem is that there isn't a doorway between your gun-cabinet room and our bedroom," she stated quite firmly. Stephen lowered his eyebrows.

"Why would you need a doorway between our bedroom and the other room?" he asked.

"Well, I'd have to walk all the way through the living room, and besides, I couldn't hear Laura very well when she cries," Lizzie said.

Stephen didn't say more after that. He just got up and walked into the living room, sitting heavily on the brown recliner and picking up a fishing magazine. Lizzie crossed her arms and glared at him. Of all the nerve! There he goes, tuning me out and refusing to talk. Well, she wasn't finished yet, so she'd talk anyway. Sitting opposite him on the sofa, she leaned forward and began speaking in a sweet voice. Or so she hoped.

"But listen, Stephen, we can't get a full-sized crib in our bedroom. It's too small. You know that. I know you don't want to give up your hunting room, but you're going to have to anyway. You can't just have that room for your stuff if we need it for the baby. And besides, you can keep all that junk upstairs."

Stephen sat straight up.

"Junk! My hunting stuff isn't junk!"

"Well, kind of."

"That does it, Lizzie. I'm not moving out of there. We can arrange a big crib in our bedroom somehow."

Lizzie sat straight up, gripping a small square pillow with both hands, her eyebrows reaching for her hairline, her eyes wide with disbelief and sorrow.

"You have to, Stephen!" she wailed.

"I don't have to do anything," he said, very quietly, but very determinedly.

He may as well have been a judge in a courtroom, raising his gavel, banging it down, and passing a sentence that would send her to prison, Lizzie thought wearily. All her dreams of pink gingham curtains and a little changing table flew out the window, disappearing somewhere above the sun.

She was afraid of the firmness in his voice, so she sighed as loud as she could, hoping her eyes would convey how hard it was when he refused to do her bidding. When he didn't respond, she slowly returned to the kitchen. Cleaning all the dishes off the table in slow, sad, little movements, she watched him out of the corner of her eye to see if he felt badly. She fervently hoped so.

There was nothing to do but give it up. Well, there was half of a small saucepan of macaroni and cheese left. She got a clean fork from the drawer and ate great comforting mouthfuls of the gooey, cheesy dish. She didn't care if she gained five pounds. Actually, if he was going to be so mean, maybe she'd just keep eating macaroni and cheese until she gained 20.

Turning on the hot water, she grabbed the bottle of dish soap and squeezed it angrily, creating way too many suds. She had to rinse the dishes twice as long, and there were suds over everything. She had always loved that feeling as a little girl, but now, the bubbles only irked her more.

After she wiped the counter clean, she felt very thirsty. She drank a large glassful of cold water from the refrigerator, then felt fat and uncomfortable and worse than ever. She didn't want to join Stephen in the living room, because she wasn't planning on talking at all. All evening—not one word.

She supposed she could go sit in the bedroom, but Laura was asleep, and she certainly did not want to wake her. She had two options: continue to stand right where she was, against the kitchen counter where he couldn't see her, or sit in the bathroom, which would seem a bit suspicious.

Maybe she could pretend to be sick and make terrible retching noises, and he would become extremely alarmed and so sorry. Then he would put his arms around her and tell her he loved her and would do anything she wanted. He couldn't bear the thought of living without her.

Well, knowing Stephen, he'd go right on reading his fishing magazine without worrying about retching noises in the bathroom. She sighed and then blew her nose, which sounded a lot dryer than she had hoped. She wanted desperately for him to think she was crying, standing all alone in the kitchen, sobbing so pitifully. Taking a few soft steps, she peeped around the partition, wondering if he looked her way at all.

He was lying back against the extended recliner, his eyes closed, looking very, very tired. A wave of love and pity washed over her then. She knew she was acting very spoiled and immature. But the thing was, her dream of a nursery far outweighed her guilt from being childish. If you put the nursery on one side of the scales, and her guilt on the other, the nursery won by a long shot. So what was she supposed to do?

Persuading a husband to do something he didn't want to do was an acquired skill, she thought. Certainly with Stephen. He could act exactly like a donkey when he wanted to.

Suddenly she brightened. She would wait a few days, and then when he was in a better state of mind, she would buy him a new shirt or tell him he could get a dog, or something like that, and he would give in. She told herself, Never, ever call your husband's hunting gear junk again.

So she walked into the living room, picked up her unfinished dress, folded it neatly on the sewing machine, and cleared her throat. She picked up the corner of the rug, pulled it into place, and cleared her throat again. Stephen stirred, then opened his eyes, raising his eyebrows as he straightened his chair.

"You know why I'm grouchy?" he asked, in his straightforward manner.

Glory Hallelujah! He wasn't angry!

"Why?" Lizzie responded, eagerly.

"Because I'm tired of working with your Dat and Jason."

"But ... but ..." Lizzie floundered, her heart sinking. Dat was their paycheck, their security, their house payment and groceries and ... and ... everything.

"I want to start my own business with my brothers."

This was too much. Lizzie's thoughts filled with a hundred unnamed fears, which whirled around inside her head like a whole flock of frightened blackbirds. She was unable to comprehend much of what he was saying.

"What do you mean?" she finally managed, a bit weakly.

"Just that. I don't have anything against Dat and Jason. I just feel as if we'll always live here and never get ahead as long as I'm only being paid by the hour."

"But ... I mean ..." Lizzie simply didn't know what to say, so she stopped and sank into a rocking chair.

"But, Stephen," she finally said, in a very small voice. "It's so scary."

"Not really."

"But ... what about Dat? What does he say?"

"I haven't said anything. And don't you say a word to anyone, either. I'm not sure exactly what I'll do. I like to make furniture, too, so maybe I could build a small shop, attach it to the barn, and work there in the evening."

Oh, that sounded like the perfect solution to Lizzie and she told him so instantly, adding that it seemed so very much safer to stay with Dat and build furniture in the evening.

They sat for quite a while, discussing both ideas.

Stephen became more enthused about building a small furniture shop as additional income. After Lizzie realized he was now in a much better state of mind, she asked a bit timidly if he really meant what he had just said about putting a doorway between the two rooms.

"Are you still chewing on that?" he asked, amazed that she had not forgotten one bit.

"Well, yes, Stephen. I want a nursery for Laura. The only thing in that room is your desk and gun cabinet, and the desk will fit nicely in the dining room. How often do you use your guns? Huh?"

"A lot," Stephen said, scowling.

Determined to have her own way, Lizzie pushed on, fueled by her single-minded desire to have that nursery.

"You don't. Only in the fall. Deer season, and that's it."

"Turkey, squirrel, pheasant, dove, rabbit," Stephen said, loudly.

"So? That's in November and December."

"October!"

"Well, whatever. But that gun cabinet could go upstairs. I'll fix up a room for it and everything. The only difference is you'll need to climb the stairs."

Stephen said nothing, only picked up his fishing magazine again.

"Stephen, if you're going to sit there and read that thing without answering me, I'm going to go get a saw and cut a hole in that wall! Put it away!"

Stephen put the magazine away and looked

straight at her, giving her his undivided attention.

"Okay, and how do you plan on sawing through that wall?" he asked.

"With a saw," she said archly.

"Once you set your mind to something, you just don't give up, do you?"

"Sometimes I do."

"When?"

"I don't know."

"I don't either. I'll tell you what. If you help me in my new shop in the evening, I'll put my gun cabinet upstairs. I'll cut that much-needed hole in the wall if that's what it's going to take to keep my very determined wife happy."

Lizzie could not believe her ears! She was so happy, she shrieked like a little girl, hugging Stephen and waking the baby. She talked nonstop as she ran into the bedroom to pick up a bewildered little Laura. She told her she would soon be sleeping in a big crib in her very own room, and wouldn't that be the most delightful thing ever?

The days that followed were busy, happy ones for Lizzie. Stephen helped her move the furniture, and then, true to his word, he brought his tools in one Saturday morning and cut a door in the bedroom wall. There was a lot of noise and dust everywhere, but she did not complain about anything, not ever. She was far too happy to have the nursery she had dreamed about.

She even stood beside Stephen, telling him he was very handsome in that gray shirt. It made his eyes look almost silver. He grinned, then told her she was just saying that because she was getting her own way. Would she stand beside him right now and tell him he looked handsome if he lay on the recliner and refused to cut this door?

Lizzie said of course not. Husbands who refused to do anything nice for their wives never looked handsome. Stephen said they looked exactly the same, just not in their wife's eyes. "You always look the same, no matter what you did," he said. Lizzie laughed and laughed, and then Stephen grinned, and they sat on the floor and talked a while about other things.

Those were the times Lizzie was glad she was married and lived with Stephen in the little brown house on top of the hill. If your husband was kind and did a nice favor for you like cutting this door, life was so happy and rosy, and your husband looked very nice when he worked.

But if you sat in a buggy beside him and the rein was too tight on the horse, and he didn't think so and refused to loosen it, your husband didn't look nearly as handsome. Actually, on Sunday on the way to church, Lizzie thought Stephen's nose was really growing and that his hair was cut too square in front of his ears. It was amazing how his looks changed when he was kind.

The nursery turned out just as pretty as Lizzie had imagined a few weeks later. She painted the walls a pale pink color. Stephen read directions from a small white manual and assembled the crib without once losing his temper. Lizzie sewed the pink gingham curtains and covered a bumper pad she had bought at a garage sale with the same fabric.

They went to town and bought a nice dry sink at the used-furniture place, which they probably should not have bought, since it was over a hundred dollars. But Stephen said it wasn't too bad, so Lizzie thought he was surely the best husband anyone had ever had.

The closet in the nursery was one of the things she was most thrilled about. She arranged all the little dresses on little pink plastic hangers, then hung them on a silver rod in a colorful row. On the shelf above it, she placed Laura's little black shawl with her navy blue bonnet on top, and then the diaper bag which she used to go everywhere, except to church when she used the little woven basket *kaevly*.

On the floor of the closet, Lizzie put the blue stroller that folded up neatly.

Now all she needed were some rugs. She still wanted soft, fuzzy, pink rugs, one to put in front of the crib and another to put in front of the dry sink, mostly because the floor was a stone-patterned linoleum. When they built the house, they planned this room for Stephen's things, not a baby's, which, if you really thought about it, wasn't too smart. They should have thought of having babies, but, then, some people never had any. You just never knew about that kind of thing, which, Lizzie supposed, was completely up to God.

Sometimes she wondered why God was the way he was. Why he let some people have a whole pile of babies. Others, who desperately wanted children, he left childless, and they had to adopt someone else's babies if they wanted any. It was hard to figure God out sometimes, never knowing what he would do next. But then, Mam helped Lizzie to understand that nothing was stressful as long as it was the way God wanted it to be. Most likely everything was the way he chose anyway. Good or bad, it was God working in people's lives, which was a calming, very restful thing for Mam, but just as scary as could be for Lizzie.

The real issue here was the idea of having more babies. As Lizzie finished placing all the cute baby things where she wanted them, she wondered if Laura would be their only child for a long, long time. She certainly did not want another one, not now, not ever. But she could not tell Mam that. Or Stephen. Or anyone, really. For one thing, Mam would start in about God's will. He meant for women to complete a family with children, she would say. But Mam loved all babies—homely ones, fat ones, even noisy, slobbering babies that weren't a bit cute. She loved them all.

Of course, Lizzie loved Laura, but she wanted only her for now. Maybe when Laura went to school, she could think about having another one. Lizzie really wondered what the Bible said about having babies. How many was a good number, how many was an excellent number, and how would only one look to God?

English people didn't have 10 children. They had only two or three, and sometimes, only one. But Amish people had a whole pile. Some families had 14 children, or 12 or 10 or whatever. So did that mean the Amish woman would have it nicer in heaven? Or find more grace in God's eyes?

She would have to get her Bible and figure this out. So she did. Stephen eyed her warily as she searched her Bible each evening before she went to bed. He thought that if she wanted to talk about whatever was on her mind, she would. And sure enough, one evening she started in with dozens of complicated questions and reasonings about having a large family versus a small one, and did it make a difference to God in the end?

Stephen shrugged his shoulders and said he didn't know, but the truth was, her endless questions about life made him tired. Why did she need to make a relatively simple existence so complicated by having to understand every tiny little thing? But that was Lizzie, and she was his wife, so he guessed he'd better learn to live with it.

Chapter 22

LIZZIE COULD NOT LET THE MATTER OF having more babies rest. She thought about it constantly, always resisting the idea. She searched her Bible until she became quite frustrated with the lack of direction it gave about the proper number of children God wanted in each family.

Stephen never said much about the subject. He rolled his eyes and sighed loudly whenever she approached him yet again with her endless wondering about having a large family, especially if you didn't want one.

Lizzie finally decided he was no help at all and marched down the hill with Laura in her arms to visit Mam. Mam was puttering around in her flower beds, carefully clipping the brown leaves off her picturesque "cheraniums."

KatieAnn and Susan came running for Laura, who started waving her arms and wriggling all over the minute she saw them approaching. KatieAnn held her while Susan looked over her sister's shoulder, both talking to her at once while Laura squealed with excitement. Lizzie watched and decided that it was amazing how much the twins loved Laura. She wasn't even their own baby. Maybe KatieAnn and Susan were like Mam, truly loving all babies, constantly wanting to hold them when they were around her. Mam straightened her back and wiped the sweat from her brow, her face red with exertion.

"Come on in, Lizzie, and I'll fix us a cold drink," she said.

"You go on working in your flower beds, Mam. You don't need to stop because I'm here."

"Oh, no, I'm not that busy. I always have time for you girls," she said, smiling.

Lizzie thought things really changed after you got married and moved away. Mam treated you more like company, becoming more smiley and polite when you came home. That was because you were no longer a real daughter, but now partly Stephen's wife, so Mam was much kinder and didn't boss you around anymore. That was nice.

Mam opened the door for Lizzie and got out two glasses from the cupboard, filling them with ice cubes and grape Kool-Aid, which tasted like Lizzie remembered home to taste. Suddenly she had a sharp pang of homesickness, and she wanted to sit around the kitchen table with Emma and Mandy and drink grape Kool-Aid while Mam bossed them around.

"What's on your mind, Lizzie?" Mam asked,

noticing the worried arch of her brows, accompanied by a most troubled expression.

"Oh, not much. Well, yes, a little."

Mam waited.

"Why do Amish people have so many children?" Lizzie finally asked.

Mam raised her eyebrows, then took a long drink.

"That's a good question, Lizzie," she said.

"Is it?"

"Yes. And you know, I don't really know how to answer it. I wanted all my babies, every one of them, even if they were born almost every year."

"But you're not normal, Mam. Not where babies are concerned," Lizzie said.

Mam laughed and laughed, her round stomach shaking as she did so, until she looked quizzically at Lizzie and shook her head. She took off her glasses to wipe them with the corner of her apron, the same way she always did.

"Oh, now, Lizzie, I think I'm quite normal."

"Then I'm not. Mam, I don't want another baby. Not ever, and it's so hard to find anything in the Bible about that subject. It doesn't say anything about the number of babies you're supposed to have," Lizzie said.

"Lizzie, now listen. The Bible doesn't say one thing specifically about the way we dress. It doesn't say we're supposed to wear capes or make our dresses a certain way or any of that. Someone hundreds of years ago decided this is the way we should dress so we remain modest, and the tradition has been maintained all these years. Having babies is very likely much the same. Did you find the passage in the Bible where it says about women reaching their salvation through childbearing? I forget exactly where it is, but it's there."

"Mam, the preachers say grace is free. A gift. Isn't grace our salvation? Then how come we have to have a whole pile of babies to get to heaven? That's trying to earn our way in—you know that."

Mam was quiet, turning her empty glass around and around.

"Lizzie, you think too much," she said. "Why don't you just stop trying to figure everything out and learn to accept whatever God sends? No matter what, and it's hard to explain this, but having babies is a very good method of learning to give up our own will."

"So, when you say that, you're saying you had to give up every time a baby was born? Right? Huh?"

"Well, not really. I looked forward to each one, wondering if it would be a boy or girl, what it would look like, how much it would weigh. I was always happy with my babies."

"Not Jason."

"Yes, I was, Lizzie," Mam said, becoming slightly perturbed, Lizzie could tell.

"He was homely-looking, you know that. And you cried in the bedroom, all by yourself, because he cried so much. I saw you."

"Lizzie, with each baby you have, your motherly instincts become better. You become more relaxed, more focused on the baby's needs and less and less on your own. That's why it's a good thing to just let God direct in your life, bearing children, learning through that to become more and more unselfish as time goes on. It is good for a woman to have children."

Lizzie thought of the hospital and the grouchy nurses, her inability to nurse Laura, her overwhelming feelings of inadequacy. She had cried constantly, feeling as if she was washed overboard in stormy seas and would surely perish, all because of having had a baby. It was definitely not something she wanted to do ever again if she could help it.

"But then, what if I don't have more children? What if I would be one of the first Amish women in the world to have only one? Does that mean God would be mad at me?"

"Ach, Lizzie, you make me tired. Sometimes I don't know how to answer your questions."

"So, you don't know, right?"

"No, not really."

"Look at Aunt Vera, in Ohio. She had two children, Leroy and Mary Ann. And I'm pretty sure she'll go to heaven, Mam, as kindhearted as she is."

Mam laughed. "Ach, yes, Lizzie. Vera is one person who had only two children. She had Leroy and Mary Ann and decided that's enough of that. Bless her dear heart, I miss her. It's time we go for a visit again. Did you know Homer bought a coal business now?"

"He did?" Lizzie said absent-mindedly, still worrying with the baby subject.

"Well, if I do have more babies, I'm not going to the hospital. I didn't like it there. That one nurse was so mean, and I still think that's what got me started crying," she said.

"Lizzie, I've been to the hospital many, many times, and I've never had a nasty or mean nurse. Are you sure it was as bad as you say it was? Maybe you were overly sensitive."

Lizzie shook her head.

"Huh-uh, Mam. She scolded me terribly for laying Laura crossways on the bed. I'll never forget how that only added to my feeling of being overwhelmed with the responsibility of a new baby. She made me feel as if I wasn't fit to have a baby, which, I suppose, I wasn't, because she wouldn't nurse right."

"Your next one might be so different, Lizzie. You know and have learned a lot with Laura. Stephen wants a little boy, and after that, you'll want more. You'll see."

On her way back up the hill, Lizzie was glad Mam didn't have better answers She couldn't prove that having a large family instead of a smaller one was a rule enforced by God. Big families were just an Amish tradition, the same as her clothes.

But, if she was quite honest with herself, the traditions of the Amish—of the forefathers, as the ministers said—was not something she took lightly. She supposed a church was the same as a school. You had to have rules or else everybody would just go out and do their own thing. What sense of structure and order would there be otherwise?

Yes, she would continue to wear a black shawl and bonnet to church, to wear black shoes and stockings, to comb her hair sleek and flat, to light her propane gas lamp and trim the wicks. She would wash with a wringer washer propelled by a gas motor, keeping up the old traditions and way of life because she wanted to. She never really wanted to change. Never. She loved her way of life, and she wanted to do these Amish things. She loved belonging to a group of people who believed in the same order.

Not that she perfectly followed every tiny aspect of the rules and regulations. She was supposed to wear a shawl and bonnet wherever she went in the wintertime. Even to town, when she went shopping. But a large woolen shawl was quite cumbersome in a store, the trailing fringes sometimes knocking things down.

Once, a little English girl had been terrified by Mam's shawl and bonnet, running to her mother and hiding. Lizzie had been embarrassed, knowing the little girl was not used to seeing someone dressed in all black, especially with a long flowing shawl. Lizzie just wore a sweater, or a coat and a bonnet only when it rained or was very cold. Most of the young women did the same.

Well, she would wait and see. She would pray about this matter of children and, like Mam, leave it to God. Perhaps she would come to want one more baby, in time, and never any more after that. She bet no one except God knew how she dreaded the thought of having another baby.

Maybe God keeps record of families in the Book of Life. Kind of a report card for mothers. If you have 14 children you get an A+, if you have 12 an A, and on down to an F for having only one. But still, with report cards you can get away with an F if it's only in one subject, as long as you have A's or B's or even C's in other areas. Perhaps if she was as kind as she could be to Stephen and would not say one nasty thing if he got a dog, or call his hunting gear junk, she would earn an A in that category. Then if she only had two children, she'd still pass.

All these thoughts were silly and unnecessary, Lizzie decided, especially if salvation was a gift and was handed down free of charge. This was about the most confusing thing ever. If salvation was so free, why did you have to bother to live right and plain and simple? Why couldn't you go out and do exactly anything you wanted and never have to worry if anything was right or wrong?

How nice were you to your husband if you gave him all he wanted, but refused to have more children? What if he was much too kindhearted to tell you he wanted a baby boy more than anything? A childish, selfish girl who didn't want any more babies would probably earn a grade lower than an F on her report card, maybe a G, if there was such a thing. Someday, when she had the courage to approach Stephen about this subject, she would.

Not too much time elapsed until Lizzie had a good opportunity to ask Stephen that very question. He was sitting on the front porch, relaxing after his shower, tired from the day's work, and glad to have the company of his wife and baby daughter. Lizzie settled beside him, and he reached for Laura, who gurgled happily and nestled against his shoulder. He patted her little bottom and smiled at Lizzie.

"She's growing so fast. Can you believe she's nine months old?"

"I know," Lizzie said tightly.

"Is she crawling all over the place?"

"Not really all over the place. She doesn't like the hardwood floor in the living room. It's too slippery, and she flops down on her stomach and yells as loud as she can."

"She's some Maidsy," Stephen said, grinning.

Maidsy was the pet name they used for Laura, and she recognized the word, lifting her head and looking at them when they said it.

Without warning, Stephen said, "About time for another one." It wasn't a question. It was a statement.

Lizzie's heart jumped, flipped, then resumed beating normally, only a bit faster.

"You think so?" she breathed.

"Oh, yes! I'd love to have a little boy. An Andy!"

Lizzie swallowed, then looked away from Stephen, out over the hilltop, down to the tree line by the creek. For once in her life, she had absolutely nothing to say.

There it was. Stephen, Mam, God, and the Bible were all on one side, and she was on the other. She was pretty sure Emma and Mandy would stick with that first group of people and tell her the same thing Mam did. Men wrote the Bible, not women.

She knew what Mam would say about that, too. It wasn't humans that wrote the Bible, it was the Holy Spirit. It was inspired by God, so really, those men, Malachi, David, Peter, John, all of them, were only vessels God used to write things he wanted everyone to know.

She may as well forget arguing about any of that.

"You're not saying anything, Lizzie," Stephen said gently.

"No. I'm not."

Her words were sharp, a bit too loud, and very certain.

"Why not?"

"I...I...Stephen, we don't want another baby!" she burst out.

"Not ever?"

"No!"

She got up, flounced into the house, and sat heavily on the sofa, feeling more miserable than she could ever remember. Why did everyone have to be so mean? Now Stephen, yet! At least Mam could be on her side if Stephen wasn't. She was surprised to hear the front door opening. Stephen came in and sat beside her, handing Laura to her.

"Lizzie, don't be upset. I didn't mean anything by it."

Those were tender words, coming from Stephen, and they melted her heart into tiny little droplets that formed into real tears as she turned to him gratefully.

"I'm not upset, really. I just…well, I need a bit of time to think this thing through. I wish I would like babies better, and I wish I was a better mother, and I wish the Bible would say more about babies," she said, tearfully.

"The Bible doesn't spell things out in black and white, Lizzie. We have to figure out what makes us feel right with God and what doesn't. We have choices."

That statement from Stephen held a wealth of peace for Lizzie. Why, of course! He was so right. It was so simple and uncomplicated and worry-free! You could soon tell whether you had made a wrong or a right choice, simply by the way your conscience bothered you. She had often experienced that in her life.

So Lizzie calmed down and forgot about her anxiety at the prospect of having another baby. She figured she'd let the whole thing up to God. Like a heavy backpack strapped to her back, she loosened it and left it by the wayside for God to pick up and take care of.

The next morning, Lizzie was walking down the hill with Laura when she met Dat coming from the barn, his face lighting up at the sight of them.

"Hello, there! How's our Maidsy?" he asked, grinning happily, and then stumbled on an uneven patch on the driveway. He fell heavily on his side as his legs gave way beneath him.

Lizzie rushed to his side.

"Dat! Oh, my word, Dat! Are you all right?" she asked, as she retrieved his straw hat from where it had rolled.

Grunting, Dat turned over and sat up, shaking his head in dismay.

"I'll be all right. Just give me a hand."

Setting Laura on the grass, Lizzie hurried over to grasp his hands, alarmed at the amount of strength it took to pull him up. For a terrifying moment she thought she wasn't able to, and they would both fall heavily back down on the gravel.

Standing straight again, Dat gave a low laugh.

"Ach my, this M.S. is about as hard on my will as anything I've ever seen. I don't have a choice. Suddenly, without warning, my brain doesn't tell my legs to do what I want them to, and bang! Down I go!"

He shrugged his shoulders.

"Nope, don't have a choice. God decided to give me multiple sclerosis, and here I am. I gotta deal with it."

He sighed, looking off into the distance.

"I don't know what the future holds, but I know God will help me handle it. Me and Annie."

He said this with so much pride in his beloved wife, and with so much courage and assurance that

God would be there, that Lizzie felt inspired to the core of her being. Surely, if Dat could handle this dreaded disease, this loss of muscle control that would steadily worsen, she could give up enough of her own will about having a family.

Dat's eyes were very blue and kind as he looked at Laura.

"She still looks like she's been in the sun too long. She's the cutest little thing. Bring her in and we'll have a piece of shoofly pie, Lizzie."

Lizzie loved Dat with all her heart. If Dat could look at his grim future with that much confidence, couldn't she? She was, after all, his daughter. Slowly Lizzie was softening her grip on her own determination to have only one baby.

Chapter 23

AND SO, ONE GLAD DAY IN AUGUST, LITTLE Andrew Lee was born at a midwife's home-birthing center in Jefferson County. The midwife and her unmarried sister were Amish. Mam was a bit unenthusiastic about the prospect of having Lizzie go there, but Lizzie maintained her aversion to a hospital, telling Mam there was no use arguing, she simply was not going back to the hospital.

Stephen had his wish, a baby boy named Andy, and his smile was wide and genuine for a long time after Andy entered the world. Lizzie was a bit disappointed, surprised at the sight of her little boy. Laura had been so adorable, with dark skin and a nice amount of hair, but Andy was very white with only a bit of hair on top of his head. She didn't say anything about it, of course, especially not to Stephen, but Andy just wasn't very cute.

It was a great consolation to think of Jason, her brother. He was about the homeliest baby she had ever seen. Now, as a teenager, he was so handsome with his curly brown hair and crinkling blue eyes.

Mary and Barbara Swarey, the midwives, were the exact opposite of that grouchy nurse at the hospital. They were quiet, encouraging, and often smiling. They held little Andy for no reason at all, except because they wanted to hold him. That was so inspiring to Lizzie, because he wasn't really a cute baby. Mary would come to Lizzie's room, wrap Andy warmly and securely in a fuzzy blue blanket, then sit down in the little wooden, armless rocking chair and rock him, all the while talking to Lizzie about babies and children and life in general.

Oh, it was truly the greatest blessing to be there, and Lizzie valued every hour she spent with the midwives. At night, when Andy would become restless and cry, one of them would appear like some magical person in a light-colored housecoat with a white scarf tied around her head and quietly murmur to the baby. She expertly scooped him up and took him away, cuddling and consoling him as she went. Lizzie drifted off into another few hours of blissful slumber.

Sometimes they brought him to be fed and then stayed to help her. They arranged the pillows, quietly encouraging her, telling her over and over to relax and hold her baby gently, until she had truly mastered this hopelessly difficult art of breast-feeding.

It was the most wonderful, rewarding feeling to know she was quite adept at feeding her baby. He would burp soundly and go right off to sleep, warm and contented, trusting her for all his needs. It was so different from Laura's birth, this feeling of accomplishment. She had a newfound confidence that taking care of this baby was something she would be perfectly able to do.

When one of Mary's girls brought her supper tray, Lizzie opened her eyes wide as a smile of appreciation spread across her face. On the tray were two large yellow ears of corn, perfectly cooked, with a small dish of salad full of sliced tomatoes, carrots, and other fresh vegetables from Mary's garden. Alongside was a thick slice of homemade oatmeal bread and a small dish with a pat of bright yellow butter made from the cream of their own cow. There was also a small glass dish of golden honey from the midwives' own beehives down by their orchard, which Lizzie thought was simply the most extraordinary thing she had ever heard of.

When Lizzie began to eat, she wished there were two slices of bread on her tray and two more ears of corn. Salad wasn't very filling, but then Mary and Barbara ate healthily and weren't overweight. They knew that good nutrition without a lot of unnecessary calories was the best for a nursing mother, especially when she tended to be on the heavy side the way Lizzie was.

After Lizzie had eaten everything, Barbara brought a pretty glass dish piled high with ice-cold chunks of watermelon. The fruit was delicious. So good, in fact, that Lizzie resolved to turn her own dry, little hilltop garden into a garden just like Mary's. She would plant plots of herbs and teas and have different flowers and vegetables all growing in neat squares, one complimenting the other like pictures of gardens in seed catalogs.

She even wanted a cow to make her own butter. She would ask Stephen to get a few hives of bees, and she would get the recipe to make this light, spongy, oatmeal bread. She had, quite simply, never been as inspired to eat healthy things and grow them in her own backyard as she was now with this supper tray.

That evening Stephen brought Laura to meet baby Andy. She was not quite two years old, and her eyes were very large and scared as Stephen carried her into Lizzie's room. She had gotten carsick on their trip across the mountain. Stephen had cleaned her up as best he could, which tugged at Lizzie's heart. Laura was so brown and smelled bad and was so afraid, seeing her mother in such a strange place. Mam walked behind Stephen, barely able to conceal the urgency she felt to see the new baby boy.

Lizzie reached for Laura, but she turned her face away and clung to Stephen.

"Maidsy!" Lizzie said pleadingly. Laura turned her head a tiny bit so that she could peep out with one eye from her position on Stephen's shoulder.

Mam picked up Andy, whom she had finally found in the little wooden crib, and was delightedly pulling on the blankets, trying to have a better view of his face.

"Oh, my goodness!" she chuckled, laughing the way she always did when she saw a new baby for the first time.

"Ach, my! Isn't he cute, Lizzie? Why, he's about the prettiest baby I've ever seen!" she exclaimed, clearly enamored of this pale little grandson.

Lizzie's heart was filled with gratitude.

"Do you think he's cute, Mam? Really?"

"Why, of course!"

She said this as if there was absolutely no question that anyone would ever think he was a homely baby. Why, of course he was cute with those adorable big blue eyes and that wispy hair which would grow in thick and blond. Mam laughed and laughed, her stomach shaking the way it always did, as she unwrapped Andy, checking him fully from head to toe, while Stephen held Laura and peered over her shoulder and laughed with her.

Stephen liked Mam. He always had. Lizzie thought it was very nice to have her husband like her mother. Weren't there a whole pile of mother-in-law jokes around? They didn't apply to Mam and Stephen, which always made Lizzie feel secure and happy.

When Laura finally did leave the safety of Stephen's shoulder, she sat a bit stiffly on Lizzie's lap. Mam brought the new baby for her to meet. Lizzie couldn't help but notice the haughty indifference with which she met her new brother, her back held stiff and straight. She glanced at him with no emotion before burying her head in Lizzie's shoulder and crying her little heart out.

Lizzie quickly bent her head to console her. Stephen reached for her, and Mam laughed some more, telling them that Laura's behavior was perfectly normal for a child. She would likely be a bit difficult for a few weeks until she became accustomed to the idea of sharing her parents with someone else.

After her family left to go back home, Lizzie had a few moments of unsteadiness, knowing those feelings of inadequacy would return unless she was strong. Right now it was very much like keeping a boat afloat on choppy seas, bravely keeping her eyes on the lighthouse. God was there, she supposed, and would keep her from sinking whenever a wave of despair hit. She would not allow herself to sink or to be intimidated by feelings of inadequacy.

Mary and Barbara were a great help. To them, there was almost nothing that rivaled the blessings of motherhood and babies. It was all a gift from God and not something to allow to bury you. They didn't think the way Lizzie did. They had a whole bright attitude about having children, which amazed her.

They actually thought of babies as a very special gift, a blessing straight from heaven. Why wouldn't someone want lots of precious babies? They were so cute and special and sweet, binding a family forever with bonds of love.

So was it any wonder then, that Lizzie felt very much like a queen in her own little world when she slipped on her navy blue dress, pinned her black apron around her waist, adjusted her white covering, and bade Mary and Barbara good-bye? They had helped her view motherhood in such a different light so that the resistance that had made her first year with Laura quite miserable completely vanished.

She was a mother now, a real mother with two children and a house. She had a husband beside her, and, if things got really scary and crazy, a mother who laughed at babies and said they were a lot tougher than they looked. New babies never frightened Mam, even when they choked or got sick or wouldn't nurse or had diarrhea. There was always something that worked, and if nothing else, you whisked them off to the doctor in town and he'd know what to do.

In the weeks that followed, Lizzie found it so much easier to cope with having this second baby. On one afternoon, however, Laura simply refused to cooperate with anyone, even Mam, throwing fits until Lizzie spanked her. Afterwards, Laura cried brokenheartedly, and Lizzie pitied her so much she started crying herself, telling Mam she was going to take a nap. But in truth, she lay on her bed with little, stubborn, angry Maidsy beside her and cried and cried and cried.

But that was it. Never again did she come close

to feeling so overwhelmed. She found that when she got up in the morning, her first thoughts were with the children and not of herself and how she felt.

She also found that you could survive quite well on five or six hours of sleep. And Laura learned to love Andy more with each passing day, which made Lizzie's life quite a bit easier. Stephen was so kind and attentive. He was a very good father to Laura, even if he felt clumsy and ill at ease with newborn Andy. He could do almost anything with Laura, and she would listen amazingly well.

Stephen built his furniture shop as an addition to the barn. He made different articles of furniture in the evenings. He loved the work, learning as he went along, making hutch cupboards and desks, among other pieces. He would start a fire in the woodstove, then bundle Laura up in her coat, the little navy blue one with a round collar that his sister, Sharon, had made for her. He tied her little white scarf securely around her head, straightened up, and took her small brown hand in his bigger one. Together they would go to the shop while Lizzie cleared away the supper dishes.

Laura would play quite contentedly beneath his worktable for hours. She played with blocks of wood or shavings, along with any tool he would allow her to have. When they returned, smelling of wood shavings and wood smoke, Laura would smile happily and have her bath willingly, telling Lizzie in her halting language about her evening with Dat.

Andy, however, was a bit of a problem when it was time for his feeding. He would not always nurse well, so Lizzie became a bit flustered about it again. She tried different ways of holding him, but she became increasingly frustrated at his lack of skill. He refused to take a pacifier.

One day when Lizzie was feeling particularly stressed, she heard footsteps on the front porch and then a small knock. The door opened a bit and someone called, "Are you home, Lizzie?"

Edna! Lizzie recognized her voice immediately. Her cousin Edna from Jefferson County!

Instantly she was at the door, warmly greeting her favorite cousin, Edna, who had walked up the hill from the farm where Uncle Elis had gone to pay a visit to Dat and Mam. Edna was also married and had two children, and because she lived in Jefferson County, Lizzie did not get to see her or her family very often. So it was a special treat for Edna to come to see her new little boy.

They settled themselves in the living room, talking as fast as they could until they both laughed, suddenly unsure if they were actually listening to what the other was saying. Edna exclaimed over Andy, then sat back on the sofa as Laura began to nurse him.

She clucked in her usual frustration, then looked at Edna. "Why can't I nurse a baby right?" she asked.

Edna's eyes narrowed as she watched Lizzie's hurried attempts.

"Well, for one thing, sit back. Relax. Put up you feet and sing as loud as you can!"

They both burst out laughing, although Lizzie felt like crying.

"I'm serious, Lizzie. You're way too nervous. No wonder he doesn't nurse. You're holding him as tightly as you possibly can!"

"I'm just not good at this," Lizzie wailed.

"Yes, you are. Learn to relax and then try it."

With Edna's guidance, Lizzie did begin to see what she meant. Frustrated, she was holding her baby much too tightly. He kept squirming and crying, trying to free himself from her hold.

After Edna's visit, the situation vastly improved. By the time Andy was a few months old, Lizzie could finally understand why mothers nursed their babies and didn't use formula. Lizzie guessed she was just not quite a natural mother the way some women were, like Emma and Mandy. Or Mam. Or almost anyone else.

She had to learn by trial and error and lots of self-inflicted hardships. She wasn't naturally inclined to be a calm, serene person when it came to having babies, no matter how Mary and Barbara made her feel. But she was learning. She no longer thought that having a baby was an affliction, something terrible that you tried to avoid as determinedly as possible.

It was just all in one's head. She had to stop

worrying and relax, as Edna had shown her, and each new problem would eventually take care of itself. That thought was extremely comforting.

Chapter 24

THE YEARS PASSED, MUCH AS TIME PASSES FOR any family. The day came when Lizzie had her fortieth birthday, which made her feel very old. In fact, the thought of being halfway through her years here on earth was quite alarming. Didn't most people die between 70 and 90 years of age? She had better do some very serious thinking, that was all there was to it.

Was she prepared to die anytime soon? Didn't people say it was all downhill after 40? Her side often hurt a lot; in fact, quite often and severely, now that she thought about it. She was at the age where people got cancer or pneumonia or arthritis and became quite sick and died.

She didn't know exactly how one went about preparing to die. Just walk into the living room, sit down on a chair, look up at the ceiling, and ponder all your sins, she supposed. But when she did that, she felt so hopeless, the amount of sins that piled up.

Her worst sins, she felt quite sure, were her lack of patience, her love of beautiful things, and wanting everything perfect all the time. She yelled at the children, six in total now. She also talked about people behind their backs. Honestly, Lizzie thought, she was hopeless, she really was.

She had often decided to stop saying anything negative about a person, ever, but it had only lasted for a day, maybe less, before she started gossiping again. The same thing happened when it came to yelling at her children, although, she reasoned, that was getting better as she became older, so she didn't really know how serious that was in God's eyes.

So, as hopeless as it all seemed, this trying to be good enough to get to heaven on your own, fortunately there was grace. She did believe Jesus died on the cross, shedding his blood for everybody. That was the only hope of salvation, the only boost to Lizzie's confidence when she thought about dying. It was tremendously reassuring.

So turning 40 years old increased her faith in Jesus' power of salvation. She grasped more fully the futility of trying to be perfect so God would like you, as she had so often tried in her younger years. She guessed God knew her nature. After all, hadn't he given it to her? He would mold her and shape her the way he saw that was best.

That was comforting but often hard to grasp, although Mam insisted that was how it was. Mam knew a lot about the Bible because, for as long as

Lizzie could remember, she read it every morning. Lizzie could never get into the habit of reading her Bible every day. Sometimes reading your Bible was boring, and you just read it to ease your conscience because you knew it was a good thing. Sometimes when you sat down to read it, instantly pressing thoughts or worries crowded in, and you were reading but not even comprehending one tiny little thing. Lizzie supposed that was the devil trying to keep you from doing something that was right and good.

That spring, on the third day of April when Andy was not quite 16 years old, Christopher James was born. He was a big boy, weighing almost 10 pounds, with large wide-set eyes like Stephen's.

Lizzie was still, at the age of 40, as happy and appreciative of Mary Swarey, the midwife, as she ever had been. Mary's sister, Barbara, the other midwife, had married a widower from another community and went to live with him and his family. Mary's daughters had come to help her, which was much the same as having Barbara there.

Stephen wanted to name his little son Neil. Lizzie thought she had never heard of such a dull name as Neil, but she didn't make too many arguments against it, not wanting to hurt his feelings. Stephen was so proud of his new son. As it was, they soon agreed on Christopher as his name, but then, when they returned home, Laura was a bit miffed because she wanted that name for her own son someday. She was 17 years old now, and, of course, was thinking about these things, although Lizzie thought that was a bit dense. What if she chose not to get marry until she was 24 or more?

And so Christopher, a strapping little boy, joined the family. Andy was thrilled to have a brother, although it hardly seemed as if he was a real honest-to-goodness brother with the age difference. When Andy held Christopher he seemed a bit unsure of himself, uncomfortable even, and was glad to hand him over to one of his eager sisters who were much happier holding a baby.

"Babies just aren't my thing," he admitted rue-fully and went on his way.

Lizzie felt as if seven children was the right amount. Her quiver was full, as the Bible said. Stephen was more than thrilled to have another son, a small boy to tag around with him when he was actually old enough to have a grandson.

And wasn't life like that? Lizzie mused. As you aged, you naturally became mellower, more patient, not as quick to lose your temper when things went wrong. If you thought about it, the youngest person in the family profited by having parents who were more willing to accept the ways of a child. Before, when she was younger, she hadn't quite realized that a young child is exactly that, a little person who is not perfect. She had expected perfection from her older children, even when it seemed to be a losing proposition.

So she had teenagers, school-aged children, and a baby. Her daughter, Emily, was six years old and would be attending school in the fall, and here was Lizzie, 40 years old with an infant to care for and no little ones to run for a diaper or a pacifier.

Laura was a schoolteacher now at the new school the community had built on Stephen's parents' land along the winding country road that passed in front of the big house. Stephen had been dead set against Laura teaching school, saying she would never make a teacher with her lack of self-confidence. He reminded Lizzie about the fact that Laura couldn't say a poem at the Christmas program in school without crying. How in the world did Lizzie expect her to teach school?

Lizzie insisted that Laura was quite capable. Didn't she have the same Mennonite teacher for all eight years of school? She was taught well, consistently having been given work that challenged her. Of course, she could teach school.

And Laura did. She taught school for eight years after that and enjoyed her time in school immensely. Andy went to work on Stephen's construction crew. Lizzie and Stephen's daughter, Becky, taught school for two years, then worked for a landscaper after that. Trials and troubles, laughter and tears came and went in the big house. Life was much the same for Stephen, Lizzie, and the children as it was for everyone else.

The wooden rockers on the front porch were filled with friends, neighbors, Lizzie and the girls, and sometimes Otis, the big black Labrador Retriever. Crocks and other planters filled with impatiens and geraniums lined the porch, the sun rose and set, each day bringing new challenges and inspiration.

As Lizzie grew older, she often sat on the porch to unwind. Every morning in good weather she drank her coffee on the rocker that faced west, thinking about things and musing about life in general. That porch corner was her mainstay, her sanctuary before starting the day.

Sometimes Stephen joined her, which reminded Lizzie that they were getting older. Hopefully, they would be able to live the remainder of their years growing old together, sitting on these very same porch rockers, finding greater portions of peace as they aged. Wasn't that what life was all about, learning to love more fully, becoming a person who quite naturally became more loving and closer to God?

Things like open stairways and neck reins on horses' harnesses and porch railings and everything Lizzie had cared so intensely about no longer held quite the significance they had in the moment. That was just how life was.

She was even making peace with her weight, that ever-present source of consternation and serious frustration. How could a person weigh so much and feel so skinny and hungry? It was one of the biggest mysteries of life. It wasn't that she sat down and ate a whole package of Oreo cookies or anything like that. She tried to eat healthfully and responsibly.

But she couldn't really help it if she wasn't quite full after having eaten a sandwich and ended up making part of another one and eating that, too.

Food was such a comfort, such a cozy thing to have when worries assailed you. All you had to do was make a toasted cheese sandwich with plenty of butter, the Velveeta cheese dripping off your fingers as you ate it, and the world instantly became a better place. But if you weighed a lot, then eventually you'd just have to accept that you were fat. Lizzie was not an accomplished dieter. She could cut way back on her food intake, lose five pounds with the best of them, eat a piece of cake, and regain the entire five pounds in no time flat.

She faced a losing proposition from the start, that's all there was to it. Mam and Dat Glick had both been heavy in their early years, and large uncles and aunts abounded everywhere on Lizzie's family tree. Right there you had it, and she didn't care what anyone said. If your ancestors had a weight problem, nine times out of 10, so would you. That was the way it was. So to try and be thin when you knew it meant that you'd never enjoy the foods you loved was far too depressing, and anyway, what did it matter?

Stephen loved her the way she was, which was a huge blessing right there. She would absolutely hate to be married to someone who watched every bite she put in her mouth, raising his eyebrows and sniffing, the way men do when they don't approve of someone.

Stephen never made her feel unattractive, although she knew full well she often was. Especially when she wore a *dichly*, that small triangular piece of handkerchief, to do work around the outside. When Lizzie wore that, her whole ears were exposed, and not just part of them as they were when she wore a covering.

Ears continued to grow as long as you live. So did your nose. But especially ears, and Lizzie's were not small. In fact, her earlobes were rather long and fat, which that made her feel very homely. But that was all right. Stephen didn't think she was homely, but Lizzie knew her girls thought so, the way they tried to help her pin her *dichly* on just so, sniffing a bit and trying not to laugh.

That was the thing about having teenage girls. They certainly kept Lizzie humble, or tried to. But she didn't go down easily. She was like a balloon that is squeezed, but just keeps popping up some other place because it still has air!

Lizzie supposed that's just how it was for everyone with daughters. They just kept on correcting you all the time. Even the way you pronounced words. She had always been proud of the fact that she could pronounce words correctly. She had been very good at vocabulary in school, read books all her life, and, actually, always thought of herself as fairly intelligent. Until Laura grew up. Then it was one correction after another, and Lizzie lived for the day when she could correct Laura about how she pronounced a word. It was all in good humor, and they didn't actually fight about it. They just let each other know when the other said a word and it didn't sound quite right.

And so, Lizzie had large ears, was overweight, and seldom pronounced all her words correctly, according to Laura, who really didn't know everything. Lizzie sincerely hoped she would always remember to laugh at herself, because life is so much easier if you didn't get too dead serious about trivial things.

That's what caused big bad feelings, she decided, and so she hoped to enjoy the rest of her journey of life with a good sense of humor about most things and a smile on her face. Anything else was of the devil, Mam would say. And, whether Lizzie admitted it or not, even at age 40, she knew that what Mam said still counted.

Dat was nearly a complete victim of multiple sclerosis now, spending his days in a hospital bed by the low window where they wheeled him each morning. He was able to watch the birds at the bird feeder, the traffic on the road, or whatever caught his attention. His patience was a constant reminder of the resilience of the human spirit and gave Lizzie courage to face the future. You just did what you had to do, she had learned. Some people said that was God-given strength once life got really serious, and she supposed they were right.

Dat was amazing, the way he spent his days in bed, often miserable but seldom complaining, waiting for the hour when angels would come to take him home.

And so, with the love of family, especially from Stephen and her children, Lizzie would enjoy the remainder of her life with a smile on her face, large ears and all.

The Recipes

Lizzie's Favorite Recipes

Chocolate Cake

Makes 15 servings

CAKE:
   2 cups sugar
   ¾ cup vegetable oil
   3 large eggs
   2 cups flour, sifted
   ¾ cup cocoa powder
   2 tsp. baking soda
   2 tsp. baking powder
   1 cup sour milk
   1 cup hot coffee

1. In a large bowl, beat sugar, oil and eggs together until well mixed.

2. In a separate bowl mix together dry ingredients.

3. Alternately add sour milk and dry ingredients to creamed mixture.

4. Last, add 1 cup coffee. Beat all together until thoroughly mixed.

5. Pour into a greased 9 x 13 baking pan.

6. Bake 45 minutes at 350°, or until tester inserted in center comes out clean.

CARAMEL FROSTING:
1½ cups brown sugar
1½ sticks (1¼ cups) butter
2-3 cups confectioners sugar
1 tsp. vanilla
⅓ cup milk

1. Cook over low heat until bubbly, stirring continually. Then boil 1 minute, stirring constantly.

2. Add ⅓ cup milk carefully, and bring to boil again.

3. Immediately remove from heat.

4. Cool to room temperature.

5. Stir in vanilla and confectioners sugar until frosting is of spreading consistency.

Cinnamon Rolls

Makes about 2 dozen rolls

ROLLS:
½ cup milk
½ cup sugar
1½ tsp. salt
¼ cup shortening
½ cup lukewarm water
2 tsp. sugar
2 Tbsp. dry yeast
2 beaten eggs
4 cups flour
half a stick (4 Tbsp.) melted butter
1 cup brown sugar
2 Tbsp. cinnamon
⅔ cup raisins, *optional*

FROSTING:
1 cup confectioners sugar
¼ tsp. vanilla
enough milk to make a spreading or
  drizzling consistency

1. Scald milk in 1- or 2-qt. saucepan.

2. Add ½ cup sugar, salt, and shortening to scalded milk. Pour into large mixing bowl.

3. Cool to lukewarm.

4. In a separate small bowl, sprinkle yeast over ½ cup lukewarm water in which 2 tsp. sugar has been added. Let stand 10-15 minutes.

5. Stir and add to milk mixture.

6. Add the beaten eggs.

7. Work in about 4 cups flour by stirring, and then kneading until dough can be easily handled.

8. Cover and let rise in a warm place until double in bulk.

9. Divide the dough and roll each half into a 9 x 12 rectangle.

10. Brush each rectangle with melted butter.

recipe continues on next page

11. Sprinkle each half with half the brown sugar, cinnamon, and raisins if you wish.

12. Roll up each rectangle like a jelly roll.

13. Cut in 1"-thick slices. Lay slices about 1 inch apart in greased baking pans.

14. Cover and let rise until double in bulk.

15. Bake at 350° for 35 minutes.

16. Frost while warm.

Broccoli Cauliflower Soup

Makes 6-8 servings

4 cups chicken broth
2 tsp. chicken bouillon granules
1 large bunch broccoli, diced
2 cups cauliflower florets, diced
2 cups milk, *divided*
1 tsp. salt
2 cups cooked chicken, cut up
6 Tbsp. cornstarch
6 slices white American cheese, or other
    cheese that you prefer

1. In 4-quart saucepan cook broccoli and cauliflower in chicken broth and bouillon until soft.

2. Add 1½ cups milk and salt.

3. In a small bowl, stir cornstarch into ½ cup milk. When smooth, stir into saucepan.

4. Cover and heat over low heat, stirring frequently.

5. When soup is hot through and thickened, stir in cheese until blended into mixture.

Potato Chowder

Makes 8 servings

2 Tbsp. butter
¼ cup onion, diced
½ cup celery, diced
3 cups potatoes, diced
1 carrot, shredded
6 cups milk
10¾-oz. can cream of celery soup
14-oz. can chicken broth
6 slices white American cheese
salt and pepper to taste

1. In a large saucepan, sauté onion and celery in butter.

2. Add enough water, a cup or more, to cook potatoes and carrots until soft.

3. Add milk, cream of celery soup, and chicken broth. Cook over low heat until very hot.

4. Add cheese, stirring until melted.

5. Salt and pepper to taste.

Farmer's Market Tomato Casserole

Makes 3-4 servings

2 cups stewed tomatoes
½ tsp. salt
¼ tsp. pepper
a bit of onion powder, garlic, and
    oregano to taste
1 Tbsp. sugar
1 cup croutons
4 oz. sharp cheddar cheese, grated
Parmesan cheese

1. Mix all ingredients except Parmesan cheese in a greased baking dish.

2. Sprinkle with Parmesan cheese.

3. Bake uncovered at 350° for 30-45 minutes, or until heated through.

Barbecued Meatballs

Makes 10-12 servings

MEATBALLS:
3 lbs. ground beef
12-oz. can evaporated milk
2 cups dry oatmeal, old-fashioned or quick
2 eggs
1 cup chopped onion
½ tsp. garlic powder
½ tsp. pepper
2 tsp. salt

1. Mix together well.

2. Form into 1" balls.

3. Place in lightly greased baking dish.

4. Cover Meatballs with Sauce. Bake uncovered for one hour at 350°.

SAUCE:
   3 cups ketchup
   1¼ cups brown sugar
   ½ tsp. garlic powder
   ½ cup chopped onion
   1 Tbsp. liquid smoke

Mix together in a bowl.

Spaghetti Sauce

Makes about 44-46 cups

½ bushel fresh tomatoes
3 garlic cloves, diced
3 lbs. onion, chopped
4 green bell peppers, chopped
1 pint vegetable oil
4 12-oz. cans tomato paste
1 Tbsp. dried oregano
1½ cups sugar
1 Tbsp. sweet basil, dried
⅓ cup salt

1. Cut stem ends out of tomatoes.

2. Cut tomatoes in half.

3. Cook tomatoes and garlic in large stockpot over medium heat, covered. Stir frequently to prevent sticking.

4. When tomatoes are very tender, put through tomato press.

5. Cook chopped onions and peppers over low heat for ½ hour. Stir frequently to prevent burning.

6. Combine all ingredients in stockpot over low heat. Bring to a boil, stirring frequently.

7. Put in jars and seal, following instructions for using your canner.

Bread and Butter Pickles

Makes 4-5 pint jars

1 gallon thinly sliced cucumbers
2 large onions, thinly sliced
½ cup salt

1. Mix together well in large pot or crock.

2. Cover with ice water.

3. Cover with a heavy plate for three hours.

4. Drain thoroughly and pack in pint jars.

5. Mix in large bowl:
    4 cups vinegar
    4 cups sugar
    4 tsp. mustard seed
    1 tsp. celery seed
    1 tsp. turmeric

6. Fill jars with this mixture.

7. Process in boiling water bath, following instructions for using your canner.

White Bread

Makes 2 large or 3 medium loaves

½ cup lukewarm water
1 package yeast
1 tsp. sugar
2 cups lukewarm water
1¼ tsp. salt
⅓ cup sugar
1¾ Tbsp. shortening
7-8 cups flour

1. Dissolve the yeast and 1 tsp. sugar in the ½ cup lukewarm water.

2. Mix the 2 cups water, salt, ⅓ cup sugar, and shortening in a very large mixing bowl.

3. Add the yeast mixture and, gradually, the flour.

4. Knead until smooth and elastic.

5. Place in greased bowl, cover, and set in a warm place to rise until double.

6. Punch down. Let rise again.

7. Put in two large loaf pans or three medium ones. Let rise until double again.

8. Bake at 350° for ½ hour.

The Glossary

Ach, voss machts aus? — A Pennsylvania Dutch dialect phrase which means, What does it matter?

Bobbies — A common hairstyle for little Amish girls. Bobbies are two small, tightly rolled knobs of hair, designed to keep their uncut hair off their faces.

Broadfall Pants — Pants worn by Amish men and fastened with buttons, rather than a zipper.

Cape — An extra piece of cloth which Amish women wear over the bodices of their dresses in order to be more modest.

Combine — A hutch or piece of furniture where dishes are stored.

Covering — A fine mesh headpiece worn by Amish females in an effort to follow the Amish interpretation of a New Testament teaching in I Corinthians 11.

Dat — A Pennsylvania Dutch dialect word used to address or refer to one's father.

Der Saya — To wish someone God's blessing.

Dichly — A Pennsylvania Dutch dialect word meaning head scarf or bandanna.

Dochveggley — A Pennsylvania Dutch dialect word meaning buggy.

Doddy — A Pennsylvania Dutch dialect word used to address or to refer to one's grandfather.

Driver — When the Amish need to go somewhere, and it's too distant to travel by horse and buggy, they may hire someone to drive them in a car or van.

Eck — One corner of the room reserved for the wedding party during the wedding reception.

English — The Amish term for anyone who is not Amish.

Gehorsam — A Pennsylvania Dutch dialect word for obedient.

Gros-feelich — A Pennsylvania Dutch dialect word for conceited.

Hold Conference — A time during the wedding ceremony when the bride and groom meet with the ministers (away from the congregation). Traditionally the ministers offer the couple words of encouragement and advice.

In-between Sundays — Old Order Amish have church every other Sunday. This is an old custom that allows ministers to visit other church districts. An in-between Sunday is the day that a district does not hold church services.

Kaevly — A Pennsylvania Dutch dialect word for a little straw basket with a lid on it. Lizzie fills her *kaevly* with Laura's toys.

Mam — A Pennsylvania Dutch dialect word used to address or to refer to one's mother.

Maud — A Pennsylvania Dutch dialect word meaning a live-in female helper, usually hired by a family for a week or two at a time. *Mauds* often help to do house-, lawn-, and garden-work after the birth of a baby.

Nava-sitza — A Pennsylvania Dutch dialect word that refers to a bridal party.

Ordnung — The Amish community's agreed-upon rules for living, based upon their understanding of the Bible, particularly the New Testament. The *Ordnung* varies some from community to community, often reflecting the leaders' preferences and the local traditions and historical practices.

Risht dag — The day of preparation for an Amish wedding. Since Amish weddings typically take place at home, this is the day when the family prepares much of the food for the wedding and sets up the benches and tables used during the ceremony and the meal that follows.

Roasht — Chicken filling. Mam prepares both a Lancaster County and a Ohio *roasht*.

Shtrale — A Pennsylvania Dutch dialect word for a fine-toothed black comb.

Siss ken fa-shtant! — A Pennsylvania Dutch expression which means, It makes no sense.

Snitz Pie — Made from dried apple slices, Snitz Pie is often served at the lunch which follows the Amish Sunday church service.

Whoopie Pies — Two round, soft cookies filled with a sweet, creamy icing. Whoopie pies were originally chocolate, but pumpkin and oatmeal varieties are also common.

Young Married Ones — The couples who are recently engaged. They receive special treatment during their engagement, especially at weddings. In some areas, after these couples are married, they visit members of the community together, sharing meals and receiving gifts.